HARD COUNTRY

A ROGUE WARRIOR THRILLER

IAN LOOME

INKUBATOR
BOOKS

Published by Inkubator Books
www.inkubatorbooks.com

Copyright © 2024 by Ian Loome

Ian Loome has asserted his right to be identified as the author of this work.

ISBN (eBook): 978-1-83756-419-4
ISBN (Paperback): 978-1-83756-420-0
ISBN (Hardback): 978-1-83756-421-7

HARD COUNTRY is a work of fiction. People, places, events, and situations are the product of the author's imagination. Any resemblance to actual persons, living or dead is entirely coincidental.

No part of this book may be reproduced, stored in any retrieval system, or transmitted by any means without the prior written permission of the publisher.

1

PAHRUMP, NEVADA

Bob Singleton scratched at his beard as he leaned against the outfield rail and the stock car roared past, tires kicking up dust as it skirted the high dirt bank of Valley Speedway's northeast corner.

The car's back end slid out, the driver taking the right 'line' around the corner but going in too fast.

"HEEL AND TOE, SON! HEEL AND TOE!"

He looked to his right. The man yelling looked thirtyish, in an "AC Delco" ball cap, with shaggy light brown hair and sunglasses. He was watching the ride intently. "Dang! Pushing the line again," he muttered.

He pulled off his cap and slapped it against the rail.

Bob nodded toward the vehicle. "Friend of yours?"

Annoyed, the man put his cap back on and nodded. "My younger brother. His ride, his team. But I taught him to drive. Or I thought I did, anyhow."

"Big racing town?" Bob asked. A pink, heavily sponsored Nitro Funny Car sat in the infield, next to its trailer. Between various corporate logos, the word "JENKINS" was spray-painted on the hood in futuristic, boxy italicized capitals.

The other man followed Bob's line of vision. "Yeah... not at the Valley. No, sir. They just race stocks here, modifieds. Too rough for Nitro, too short on the straightaways. That's just a promo the Jenkins team does." Then the man frowned, puzzled. "Mind, they do fuel it up here sometimes. Have that big ol' tanker in the lot on Fridays. That's kind of weird, 'cos it don't run here, just down at Ron Fellows..."

Bob let his ignorance show. "Ron Fellows...?"

"Spring Mountain, the operation down the road," the man said. "Long story short, Ron Fellows is a driver, ran in NASCAR, endurance races like Le Mans. He's got a school based out of it. Anyhow... real nice place, real good layout, lots of different track setups, clean concrete surfaces to handle the heat. So all the high-level stuff, when it comes into town, goes there. Team Jenkins runs Nitro there, does testing and driver training."

It couldn't be a coincidence, Bob supposed. "Jenkins... is that related to Jenkins Mechanical, in Bakersfield?"

"One and the same. Dick Jenkins is old school."

"I have a friend working there."

"Uh huh." The man directed his attention back to the track. "OH, HEY NOW! COME ON, LES! FOOT DOWN!" He glanced back at Bob. "Takes the perfect line out of the second turn, barely steps on it coming into the straightaway. I swear, he's got talent, if he could ever learn to concentrate."

Bob nodded, but had half-tuned him out.

If his friend Dawn had had her way, he'd have gone to Bakersfield instead of heading to Seattle by bus via Pahrump. She wanted him to see Marcus, her adopted step-son, give him some encouragement from another male voice.

He was apprenticing at Jenkins, a daunting first trip for the nineteen-year-old.

"He's a sensitive kid, and he looks up to you," she'd said. Then she'd gone quiet for a moment, the way she did, and said gently, "He talks about you all the time. I think he sees you as family now, and he needs one. We all do."

Dawn and Marcus had seen him at his worst, when he was living on the street, and then when they'd been on the run, fleeing the killers of Marcus's parents and Bob's CIA past. But she didn't believe there was a risk anymore; he could sense it.

Even though he'd been on the road for nearly a year, she fixated during their calls on the fact that no one hired by his former bosses had tried to kill him since Memphis, six months earlier.

"If I didn't care about both of you," he'd reminded her, "this wouldn't even be a discussion. There's a reason we use burners and don't see each other."

And so it had gone, Dawn trying to erode his will to keep moving, urging him instead to settle and build a life for himself; Bob trying to get her to understand that he didn't want to keep running but he had no choice.

Thus, Seattle.

He watched the stock car complete another lap, the older brother clapping and cheering an improved performance. Seattle was for a second opinion. The specialist in Las Vegas, Dr. Michael Strong, had diagnosed him as having ADHD and complex PTSD.

The first part he could handle. *That was all fine, such as it was.*

He watched the stock car break too late, almost skidding out. The chatty brother was wringing his hair out.

But then he kept on with the PTSD nonsense.

The stock car was pulling up to the pits. The bearded man hopped the rail and headed in its direction, leaving Bob on his own. He looked around, realizing he hadn't checked his perimeter in ten minutes.

He scolded himself for being so lax.

He headed towards the parking lot and exit. The speedway had been a distraction, but he still had two hours before his bus was due to leave.

Pahrump made sense. There were more direct routes from Las Vegas, but anyone hunting him would check larger destinations as a matter of course. Most people hide out in crowds.

Being counterintuitive—using buses, avoiding traffic and airport cameras—had served him well for close to a year. But eventually, someone would cotton on.

The town was an hour northwest of Las Vegas, perched on the edge of Death Valley, where the daily temperatures bleached bones until they cracked. A pastiche of small homes with zero-scaped front yards and red-grey dirt, the only greenery easily visible was the odd cactus.

It didn't exactly scream "friendly." There wasn't much there, that he could tell: some housing developments, a Walmart, a few casinos, a couple of brothels. If the town had thirty thousand residents, it was hard to see where.

Or, maybe, why, Bob figured. It was the kind of frontier town that usually died out with the closure of a local mine or rerouting of a rail line, long before the Great Depression. It was dusty, scorched daily by temperatures above 110 F.

People didn't go to Pahrump to draw attention, Bob figured. They went there to disappear. *Maybe that's the real reason you chose this route; maybe you were looking for another Tucson.*

Somewhere to just disappear.

The speedway was a twenty-minute walk from the bus stop. Bob had always been curious about stock cars. He'd figured they'd have burgers, at least.

But he'd found on arriving it just wasn't that busy, the track often rented during the day by individual outfits like the chatty brothers.

The dirt-and-gravel parking lot was almost empty, a half-dozen cars set back a few dozen yards from the back of the bleacher seating. A couple of pickups, a sedan and...

Bob whistled under his breath. The Dodge Challenger had arrived while he was watching the run, its throaty engine drowned out by the stock car. It was near the entrance, a '73 in bright yellow, with black rally stripes.

Serious muscle. He approached it and crouched slightly to study its lines. *So pretty,* he sighed.

The voice came from behind him, slightly nasal and nervous. "Now, you all are going to want to put your hands up, real slow, and clasp your fingers behind your head."

2

Bob glanced over his shoulder. A police officer in a tan tunic and brown slacks was approaching him slowly, slightly crouched, his service weapon braced, his badge gleaming in the desert sun.

He did as he was ordered. Rural cops were, in his limited experience, the height of unpredictability.

The officer crept a few steps forward. "Nye County Sheriffs!" he announced. "Okay now, you're going to want to drop the bag, then kneel down and put your hands right there on the rail in front of you. Lay 'em flat, so's I can see 'em, and spread your fingers."

Bob complied. "Like that?"

"Yep." The officer kept his pistol trained on Bob. He reached down and snapped half a set of handcuffs around Bob's left wrist, then used the same hand to cuff the other bracelet to the right wrist.

Bob glanced over at the parking lot, then back to the handful of people trackside. Nobody was paying them any attention.

"Now I'm going to go on and search you, there, big fella, and you just stay real still, like," the deputy said. "You carrying?"

Bob nodded. "FN five-seven in my bag."

The deputy frowned, puzzled. "Nothing on ya?"

"Nope."

"Huh. Weird." He began to frisk Bob's coat. "Figured you'd just up and get yourself some spending money while out on the road, huh, mister?" the officer suggested.

He took Bob's wallet out of the coat as he moved into Bob's line of sight again. His tag read 'Deputy D. Buckwalter'.

The officer withdrew his license and studied it, then put it back into the wallet.

"Robert MacMillan of Las Vegas, huh? You been keeping busy, ain't ya, Mr. Robert MacMillan of Las Vegas."

"I have no idea what you're talking about," Bob said. "I can account..."

"WHY... why don't you just go on and shut it," Buckwalter said. "Unless maybe you want to go and confess..."

"Confess to what?" Bob said. "I literally got off a bus, walked around town for a while, then came here to check out the track."

"And in the meantime, you just went ahead and robbed Mike's Gas Bar, didn'tcha? Didn'tcha!?"

"No, I didn't."

"Uh huh, sure. Seems awful convenient, though; you know... you coming into town right on the day he gets robbed by some dude he didn't recognize—a guy he said was dark-haired, carrying a soft-sided bag. You've got a soft-sided bag right there. You want to explain that one?"

He can't be serious. "You can't be..." Bob caught himself.

The dude was a power-mad yokel nervous about outsiders, clearly. Irritating him wasn't going to end well. "I get to call a lawyer at some point, right?"

The deputy grinned. Bob's reflection warped in the man's mirrored Aviator shades. Buckwalter's teeth were gapped, a fleshy lump on his lip suggesting he liked dip tobacco. "Well now, sure... at SOME point."

He crouched and picked up Bob's bag, opening it and throwing the wallet inside. Then he began to rifle through it.

He withdrew the FN in its speed holster and dropped the bag casually at his feet. "What the fuck?" he grumbled, standing and holding the gun's grip daintily by one thumb and forefinger. "I seen this piece before online. It's used by NATO globalist types. Super-small bullets but real accurate."

"Whatever you say, man."

"Yeah... you're darn right. It's light, too... like a lady gun." He dropped it back into the bag and it clunked off the cement.

Bob winced slightly.

Behind them, Bob heard brakes squeal, the desert dust creating friction. Buckwalter glanced that way. "HEY THERE, BOSS MAN!" he called out.

Bob turned his head to look northeast, towards the Lockspur Avenue entrance. A police cruiser had pulled up twenty feet behind them, an older man in uniform leaning out the window. "You need a hand there, Dobie?" he asked.

"No, siree, Sheriff! I'm just going to be Mirandizing this here miscreant shortly, then taking him over to the office. Mr. MacMillan up and robbed Mike's."

"I heard that." The older cop squinted at him curiously. "That was just about an hour ago, I reckon. Found him awful quick."

"Learned from the best," Buckwalter said. He leaned Bob's way slightly. "Deputy Sheriff Parnell has twenty years in law enforcement."

"Uh huh."

Buckwalter turned back to his boss. "Sure can tell he's a bad'un just by looking at him." The officer sniffed.

Bob tilted his head and peered up at him incredulously. He looked over at Parnell. "Is he for real?"

"Aw... don't mind Deputy Buckwalter. He's got what you call a flair for the dramatic, I guess. Now... you got something you want to tell us, Mr. MacMillan?"

"Yeah: I'd suggest you check the gas bar's security camera. If you charge me, I imagine it's going to come up at some point."

"You'd like that, wouldn't you?" Buckwalter sneered.

"YES!"

The officer ignored his vehemence. "You'd like us to waste our time tilting with Mike about warrants for cameras and what not."

Bob sighed loudly. "My phone call."

Parnell's attention shifted from his officer to Bob. "Impatient sort of fella, ain't ya?"

Bob winced again. Everything about Pahrump was beginning to irritate him. "What *is* that? What is that accent? Why does everyone here sound like they stepped out of a documentary about an Ozarks blood feud?"

Parnell frowned. He looked slightly taken aback, leaning back and straightening up slightly in his car seat. "Well now, that's just kind of hurtful, sir. Like many folk in this community, I'm from inland Cali-for-nye-aye, born and raised. Bakersfield in my case, and I believe Deputy Buckwalter..."

"Barstow," Buckwalter said.

"But, like lots of folks from the area, our families come west from Oklahoma."

"And Texas,' Buckwalter added.

"And Texas. You'll find we tend to cling to that independence and southern hospitality," Parnell said. "When warranted."

"Don't take kindly to rudeness, though," Buckwalter sniffed.

"My phone call," Bob repeated.

Buckwalter wiped his nose on his sleeve. "Law says we can hold you for forty-eight hours before we even get a whiff of trouble for it. Ain't that right, Sam?"

"I believe so, *Officer* Buckwalter." His officer's informality clearly bugged him, Bob figured. "Though I imagine it won't have to come to that, assuming Mr. MacMillan behaves himself." He nodded Buckwalter's way once more. "You sure you're good?"

"Right as rain, boss."

"Well, I'll see you back there, then." Parnell's cruiser pulled ahead a few yards, before executing a U-turn and leaving the parking lot.

Bob looked up at Buckwalter. He was avidly following the deputy sheriff's car as it disappeared. Then he looked down at his captive.

"Well now, you just got quite the big mouth on you, don'tcha? That ain't no local accent, neither. Where you from originally, Big Slim?"

"Michigan."

"Uh huh. Well... you a long dang way from home."

The gravel nearby crunched, catching both men's attention. Two other men were approaching, both in civvies, blue jeans and work shirts.

"Ricky, Zeke," Buckwalter said.

Ricky stopped five yards short. He had ginger hair and a neat, short beard. He looked like he'd been working hard, his face smudged with dirt, his cheeks burnished by the sun. He took a pack of Marlboros from his chest pocket and lit one. "Who's the little bitch?" he asked.

"Some vagrant thief out of Vegas." Buckwalter looked both ways suddenly, as if checking for eavesdroppers. He nodded towards his friends. "You fellers up for a little fun?"

3

They walked Bob towards the two pickups at the back of the lot, a man under each arm, both escorts checking their surrounds for any potential problems, Buckwalter carrying his bag.

They moved him between the two trucks, to an empty space facing the exit, seventy yards away.

"Sure is built solid," the man on his left arm muttered.

"You want to date him?" Ricky jeered.

"This is really, really stupid," Bob said. "Surely there are cameras on this lot. And someone could just walk over from the track..."

"Eh... I get along real well with the head of security here," Buckwalter said, dropping the bag a few feet away. "Came to my wedding. And there ain't nobody around, like you said, Big Slim." He clapped Bob on the shoulder. "A man on his own, causing hassle in someone else's town, showing a guy up to his boss, robbing honest businesses? He's liable to trip, hurt hisself. Or have a eeh... ah eeh..." He paused, the term not coming to him. "What'd you call it again, Ricky?"

"An epiphany," his Marlboro-smoking friend said. "Like, a big idea and such. See the light."

"Yeah... He's liable to just up and see the light, start confessing to all sorts of things." Buckwalter crouched beside Bob, garlic breath hot on his cheek. "It's the strangest thing how that happens."

On Buckwalter's belt, his mic phone began to ring.

THE COUNTY SHERIFF'S office was part of a vast single-level government complex on East Basin Ave. Like much of the town, its most prominent neighbors were desert scrub and cacti. But there was also an animal hospital across the street, and the Second Amendment Gun and Range next door.

Deputy Sheriff Sam Parnell turned the cruiser's steering wheel right and navigated the big Ford into the parking lot.

Then he hit the brakes. He keyed the radio mic. "Car 840 to dispatch. Come in."

The radio crackled. "Dispatch to 840. Go ahead, please."

"Dotty, you got a description on that gas station robber from this morning? Over." Parnell had twigged just before he'd reached down to shut off the engine. The guy on his knees had still been almost up to Dobie's chest, which meant he was probably over six foot tall.

"Ten-four, Sam. We are looking for a Caucasian male, twenties to thirties, five seven to five nine, maybe a buck sixty, carrying a blue Nike soft-sided bag. Over."

"Thank you, dear, much appreciated. We having ham steak tonight?"

"Nothing but."

"I'll be ten-two for a while. I got a feeling Dobie's about to get himself into trouble again."

"Roger that, eight-forty. Over."

"Over and out." He hung up the receiver. The guy on his knees was not only too tall, he'd looked older than his thirties; forties easily. And his bag had been off-white.

Dang it, Dobie... He hadn't wanted to go out of service, but Dobie was family, and that meant dealing with whatever he was up to on the down low.

He took the phone off his belt and speed-dialed the officer.

"Well... hey there, boss!" Buckwalter said. "I was just thinking about you and saying to Ricky Nettles what—"

"How come you ain't rolling already?"

"I got a few things to take care of. But don't you fret, boss; thief's cooling his heels cuffed to the backseat of the Challenger. Won't be but ten, fifteen minutes."

"Did you happen to check the description before—"

"BOSS! YOU STILL THERE? Can't hear you no more."

Parnell gritted his teeth. *Is he pulling my leg?* "Now, Dobie, don't you go doing nothing stupid..."

"Can't hear a thing," Dobie voice came back softly through his handset.

The call dropped.

Ah, hell. Parnell took a deep breath to keep the stress at bay, then started the cruiser's engine again. He reminded himself he had to call his witless cousin one day and thank her for sending her no-good idiot of a son to work for the department.

But you can't fire family, unfortunately.

BOB WATCHED Buckwalter end the call.

"Parnell's so square, he'll up and believe that call actually dropped." The officer snickered.

His friend Ricky grinned broadly, removing the cigarette to quickly agree. "Probably apologize to you for the department's use of such a lousy service. 'I do most humbly apologize that you was so egregiously inconvenienced'," he mocked.

In Bob's bag, a phone began to vibrate.

Damn it. Only one phone in there set to vibrate. And we just talked.

If she's calling now, it's important.

Parnell heard it, too. "Well now... seems someone wants to yammer at ya. But they'll just have to wait."

But it couldn't wait, Bob knew. If Dawn was in trouble... "Okay... take these things off me and I'll sign whatever you need," he said, holding up his shackled wrists.

"Uh huh... I don't think so," Buckwalter said. He leaned in close and lowered his voice until it was soft and gentle. "Now... what's going to happen is, Ricky's going to go get a copy of the department's rules and regulations out of my car. It's a big sucker, about three inches thick. It's a funny thing, though, that when you hold it up against a man and hit him through the book, it don't leave no bruises but he sure as heck still feels the punch. Now... what you think about that, big man?"

Ricky took his cue, heading off toward the yellow Challenger at the end of the lot. "So... once he gets back here, you guys are planning on beating the crap out of me, then?" Bob asked.

Zeke snapped his gum. "He ain't too stupid."

"So... there's really no percentage on me being helpful, then?"

The officer sounded confused. "What?"

Bob pivoted on his left knee, putting all his weight on it, feeling the sting of the dirt and gravel as he turned twenty degrees counterclockwise. He leaned forward, using his cuffed hands flat on the ground to brace his weight as his right leg shot out, snapping a kick that caught Buckwalter in the knee joint, slamming it sideways.

The cop went down hard, shrieking from the pain of a torn tendon.

His friend Zeke turned to react, but Bob was already rolling sideways to his left, coming up on the balls of both feet and swinging his left leg in a circle at the hip, the 'coffee grinder' sweep taking the man's feet from under him.

Zeke crashed to the ground, a pistol popping out of his waistband and clattering on the hard-packed dirt and gravel.

Bob could hear Ricky running back towards them. He leaped to his feet and retrieved the pistol, momentarily thankful Buckwalter had cuffed his hands in front of him. The Team had taught him to 'hop' wrists cuffed behind by partially dislocating his shoulders, but it was painful and would've taken more time than he'd had.

Buckwalter was struggling to rise on a twisted knee, Zeke rolling over after landing flat on his back. Ricky reached for his belt as he sprinted towards them.

Bob turned the pistol his way. "Uh-uh," he cautioned. "I don't need a whole lot of free movement to shoot you."

Ricky stopped running.

"Hands up," Bob said, "where I can see them." He quarter-turned again so that he could watch Ricky and the other men. Buckwalter's hand drifted towards his holster. Bob shook his head slowly. "Not a good idea." He gestured towards himself. "Keys. Now."

Buckwalter raised a palm in protest. "Now come on, here, son... you're being real foolish! I am an officer of the law! You just give yourself up. Let's talk, sensible like."

Bob levelled the pistol at Buckwalter and glared at the man, his irritation rising by the second. "Keys. Now! Before I decide to shoot one of you rednecks out of sheer principle."

"My... my knee," Buckwalter whined. "Think you tore it. Can't move."

Bob nodded towards Zeke, who took the cue and retrieved the keys.

"Undo me. Try anything and I'll shoot you in the gut. I'm sure, being the enthusiastic sportsmen you three clearly are, you'll know what that could be like."

The wary local uncuffed him.

"Drop the cuffs on the ground and step away," Bob ordered.

Zeke did as he was told.

Buckwalter sniffed, wiping his nose with his forearm like a disconsolate child. "You realize the cameras by the main gate are going to have clear images of you. You ain't going to last long out there after assaulting a police officer."

"The Challenger," Bob said bluntly.

Buckwalter looked away, irritated.

"Keys," Bob commanded.

Buckwalter was sweating from the pain. "I ain't giving you my dang car."

"If I have to take them this could get real ugly," Bob said.

"JUST... give him the keys, Dobie, dang!" Ricky commanded.

Buckwalter took the keys out of his trouser pocket and tossed them over.

Bob gestured to Buckwalter using the pistol. "Wrist restraints."

"I don't—"

"You use them when you arrest people in groups, instead of cuffs. That means you always have some on you. Three sets now, and you avoid me having to shoot all of you to slow you down."

The officer's eyes rolled up towards the Heavens. "You just added uttering threats to the list."

"Yeah. I'll keep that in mind."

Bob left them seated on the concrete, back to back, their arms interlinked and secured with the steel-reinforced rubber wrist restraints.

He retrieved the burner phone from his bag and began to walk across the lot. The man he'd been speaking with trackside was watching with an incredulous expression.

"I'd leave them be," Bob said. "You really don't want to get involved."

He walked over to the yellow Challenger. It was hardly low-profile but by the time the three idiots could get free and had an All-Points Bulletin out for it, he knew he'd have dumped it for another.

Stealing cars was never ideal.

Right now, it's necessary.

He was about to open the door when the police cruiser pulled into the lot.

Bob pocketed the burner, which had begun to buzz once more. Whatever she was calling about, Dawn needed him immediately.

The cruiser ground to a halt, kicking up dust and gravel. For his age, Deputy Sheriff Parnell was quick, bailing out of the driver's side the moment the car stopped rolling, his pistol drawn.

"Halt!' he bellowed.

Bob turned his head slowly and peered at him, not hiding his irritation. "Is it going to help me at all if I point out your boy and his yokel friends were about to beat the shit out of me for no reason whatsoever?"

Parnell sighed, as if he wasn't remotely surprised. "Well now... it might have done, had you not done whatever you did. He glanced to their right. "That's them, sitting over in the corner at the other end there, I take it?"

"It is."

Parnell approached him, the pistol raised and trained on him. "Gun on the ground, please."

Bob tossed the Glock into the dirt.

"Hands on top of the car. Spread them fingers! Lean forward and spread your feet shoulder-width apart."

Bob complied. After a moment, he saw Parnell's booted foot poke between his sneakers, pushing his stance uncomfortably wide with a pair of short kicks to his heels.

Great. NOW I get the professional.

"So, you're actually going to arrest me for this?" Bob asked incredulously. "For defending myself?"

Parnell was clearly exasperated. "Well now, son... I know Dobie well enough to figure you're probably telling me true. But you can't go assaulting officers of the law. There's a process to this sort of thing what's got to be followed, and you didn't do that. So, while I will be having words with our officer, I must also place you under arrest on suspicion of assault causing bodily harm and resisting arrest."

Parnell patted him down.

"Hands behind your back."

Bob complied. He waited until he felt Parnell's free hand on his left wrist, the feel of skin on skin a cue to stoop slightly and throw his head backwards, full force. The back of his skull caught the officer across the bridge of the nose, snapping the bone.

"Unggh!" Parnell grunted, staggering back a few steps. Bob spun on his left heel, his right foot coming around in a spin kick, adjusting it in mid-flight slightly, the base of his heel smacking into Parnell's chin, the mental nerve crushed. The sheriff's legs gave way and he crumpled to the dirt, dazed, his service weapon tumbling from his grasp.

Parnell tried to recover, fighting near-loss of consciousness, looking around, confused, for the gun. Bob clocked the move early, taking two steps and kicking the pistol under the car.

He took two steps back as the deputy sheriff found his feet and rose slowly. Bob crouched and picked up the Glock he'd taken off Buckwalter.

Parnell shook his head and held up both hands, an attempt at conciliation. "Now, Mr. MacMillan, you don't want to make this any worse…"

"Do I seem to you, after the last few minutes, as someone easily shaken by authority, deputy?"

"I can't say you do, sir, no."

"Turn around."

The deputy did as ordered. Bob picked Parnell's cuffs out of the dirt. "Hands behind your back."

The older man complied.

"Your deputy," Bob said as he cuffed him, "cuffed me with my hands ahead of me."

He didn't need to elaborate. The smaller cop seemed to visibly deflate. "Dang. He is… Well… I should keep my opinions to myself, as this has all been a might unprofessional already. You sure you won't reconsider this, Mr. MacMillan?"

Bob shook his head casually. "Believe me when I say I've had just about enough of small-town Nevada for a lifetime. I'm going to go now; a friend of mine needs my help, and your deputy's car is conveniently located."

He climbed in and started the engine. Then he rolled down the window. "I'll leave it somewhere safe," he said.

"It's still theft, son!" Parnell said, frustrated. "I'm telling you, now... I wasn't going to let nothing bad happen to you."

Bob frowned. The man seemed earnest. His deputy was just a violent ass. "You need better hiring policies."

Parnell shrugged. "Family."

"Your problem," Bob said. "Not mine."

A moment later, he pulled the Challenger out onto the highway, heading west. It wouldn't take long for the trackside oglers to call help, he figured, so getting out of town and the state was the immediate priority.

Nonetheless...

Bob took the phone out of his jacket pocket and hit redial.

"Where were you!?" Dawn asked without pause. "You didn't pick up right away. You always pick up right away!"

"I was tied up. What's going on?"

"It's Marcus."

Bob groaned. "For cryin' out loud, Nurse Dawn, I thought you were in danger! We only just talked about him a couple of days ago..."

"No, this is new," she said. "He's in trouble."

4

BAKERSFIELD, CALIFORNIA

Marcus watched the other men in the holding cell warily. They'd come in over the course of Friday evening. The cell was ringed with cots attached to the bars, but no one slept, other than a hulking figure who'd looked so at home that he must've been a regular.

They'd picked him up in the alley he took daily, a block from his job placement at Jenkins Mechanical. They'd questioned him for three hours, demanding answers, slamming hands on tables, out-and-out yelling at times. They'd asked him why he killed a man named Singh. They'd told him they had witnesses, that there were cameras nearby that had evidence of him doing it.

They'd been surprised when he'd said he knew that wasn't true because he hadn't done it.

They'd told him what could happen to handsome young men in Lerdo, the pre-trial jail, where only his lawyer could visit him.

They told him how the District Attorney's office usually

won whether the guy did it or not, so he'd be better off telling them what he knew. They told him a real prison would make Lerdo look like Sunday School.

Then they told him they could ask him questions for two days before he got his first phone call and, since it was now Saturday, he wouldn't be arraigned until Monday at the earliest.

"We get some real winners in here," the deputy with the pencil moustache who'd arrested him had sneered.

By mid-morning, they'd realized he had nothing to say—or decided he just wasn't up to talking—and let him have his first of three calls, on a payphone in the hall beyond the cells. He'd used it to contact the only person he knew was definitely on his side.

"I didn't do anything wrong," he'd started by saying.

And Dawn had said what he knew she'd say.

"I know." She'd get him a lawyer, she'd suggested. "And Bob is on his way."

"Here? He's coming here?"

"I'll make sure. He's not far away now."

"He's going to be so angry."

"Probably, yes. Do what he says, and he'll get you out of this."

"I know. I mean... I didn't do anything."

"I know. Marcus..."

"Yeah?"

"Don't let this get to you. Don't worry... I mean, I'm guessing that's hard to hear when you're in custody but..."

"Yeah. Keeping my head down, keeping to myself. There's—"

A hand came down on his shoulder. "Time's up, let's go."

"I have to go," he said. "Thank you."

"Of course. I love you, sweetie. Stay safe," Dawn said.

The holding cell was slightly more crowded when he got back, a biker type who looked like he could cause an eclipse taking up one of the benches. He had a shaved head, a spider-web tattoo around his right eye and a nose ring through his septum. No one was sitting or standing within ten feet of him.

Marcus took the hint, making his way to the last bunk and sitting on its edge, a roomful of men trying to pretend it wasn't tense.

"HEY!" the new arrival bellowed his way without even raising his voice.

Marcus looked to each side. "Me?"

"Yeah, you. You afraid of me?"

He felt his stomach turn. "I... uh... yeah. You're pretty big."

The giant glowered at him, but only for a second. Then his face softened to disappointment. "I ain't going to hurt anyone," he said. "I just lost my head, is all."

Marcus scanned the room again. The other prisoners didn't look any nicer than the big man, just smaller. And there were a lot more of them. He got up and crossed the room, gesturing to the bunk. "Mind if I sit?"

The bigger man's expression barely changed. "Why?"

"I don't know. It's boring, yo. I've been in here for, like, sixteen, seventeen hours already. And you said I don't have to be afraid, so..."

His new cell mate extended a baseball mitt-sized paw. "Lawrence Cresswell. I have a slight problem with methamphetamine at present, and I owe my dealer quite a lot of cash. Sorry. Most people ain't nice to me, and I should be better. So... yeah. Sorry."

"Ah. Cool. Marcus Pell." They shook.

The balding biker looked crestfallen. "My wife has a slight problem with infidelity. Unfortunately for this week's boyfriend, I came home early from work and was pretty tweaked."

Marcus figured he understood. "You beat him up?"

"I chased him down the street and smacked him around a little too much, yeah. He's in hospital."

"And... how do you feel about that?"

"Less sympathy for him than I probably should. I mean, he's a dick for sleeping with a married woman, if he knew. But... mostly I'm just sad... Mostly. Wish she'd stop breaking my damn heart." A morose, distant expression overtook him. He rubbed his giant palms together nervously. Then he sniffed hard, shook it off. "Wish I'd never left Susan, my ex, for her. Worst mistake I ever made. You?"

That was your worst mistake? Not the meth problem? "They think I killed a guy."

Lawrence sat up straight. "Okay, then." He began to shuffle slightly further away, then caught himself. "Sorry... didn't mean it like that. You... didn't do it, right?"

"Nah. Literally walked around a corner, saw a car, looked inside it, Five-O rolls up."

Lawrence shook his head and leaned back against the bars. "It's a cruel-ass world, Marcus Pell, a cruel-ass world. I tell you what, though. You were nice to me, and sometimes that's what I need. So don't get too worried. I got your back."

THE DRIVE to Bakersfield had been bleak, a four-hour trek through badlands and scrub, across flat desert and through winding mountain passes. It was rare to see another car, and there were no people. The car's dash readout said it was 118 F.

He'd dumped the Challenger in Shoshone, a tiny town in the Nopah Mountains that served a handful of wilderness tourists and campers daily.

A pickup truck with "truck nuts"—literally a pair of steel bull's testicles hanging from its tow bar—had taken the yellow sports car's place.

It had carried him for two more hours, through the merciless desert terrain of Death Valley, past a string of towns long abandoned—Tecopa, Baker, Dunn. Each had been a mining center at some point. Now, they were nothing but the odd dilapidated building or trail marker. The collective memory of the Old West was long dead, descendants swept away by new opportunities like so much sagebrush.

Barstow was the only notable city along the stretch, cut out of the foothills of the Calico Mountains, where the air a century earlier had been filled with the clink of pickaxes and the promise of silver. It had been saved from obscurity by railroads, as the only stopping point between Las Vegas and Los Angeles.

But it had been decades since Barstow thrived. Route 66 was gone. The rust-mottled petroleum storage tankers on the edge of town betrayed its current role serving the businesses of the nearby Midway-Sunset fields, America's most productive wells.

He'd found a beater online, a 1996 Buick Skylark that the owner had parted with for five hundred in cash. He'd left some cash under the driver's seat of the pickup, along with a note of apology.

He stopped at a gas station, bought a razor and a pair of scissors, then visited its bathroom.

He shaved off the heavy beard, then carefully trimmed his hair slightly. Eventually, images from the track cameras could make their way back to Team Seven. The National Security Agency's facial recognition software was superb and had access to law enforcement broadly. The sheriffs would be angry, looking for payback, and would have an All-Points Bulletin out on him in short order.

It wouldn't help them much across the California border, out of their jurisdiction, where hundreds of miles of desert between the nearest city and Pahrump made chasing gas station robbery suspects awfully low on anyone's priority list.

And any attempt to bust him for the "assault" would lead to questions, viewing the track video, accusations of police brutality. Parnell had seemed the type to avoid all that.

BAKERSFIELD'S SUBURBS started in the town of Edison, a highway strip of scrub lots and hardpan dirt, broken-down industrial yards, weigh scales and truck stops. The highway split at a spaghetti junction just past it, the north leg leading him into the city proper, the road diverging into four lanes to accommodate heavier traffic.

The service stations and desert gave way to homes and businesses. Bakersfield stuck with the same theme as the rest of the inland desert towns: low rise buildings, few over three stories, many whitewashed to reflect the heat, close together to encourage shady recesses. It went on for miles, the valley home to more than a half-million residents.

A brown haze hung in the air, which Bob figured was dust from the surrounding hills. He steered the Buick towards downtown.

First order of business is to get a room at the motel, then go see Marcus.

Dawn had said the boy would be expecting Bob as his legal representative, the only way he could gain access to Marcus, with pre-trial detainees barred from having visitors.

It irked him, losing his 'Robert MacMillan' ID to the deputies in Pahrump. It had carried him across two states and been solid for nearly three months. And it had cost him a fortune from the forger in Tucson. Now, he had to start from scratch, he knew, with the only paper he'd managed to secure in Las Vegas, a brutally expensive driver's license in the name 'Bob Richmond.'

Marcus was supposed to have told his captors that his lawyer 'Bob Richmond' would be stopping in before the end of the day. It had taken Dawn twenty minutes to find a lawyer in California named R. Richmond, a real estate specialist based out of Huntington Beach, which was at least a little bit of luck. It would have to suffice, but Bob knew any backchecks would compromise the ID quickly.

He stopped the car at a red light and checked his watch. It was just after five thirty in the evening.

Still technically before the end of the day, I guess.
Now I just need to figure out how to get him out.

At the intersection's corner, a leathery, weather-beaten man in dirty denim overalls, a string vest and a wilting cowboy hat eyed him with surly deference. The man scratched his scraggly cheek whiskers as he kept his eyes on the Buick, then stooped slightly to spit out a stream of brown tobacco juice.

He was still staring as Bob's car pulled away.

5

The sergeant behind the booking desk stared at Bob with annoyance then looked past him, over his shoulder, to the clock above the main doors. "Your client has been in holding for a day already," he said. "What took you so long, counsellor?"

"I had to drive in from Los Angeles," Bob lied. He glanced sideways at the waiting room, where a half-dozen detainees, mostly cuffed, were waiting on benches to be booked.

"Your driver's license says Nevada." The sergeant tossed it back to him across the counter and Bob put it back into his wallet. The officer had a small name tag with "DYCHE" in tiny white lettering.

"Because I used to live there. Apparently, his mother was owed a favor by my partner, so here I am. Do I sound happy about that fact, Sergeant?"

The cop's face suggested he didn't want to be there on a Saturday night either, making mild irritation appropriate.

"You do not, counsellor, you do not. I'm sure our fair city

has nothing on whatever you had planned this evening, but if I was your client, I'd be annoyed." He turned around a ledger and pushed it across the raised desk. "Sign in and we'll get you a room."

"A room?" Bob said. He cursed himself inwardly. That was probably something obvious to a lawyer. *Don't ask unnecessary questions, idiot. Keep making mistakes like that and the jig is up, Bobby.*

"For your interview." The sergeant frowned. "He's still in holding, obviously. You don't do many of these, I take it."

"I'm licensed to practice criminal law, Sergeant, I... just don't get much opportunity." *Lace it with self-doubt. Let him know you're embarrassed to be here, because you're an asshole lawyer.* "I handle real estate contract law, typically, homes in Malibu. This is a little... below my pay grade. You understand."

Sgt. Dyche sucked on his tongue, a derisive expression on his face. "Uh huh. I don't reckon your client would want to know that, either. He seemed pretty nervous about being here."

"I'm sure he's a sweetheart," Bob said with dry cynicism.

From behind him, a woman's voice chimed in. "If that's the attitude you take, I wouldn't want you on my team."

Bob turned. She was tall, with copper hair, broad-shouldered, in a skirt suit, legal briefcase in right hand. She wore a stony expression.

"Mr. Richmond, this is Assistant District Attorney Margaret Swain," the sergeant said.

"Your client deserves the fullness of your attention, counsellor," Swain stated icily. "If I'm of the opinion he isn't being properly represented, I'm bound by my duty as an officer of the court to ensure that is addressed before any proceedings are tainted."

"Duly noted. And as his counsel, I'm duty bound to point out to you that his arrest is a travesty."

"A travesty!?" She practically smirked at the notion, Bob thought. "Mr. Richmond..."

"Please... it's Bob."

"Mr. Richmond, your client was caught four feet from the body with the smoking gun that—"

"No, he wasn't," Bob interrupted. "I know that kid's family, and I'd bet anything that he was set up."

She looked weary. "Mr. Richmond, just because you've read the odd story about Bakersfield police being corrupt doesn't mean you get to denigrate the entire department."

"No, but it's interesting you bring that history up," Bob said. "After all... I didn't. But I do know Marcus's family, and you'd be more likely to jail a felon if you arrested Santa Claus."

"If it looks and quacks like a duck..."

"Marcus isn't a killer, Ms. Swain. Bet if I start digging into who arrested him, I'll find something."

She nodded, lips pursed. "Well, okay then... Good luck to you, counsellor. Try to show some sensitivity to the Singh family; this is a small town, sometimes, for such a big city, and some of us have known them a long time. They don't deserve the third degree."

"Noted."

"I'll see you at arraignment and bail on Monday."

She turned and left. Behind the counter, Sgt. Dyche looked impressed. "Margaret Swain, bringer of pain," he intoned. "She has a 98% conviction rate."

Bob nodded. "Good. It just proves that nobody's perfect."

"You sounded a little more enthusiastic with her than your initial introduction," the older cop said.

"Yeah... well, like I said... this is a favor," Bob suggested, getting back into sleazy character. "I could be in Malibu sucking on a Mai Thai right now."

"Uh huh."

The sergeant hit a button on his desk. A few moments later, the steel door behind him and to his left swung open, another officer stepping into the atrium. "Officer Carbajal here will take you down to Room C, so you can talk in private. Don't worry about the camera. It does not have sound on."

They followed the hall to the end. The interview room was sterile, whitewashed, with just a desk, two chairs and an observation window. There were doors on two walls.

Bob stood and waited for fifteen minutes before they finally led Marcus in. The boy's eyes widened when he saw his friend. Bob quickly raised a finger to his lips and nodded towards the guard.

The guard led Marcus to the table and sat him down. He cuffed one of the boy's wrists and looped the other cuff around a steel ring set into the tabletop, then locked it.

"Just ring the buzzer on the table when you need me," he said before leaving.

Bob sat down opposite him. "You okay?"

Marcus nodded. "It's good to see you." He frowned. "They questioned me for hours before you got here. That's illegal, isn't it?"

"No, but they know anything you gave them could probably get tossed. They do it to soften a suspect up, see if he'll spill something big before he gets help, something they can follow up that's evidentiary, so the statement itself doesn't matter."

"It's scary in here." Marcus glanced around the interview room. "Last night was... man, I never tried so hard to keep my eyes open."

"Jails tend to be like that, even holding cells. And... it's good to see you, too, although we sure could've met somewhere nicer. Are you going to give me the quick version, or is there a long, complicated version Dawn hasn't told me? She just said you'd been arrested for shooting a guy."

"Yeah... There's not much more to it than that. I was on my work placement at Jenkins. I decided to walk my regular route back to the motel."

"About that... Why the Feeney Motor Lodge? Aren't you here for three months?"

"It was cheap. It's tough finding room rentals here for a short time. The apartments all wanted a six-month lease."

"And last night?"

"I cut through an alley and a car was parked with the door open and the alarm going off. So I looked inside and found a dead guy. I was about to call the cops and they pulled up and arrested me."

"That can't be it, surely?" Bob asked.

Marcus's eyes rolled up as he stared at the ceiling. "They also say they found the murder weapon on me, and they have security footage from the alley proving no one else entered it after Mr. Singh and me."

"Excuse me?"

"That's what the deputy said when they were booking me. He said..." Marcus affected his best drawl, "... 'How're you going to explain away having the gun what done it, smart boy? How're you going to prove someone else did it when there weren't no one else there?' Something like that."

"You... weren't carrying, I take it?"

Marcus shot him a dry look. "Really?"

"Point taken." But it complicated everything. "Marcus... if they're claiming they have direct evidence taken off you, this is a frame-up."

Marcus's head sank. "So... what does that mean, exactly?"

"It means someone involved, maybe one the deputies who arrested you, has some sort of stake in this man's death. Whether out of convenience or plan, they've picked you to take the rap for it. Young man, in town temporarily, from the big city from their perspective. You've got no clout here, which makes you a good patsy."

"That's... Man... That's bad."

"Yeah. But... we can work with it."

"Huh?"

"If they need you as a patsy, they'll want to keep you alive, at least for now. When you're arraigned on Monday, the district attorney's office will likely ask for no bail, at the officers' request, because they don't want you disappearing or working to disprove the narrative."

"And you're going to... what? Figure out who actually did this?"

"If that's what it takes. As long as they need you, you won't have much to worry about, as long as you keep your head down. Guys awaiting trial, for the most part, don't want to dig the hole they're in any deeper. So you're safer here than it feels. And the cops will need a conviction, or someone might keep digging away."

"But…" Marcus leaned in, his voice a murmur. "You're not a lawyer! What about the actual case?"

"Dawn's arranging a proper attorney in case I can't resolve this quickly. We'll figure that out, don't worry."

"You think I might be stuck in here."

"I'm not saying that. She's just being cautious. Now we need you to be, too."

"There's a big dude in holding I made friends with," Marcus said. "He's sort of mixed up but he's looking out for me, I think."

"Uh huh. Don't trust him. Don't trust anyone in here. Keep your head down and your back to the wall. Mind your business until I can find something that might spring you. Can you do that?"

Marcus shrugged. "I ain't got much choice."

Bob rose and pressed the buzzer. "Okay then." He put a hand on Marcus's shoulder and leaned in. "Remember what I told you in DC: I'm not going to let anything happen to you. Okay?"

Marcus nodded and tried to smile, but Bob knew the kid had to be terrified.

The door opened and the officer stepped inside. "All done?"

"For now," Bob said. "The arresting officers—I'd like to speak with them."

"Uh huh. Well, as you no doubt know, those arrangements have to be made through Sgt. Dyche."

"The charming fellow taking bookings?"

"One and the same."

"Then let's go have a word."

6

Sgt. Dyche looked up for a split second as Bob returned to the atrium, then went back to the newspaper on the counter.

"How'd it go, counsellor?"

"Fine. I take it you'll want to question him with me present."

Dyche shrugged. "I do not believe so, no, sir. Arresting officers have an open-and-shut case from their perspective, and video camera footage from the alley showing no one else left it before your client entered."

He reached under the counter and withdrew a brown manila envelope. "I assume you want the police report from the arresting officer. It's here, along with stills from the security camera footage."

Dyche tossed it onto the counter. Bob picked it up and undid the string holding its flap closed. "And the arresting officer himself?"

They found Officer Jeb Fowler in the station parking lot, leaning against his Ford Crown Victoria cruiser, smoking a cigarette. He was short and skinny, with straw-blonde hair, spindly arms and a pencil-thin moustache under green-tinted Aviator-style sunglasses.

He was about as undersized a cop as Bob had ever seen. Dyche introduced them.

"Mr. Richmond, this gentleman—who was just butting out that already lit cigarette he found on department property—is Officer Jebediah Fowler of the Patrol Unit. He and his partner, Officer David Czernowitz, picked up your client at the scene."

"Sarge," Fowler said, stepping on the cigarette butt. He tipped back his Montana peak Stetson slightly. "Mr. Richmond. I hope our fair city is treating you kindly."

Bob didn't want to waste time on niceties. "Your sergeant showed me the official report on our way out here. It's only fourteen lines long. For an alleged homicide scene."

"Uh huh. Stand by every word," Fowler said. "And will do so again in court when the DA convicts him."

"I'll just leave you two to it," Sgt. Dyche said, before turning and heading back towards the building.

"So... you're claiming he had the gun on him."

"Uh huh, right there in his jacket pocket."

"On the left side, I take it, since he's left-handed. Your fourteen-line report did not specify."

"Uh huh, yeah, the left."

"You're sure."

"As I'm standing here."

"Marcus isn't left-handed. Why would he fire a gun and then put it in the left-hand pocket?"

Fowler's smarmy demeanor evaporated. "You think that's real smart, don't you, counsellor?"

"Well, now... if you fellas are allowed to lie to get information from people, I figure that's just fair game. Can you answer the question?"

"Maybe because his wallet was in his right-hand pocket, leaving little extra room for a large pistol. Or maybe..." He took a couple of steps closer, until he was looking up at Bob's chin. "Maybe he's just a wrong 'un, the kind who does unpredictable, wild things. We..." he sniffed, "... we looked him up, you know, your client. He's got a past."

Hickory Hills. Newspaper stories about his parents' "murder-suicide", cover for a CIA cleanup. That had to be it, Bob knew.

"Rough business," Fowler said. "Kind of mess that'll drive a kid right around the bend, make him go and do something crazy, like rob a successful doctor."

Bob kept his voice equally hushed. "See, the thing is, Officer, I know that kid a little better than you might think, despite being a bottom-feeding lawyer. And I know not only that you planted that gun, but that you must've had a darn sight better reason than a robbery. And where there's smoke..."

Fowler smiled slightly at that, nodding, relishing the challenge. "Well, now, I do believe you're in the wrong place, Mr. Richmond. I believe you should've stopped by the fire department if you needed help on that front. If you're doing some *fire* investigatin'. Me, I have to let you take my statement, let you depose me, as the man says. But I only have to do it once, officially, with a steno. Other than that, I'm just a local officer of the law and you're... well, you're a visitor in my town. And I'll thank you kindly to keep that in mind."

He gave Bob a little wink and turned to open the door of his cruiser.

He looked over his shoulder. "As I am on time-off-in-lieu

for the next two working days, I believe I may have some place in my schedule next week, if you'd like to call legal services to set that up." He got into the car and slammed the door, then started the engine and rolled down the window. "Enjoy your time in Bakersfield, Mr. Richmond. I'll be seeing you."

The car rolled off.

"Sir?"

Bob turned. The officer behind him was stockier, a little bigger, holding his hat ahead of him like it needed inspection. He had a tight crewcut and square chin, a neatly trimmed moustache His badge read 'Czernowitz.' "I understand you've been looking to speak with me?"

Bob nodded towards the road. "Your partner just left without you."

"I'm not supposed to be working today on account of treatment for a medical condition," the officer said. "But Sergeant Dyche did indicate that you wished to speak about the Singh case."

"Yeah... Your partner was just telling me how you found the gun in the car," Bob said.

Czernowitz frowned. "I do not believe that is accurate, sir. I believe Officer Fowler found the gun on the person of the young man we arrested, Mr. Pell."

"You believe?" Bob said. "You mean you didn't actually see him find the gun."

Czernowitz scowled, appearing confused. His eyes darted from side to side as if weighing options. "I mean... I did, yes. From the accused."

"You... saw him take the gun from the kid's pocket?"

Czernowitz's head bobbed a little, as if he wanted to acknowledge the point again. Instead, he licked his lips anxiously. "I do agree with everything in Officer Fowler's official report."

Bob held up both palms in surrender. "Officer... it's okay. I'm not trying to trick you or trap you or anything. We can just talk about what actually went down."

"I've said all I can say, sir," Czernowitz stressed. "Because that's what happened. Yes, sir. Jeb... Officer Fowler, he said you will try to get us fighting over the details. I know that's what lawyers do, defense lawyers most of all. Try to trick us, make the good people seem bad."

"I just want the truth about—"

"I need to go, sir," Czernowitz said, anxiously flitting glances at the door to his left. "If you need me to make a deposition, I will do so and repeat the same thing, that—"

"You agree with everything in Officer Fowler's report. Yeah, I got that."

"Okay then. Good day and thank you," Czernowitz said awkwardly before heading for the door.

Bob watched him head inside, a memory twigged, of a guy he'd known in the Marines. He'd been a hell of a fighting man. It had taken Bob a solid six months to figure out he had the maturity of a toddler and was intellectually slower than molasses in January.

Czernowitz had given him the same vibe.

That could be good, because toddlers are pretty easy to handle. I mean... you'd have to think so, anyway.

Or... that could be really, really bad.

Because nobody sane gives a toddler a gun.

Bob walked around the building to the public parking on

Eye Street. He was almost at the Buick beater when a woman called out.

"Mr. Richmond?"

Bob turned her way. She hurried up the sidewalk towards him

"Mr. Richmond, I'm Sharmila Singh. Hap Singh is... was my father. Margaret Swain said you're representing the kid they charged."

"Marcus Pell." She was a shade over five feet tall, East Indian, in a purple pant suit and black blouse. Her hair was swept back in a ponytail, and she had no makeup on. Her eyes were darkly ringed from fatigue.

"Miss, we probably shouldn't be talking yet. He still hasn't been arraigned." The last thing he needed was to be attacked by someone's grieving daughter, but he didn't want to just blow her off. The pain was written across her face.

She nodded down the sidewalk. "You see those people on the corner up there?"

A small group of people in business wear were gathered. A few were holding small objects—phones?—but from half a block away Bob couldn't make it out. "What's—"

"Reporters. That's the cream of the local press, such as they are. They're waiting for the deputy chief to make his statement about how they nabbed a killer moments after the act, and how my father will get justice, and just how much he and the department care."

"You sound unconvinced."

She nodded, crossed her arms over her torso, pulling them in tight towards her, her jawline suddenly tense, her lips pursed, her expression glum. "It's all a show. They know that boy didn't do this. They know my father had enemies.

They don't want to catch whoever really did it. Knowing Bakersfield, they're probably working for them."

Bob nodded. He wanted to tell her about the gun, and how it fit, but he didn't know the woman from Adam. She seemed grieving and sad, but that didn't also mean she was stable or trustworthy. And no community was that black and white.

"You say that like you might have some idea on the matter."

She looked around them to see if anyone was close enough to listen. "Some folks are dirty as hell in this city, Mr. Richmond, and my father tried to clean up one corner of it. I know who killed him, and they know who killed him."

7

Bob stared at the diner menu. It was nearly eight o'clock in the evening and his stomach was grumbling. Sharmila hadn't eaten and had a lot to say, so she'd suggested a place a few blocks from the station.

But his expression spoke confused volumes. "Eighteen dollars for a hamburger!?" He shook his head. "Greed is driving this entire country into the ground." Then he realized how bad his timing was. The woman was grieving. "Sorry. You don't need my whining right now."

She frowned and shook her head slightly. "It's okay. I mean... I guess life just has to go on, right?" She sniffed a little. "Bakersfield is a tough city. There's so much money in the valley that to folks making hundreds of thousands a year in the oil industry or agribusiness, these prices don't mean much. But this whole city is just about evenly divided: about half are struggling, and about half are doing real good. And more than ten percent of the population is undocumented, so they get treated quite poorly much of the time."

"Ten percent? You have 40,000 illegals in Bakersfield? That seems... That's incredibly high, right?"

"I believe it's more like 60,000, right around thirteen percent. Something like that. When people have few legal rights... well, that isn't a situation that lends itself to fairness. If it was, people like my father would have had an easier time protecting the health of the average citizen. If it was... he probably wouldn't be dead right now."

She pursed her lips again, holding it together.

"Outside the station you said you know who killed him."

She looked around again to make sure no one was eavesdropping, before lowering her voice. "A drug dealer named Merry Michelsen. He controls a big piece of the meth trade. My father had made combatting that trade a political issue."

"How so?"

"He ran an HMO for years and had to treat kids from meth families, kids living in extreme poverty."

"He was a physician?"

"And a surgeon.

"Intense."

She nodded curtly. "Which is why I became a GP."

"And... he was taking on the drug trade?"

"He'd had enough. He heard they were planning to massively expand the trailer parks on the edge of Oildale, where much of the meth is cooked."

"And he opposed that?"

"Initially, it was sold as more affordable housing. But the more he looked into it, the more the plan seemed to shift from what he thought would be apartment blocks to another trailer park, a massive one. It bothered him. Dad was going to run for Sheriff of Kern County. He might've won, too. Everyone loved him."

Bob ignored the irony of the statement. "Bakersfield has its own police..."

"Yeah, but the trailer parks aren't in Bakersfield. They're in the county. They've got shared policing arrangements and all, but technically, the county sheriff gets a big say in everything, enforcement-wise."

"And someone didn't want him running."

"That's my guess, yeah. He hadn't even made it widely public yet, just let a few key people in the business community know. He filed last Wednesday, had a meeting with business types on Thursday, and Friday..."

"Someone killed him."

"My father... you have to understand, he wasn't around much for his kids. But he was really popular in Bakersfield. He treated generations of school kids, often on his own dime."

"And this Michelsen guy?"

"Expanding the trailer parks, adding new ones... that would mean thousands of new residents... which would mean potentially hundreds of new customers for the dealer who controls them. But... beyond that, I don't know how he's involved. Maybe he's got money in it somehow."

"I'm guessing he's not Oildale's only meth slinger."

"Not by a long shot. It's a real problem. But he's the biggest."

"Tough guy, then?"

"He frightens people. He's also hard to miss. He's a big man with dirty platinum blond hair, sunglasses. Always has an entourage of his thug friends. He showed up at a community meeting and intimidated people. That was three months ago, and the first time he threatened my father. That was when Dad started to see the affordable housing angle as maybe something untoward."

"And it continued?"

"Three weeks ago, Dad was driving home from business in San Jose and a truck tailgated him, bumped him at high speed. They basically tried to run him off the road. If a cop car hadn't passed and given him a chance to pull over, I don't know if..." She paused. "I guess it doesn't matter now."

"And you told the cops this?"

"Uh huh. Have you met the investigating officer in his shooting? Jeb Fowler? Lots of good cops in this town...but a lot of pretty dirty ones, too. Most folks who know him figure he's one of the latter."

"We talked briefly. He exudes jagoff energy."

"Jagoff?" She looked puzzled.

"Eastern thing. He's an asshole, basically."

"Yeah, that fits. I went to high school with him and he was a piece of work even then. His partner's okay, but not the brightest bulb at the bulb store, if you catch my drift."

"I got the same impression."

"Officer David Czernowitz," she said. "But everyone's called him 'Witty' since he was little."

"Because... he's not bright? Ouch."

"Yeah, well... he never seemed too bothered by it. But like I said, he's not the sharpest knife in the drawer, and I'm not sure he ever really got the joke. Even in high school, he was doing pretty much anything Jeb said. I have to admit though... he's still awful cute. Had a thing for me for a while."

She played with her necklace when she said it, and Bob had the feeling maybe the crush had run the other way. "So his partner Jeb is his buddy?"

"Sure. I mean, it always seemed a bit more abusive than that. Jeb saved him from some trouble once, when they were little. So David was always worried about hurting Jeb's feelings, or offending Jeb. And Jeb wasn't what you'd call kind to him."

"Hmm," Bob said.

"What?"

"Nothing. Well... not really, because I don't know enough about them. But there's a certain behavioral profile I learned about in the military, the low-empathy individual who befriends a slower-witted one to take advantage."

"That's about the case of it, I guess," she said. "Witty's just a little dumb. I mean, not so stupid as to not remember stuff. He can learn and such. He passed school and all, but he wasn't going on to educational greatness. He didn't make good decisions, or know how to handle stuff. He was sort of dazed. Professionally, I'm never supposed to diagnose someone from afar, but if I was forced to, I'd say he has ADHD, maybe a bit of Fetal Alcohol Spectrum Disorder, from his momma's drinking problem."

"And he's a cop?"

"There are people in every walk of life who deal with developmental disabilities, Bob, people who are otherwise gifted in all sorts of ways. So you really never can tell."

"Hmph," Bob grumbled.

"What? "

"Well... you basically just repeated how a shrink in Vegas described me. He thinks I have ADHD and PTSD simultaneously. It shows up similar symptoms to what they used to call Aspergers and now call Autism Spectrum Disorder One. So it's hard to tell them apart."

"Wow. That's difficult," she said.

Bob shrugged nonchalantly. "It seems it to you, I guess. It's all normal to me. I mean, those are two of the symptoms, being hyper-focused and unemotional. But that can cause attachment issues, not to mention a little depression, too. I don't really understand it, and I need to if I want to get the most out of my life. So I'm looking for a second opinion. That's why I was going to Seattle, before Marcus was arrested."

"It sounds complicated."

"It is."

Their food arrived and the waitress set it down and offered refills before departing.

Bob took a bite from his burger and chewed it quickly. "So assuming you've got the right guy, and this Michelsen guy is behind it, how do we prove it?" He frowned, thinking back to the arresting officer's report. "Why that alley, for one?"

She stared at her omelet, picking at it with a fork but not eating. "I... couldn't tell you. Dad and I... we didn't talk much in... in the last year." She pursed her lips tight, holding back tears, emotional weights crushing her. "I... Oh, God." She had to stop talking. She grabbed the paper napkin from the table and covered her mouth for a moment, then dabbed at her eyes, clearing tears. "I'm sorry, I shouldn't..."

"Don't apologize for crying. You're not wrong. There's nothing worse than losing someone you love."

"Except maybe losing them when you've been fighting, and aren't talking. I... I was so angry at him for placing first his career, then his business and then the HMO above his family, above retiring and being here for the rest of us. My mother died of cancer six years ago, and he wasn't there for her enough when she was in treatment. She'd insist on taking care of things herself, anyway, but he didn't have to use that as an excuse to throw himself into his business."

"It felt like he was selfish," Bob reasoned.

"I got angry. He didn't pay much attention to me after about age twelve, or to my younger sister. I... I was such a bad daughter in the last year. I went to work for a competing HMO. I wanted to punish him, force him to care, even though I knew he loved me, that he was just distracted. But... even when I was a 'rebellious' teen, we still had good talks. He was a good dad. And now I'll never get to talk to him again."

The tears began to flow freely. Bob stayed respectfully silent. He didn't want to think about how she was feeling, though. That would bring about his own memories, of losing Maggie, of the Sarge. Of the men he let down in Tehran, when Team Seven almost spun into oblivion. Of Sister Eva. Of Ellie Grainger's husband, weeping softly at her pointless, meaningless death.

So instead, he tried not to think about anything.

He chewed on his burger, and Sharmila wept.

8

OILDALE, CALIFORNIA

The man standing in front of the old wooden desk looked unwell. His light brown hair was long and greasy, his grubby string vest and black shorts stiffened by encrusted dirt. He was rail thin, bones jutting out over sallow cheeks, most of his teeth missing, the remainder shrinking from rot.

More than that, he looked ill at ease, shuffling his feet, holding his arms across himself defensively, not so much crossed as hugging himself like a shock victim.

His dark-brown dot pupils contemplated the two objects on the desk, flitting between them, ignoring the man sitting behind it. It was clear he was having difficulty deciding.

Behind the desk, Merry Michelsen shifted in his seat, a gold-painted Louis XVI knockoff wooden armchair, built for his larger frame, creaking under each shift of his four hundred pounds.

An array of gold chains and jewelry was half hidden under his open grey tracksuit top. He tossed his bleached-blonde hair a little as he studied the man.

It wasn't like he had contempt for his customers; they were addicts, and they needed their medicine.

He just didn't feel much about them at all.

Or anyone.

Instead, Merry had always enjoyed *things*. New things to play with, new things to do. Something new every day. Merry liked the visceral, anything that could make him feel immediate power or pleasure.

That's why he liked the game he played with the junkies when they couldn't pay up.

He had to make an example of them. Not paying was disrespectful. He liked to think it was giving them a chance to be brave.

"I tell you what, Critter Joe: you're going to make that decision eventually, because you know the alternative is going to be a whole hell of a lot worse," he said, gesturing to the table.

Critter Joe looked down at the two objects again. Ahead of Michelsen's left hand sat the old electronic board game Operation, a torso of a man cartooned onto a tin board in a flat rectangular box the size of a medicine cabinet. Holes had been cut out of his body over the location of vital organs— roughly speaking. In each hole was a plastic organ that had to be "removed" by metal tweezers, without touching the sides of the hole.

They'd come with joke names, but Merry had covered seven off with masking tape. Each of the remaining five had been relabeled accordingly: heart, lungs, liver, kidneys, eyes.

Normally, hitting the side of an organ cavity just set off a red lightbulb in the "patient's" nose.

But Merry had a different rulebook altogether.

"I see you looking at that there Operation game and I see

them possibilities in your mind's eye, Critter Joe. Them permutations," he said.

There was a light giggle from the other side of the trailer's open-plan living room/kitchen, where his bodyguard and a pair of goons sat, waiting to resume a card game.

"I see you doing the necessary calculations. I see you considering that with Operation, you get a chance. Pick a card, pluck an organ. But no hands! So... not a good chance, mind. However..." he leaned forward conspiratorially, "... if you can hold them tweezers real steady between them few teeth you've got left, you might get a clean pick. And then you get to walk out of here, free and clear, no debt. All that worry, gone. All that debt, gone, lickety-split."

Critter Joe drew in a breath sharply, his eyes widening at the prospect, the tip of his tongue moistening his lower lip. He owed close to three grand and had nothing left to sell; the idea of erasing his debt...

"You can buy a lot of meth with the three grand you owe me, Critter Joe. Or... well, if you don't want to take your chances, you can always play 'Spin the Sig'."

In front of Michelsen's other hand, a Sig Sauer pistol's trigger guard had been placed over top of a metal letter spike, so that the gun could be spun around in a circle. Under it was a colored card, a pie-chart of options, each triangle listing a different body part. "You play the pistol... you know you're going to get shot. But it won't be fatal, in all likelihood, and you'll still owe me my cash money, plus interest. You play Operation, maybe you get away scot-free."

Critter Joe inhaled deeply, the notion reaching down deep in him, anticipation welling up.

"But if you hit the sides of a hole and a buzzer sounds..."

Critter Joe looked down at his emaciated, grubby torso.

"I know what you're thinking. Can I make do without a kidney? Without my eyes? 'Cos you sound that buzzer, and that's what I'll take. 'Course... you pick a 'liver' or 'heart' card, your future will be real brief. Ah! I know! I know... you're worrying about whether I'll ever get my money back, good soul that you are, should you perish and depart this here mortal coil. But don't you fret none: a healthy heart can fetch a good buck in L.A."

Critter Joe's face blanched at the prospect.

Michelsen's eyes narrowed. "Mind you... you won't be around to find out how well I did. That's the problem with organs, I guess. Body don't function without 'em, mostly."

Merry was especially proud of the 'eyes' target, he'd told people. He'd clipped an extra little hole out of the tin board himself and found a tiny ceramic set of peepers on a ceramic rat model. They were precious, he'd said, just like his momma's miniature doll collection.

"So you go ahead and draw a card. Or... you play Spin the Sig, take your medicine, come back in two weeks with my cash money."

Critter Joe reached out towards the Operation game. But his hand stopped halfway there, frozen by indecision.

He frowned, staring at the hand. He was probably noticing how much it shook without his first fix of the day, Merry figured, that first acrid puff of methamphetamine smoke. He looked down at the tiny set of tweezers connected to the board by a thin wire.

The tip of his tongue traced the few mossy remaining teeth he had left. Merry could see his gears turning, trying to imagine holding the tweezers steady between his front teeth but also squeezing them together, the pressure, the chance of them slipping.

The expression shifted from hope to dread. He'd heard about Operation, everyone had. And they'd all heard about Cody Dufresne just a few weeks earlier, how he'd lost his liver but then bled out, unable to afford proper care.

He hung his head. "I'll Spin the Sig," he said, defeated.

Merry leaned on one elbow and felt a swell of disappointment. Old rich guys would pay a hundred grand through a Dark Web broker for a healthy heart to transplant. Critter Joe's probably wasn't that healthy after nearly a decade on meth—he was only in his twenties but looked fifty. But the buyer wouldn't know that, and there was no recourse if a stolen heart failed.

It eliminated buyer remorse and made it the best kind of business deal Merry could imagine: a free product, a big payday, and no recriminations.

He sighed. "Alright then. Go on, get it over with," he muttered.

Critter Joe leaned over and spun the pistol.

The barrel stopped on "left hand."

Merry felt his annoyance grow. "Dang, not even a knee?" He shook his head. "I am too goddamn kind to you, Critter Joe! Too goddamned kind by half." He stood up and slipped the pistol off the spike, working the slide to chamber a round. "Left hand, palm out like you're begging for food," he ordered.

Critter Joe held out his hand then closed both eyes. He opened one, squinting hard as he looked down, waiting for...

The bang was loud, his scream almost its equal, the bullet tearing through the center of his palm, destroying tendons and ligaments. Critter Joe collapsed to one side, moaning, clutching the wound as blood poured out onto the linoleum floor tile.

Merry nodded towards his goons. "Go on, get him a dang bandage before he bleeds out. Then get his ass out of here. I don't want to see you in Oildale again, Critter Joe! Not unless you got something for me. You feel me? You've got two weeks, by which time the interest will have it up to five grand, cash money. You come back empty, you play Operation."

His phone buzzed. He retrieved it from the track suit jacket pocket as they dragged the moaning junkie away.

The number was familiar.

He hit the green button and put it to his ear.

"What you want?"

The voice was calm, professional. "We have a matter that might complicate things. Our mutual problem was not dealt with, apparently, at least not completely. There's a new player, a lawyer named Bob Richmond."

"Uh. A lawyer?"

"Not local and no pull here as far as we can tell. We'd like him to reconsider taking the case."

"Uh huh. And how do you suppose I convince him?"

"However you choose. As usual, I have no interest in your methods, just that you get it done. But don't kill him. We don't need any more attention than this is already getting."

"And where might we find this feller?"

"I had someone tail him. He's staying at Mel Feeney's place on Eighteenth Street, room seven. Same motel the boy was at. Once we've got him out of town, we can steer a lawyer we know the boy's way, a pro bono gesture of goodwill. Even the dumbest judge can't help but convict him if we're running his defense."

"Okay then. A good scare it is," Michelsen said.

"Let me know when it's done and he's gone."

The call dropped.

"Jonah, Terry!" he yelled to the remaining card players. "Grab Diego and head on over to Feeney's. There's a feller in room seven, name of Bob Richmond. You go on down, give him a lesson, let him know what happens to fellers what get up in our business, you hear? But... don't break nothing. We want him scared, not running to Five-O."

Not that it bothered him too much if they got it wrong and beat the man to death. The real problem had been Hap Singh, not the kid they'd framed. And Hap Singh was dead.

Old news. And once the kid goes down for it, a shitload more money. Maybe get me a pad in Palm Springs, like Liberace. Get me a proper Boy Toy and a diamond-studded piano. Move on up in this world.

9

Sharmila provided a list of names, people her father had spoken with about the trailer park project. It was mercifully short, Bob noted as he parked the Buick in front of his motel room door.

He got out.

"Everything go okay?"

He looked right. Mel Feeney, the motel owner, was sitting in a rocking chair on the narrow porch, just ahead of the rooms and door to the main office. His face was heavily tanned, creased from years of sun damage. He wore a brown cowboy hat, a black leather vest over his denim shirt, and held a pipe in one hand and a book in the other.

"About as expected," Bob said. "Thank you again for being so nice to Marcus since he's been here. He mentioned you helped him get settled."

"Uh huh... My wife's passed sixteen years now, so I do have some time on my hands, and our kids... well, I'm getting on, so they're long gone. Nice to be of some help. And he's a fine kid."

"That he is."

"You find the police station okay?"

"Yeah, hard to miss. They were about as glad to see me as you'd expect."

"Uh huh." Feeney chuckled. "You'll find Bakersfield's sort of all of one and none of the other; by which I mean, they either love or they hate you, but either way, eventually you're going to find out how they feel."

"Yeah... about that, I get a lot of bleak messaging here, like being adjacent to a desert has sort of imprinted this whole stark vibe."

Feeney looked uncertain. "Yeah... I mean, I guess. When life's feast or famine, a whole lot of differing narratives spring up. I lived here my whole life, wouldn't want to live anywhere else. Mind, I've always been healthy, had good parents, never lacked for work or things to do. And most of my years were before it grew so darn big, got so polluted. Lot of folks here, they don't have it so good. But if you're doing okay, working hard, making a buck... well, then Bakersfield is a fine community."

"But with plenty of issues."

"Son, I am seventy-two years old. If I spent my entire life just focusing on raising and solving problems, I would be one miserable sonuvabitch. Change comes real slow, and will take longer than I got. So, I take the good and bad, and there's a lot of good here too: a great American tradition of country music, and rodeo, of wide-open spaces, of outdoor life and great food. Of family, and faith and looking out for each other."

Bob understood. He'd just never felt it, that level of dedication to a singular place, a geographic home. And the closest he'd come to family after the deaths of his mother and Maggie had been with his units in the Marines, and with Team Seven.

The closest I had to family was a group of trained killers.

"Still..." Feeney continued. "Can't say I like the idea of Marcus in the stir for any length of time. Meth is big business here and tweakers are unpredictable."

Marcus.

And Dawn.

Stop feeling sorry for yourself, Bob. What did Dawn always say? You make your own family, right? But only if you treat them as such, and appreciate what you have.

"And that's why I'm going to make sure he doesn't spend much time there," Bob said.

To their right, twin headlights swung across the narrow parking lot. A truck squealed to a halt, the back end sliding, fishtailing slightly, Kid Rock blaring from the cab, a country rock tune mangling the melody to "Werewolves of London."

Or possibly "Sweet Home Alabama." Bob wasn't sure which.

Who's this, now? "Friends of yours, Mel?" he suggested, as three men climbed out of the cab. They held beer cans and were laughing and hollering.

"I expect not," Mel said. He leaned forward in his chair. "I best get my Remington from the office, just in case."

Bob waved him off. "No... don't worry about that. If they're here for me..."

"You're presently our only guest, and I'm pretty darn sure they ain't here for me."

"I'll try and defuse this as politely as possible."

"Uh huh," Feeney said doubtfully. "Tell me, friend Bob, you don't happen to be carrying per chance?"

"I do, as a matter of fact. But it won't come to that. It usually doesn't."

"Usually?"

10

The three men strolled over. They were broad-chested, one in a black string vest, another in a Lakers jersey, the third in a white-and-blue Dodgers home shirt. The biggest had a straw cowboy hat, while his friends wore ballcaps.

Bob got the immediate sense they were either a whole lot of fun, or a whole lot of trouble.

Cowboy Hat nodded his way and gestured with a friendly raise of his beer can. "Howdy!" he said. "Would you happen to be Bob Richmond, by any chance?"

From behind him, Feeney intoned, "Jonah Kepler? That you, boy?"

Cowboy Hat nodded his way. "I know you, old man?"

"Uh huh. I just remember your days with the Drillers when you was a dead cert to go Division One..."

"Yeah." The cowboy looked irritated at the mention. "Long time ago now."

"What happened, son? You blow a knee out or something?"

"Well now... that ain't really none of your bees' wax, now, is it?"

"Jonah here used to be a guard for the Bakersfield High Varsity Drillers."

Jonah turned his attention back to Bob. "Like I said, you Bob Richmond?"

"Who's asking?"

Jonah grinned a little at that, nodding. He slugged back the last of his can of Stroh's, before crushing it and tossing the can over his shoulder. "You're a funny guy. He's funny, ain't he, fellers?"

"As long as you don't mean funny looking, I'll take it," Bob said. "What can I do you for, gents?"

"Well now, I think it would be better if we talked about that in private, right, boys? Maybe the old man would like to make hisself scarce right about now."

"Bob..." Feeney began to say.

Bob held up a hand. "It's okay. You go on in the office, Mr. F."

"You sure?"

"Oh... as much as anyone can be, yeah."

Feeney got up and shuffled his way over to the office door, going inside and closing it behind him.

Jonah and his two friends closed the gap until they were just a few feet away. Bob didn't see any obvious weapon bulges, but one of Jonah's friends had a buck knife sheath on his belt, the handle probably under his shirt.

"We came over to deliver a message, Mr. Richmond," Jonah said.

"Mister? How polite!" Bob said.

"Uh huh. You'll find people do sort of value that round here. We come to deliver a message."

"Yeah... you said that part already."

Jonah frowned. "We come to let you know folks around here don't like folk from up north coming down here and killing and robbing people blind. Your boy, Marcus Pell..."

"What about him?"

"He ain't your client no more," he said tersely, an order, demanding compliance. "He's going to be seeking new and different legal representation. And you are going to be driving yourself back to Los Angeles. Do you get what I'm saying? Do you understand what I'm telling you?"

"I do," Bob said, nodding.

Jonah looked puzzled. "Easy as that?"

"Of course. Absolutely." Bob kept nodding. "You gents don't have to worry about me in the slightest. I'll just go."

Jonah glanced at his friends, unsure. It was clear from his confusion, Bob figured, that he'd expected some sort of resistance, or been ordered to provide incentives. The ex-jock hooked a thumb over his shoulder, towards their pickup. "We leave and... you just... roll on out of here? Just like that?"

"Absolutely. I'll pack up my stuff."

"Uh huh." Jonah crossed his arms. "Maybe we'll just wait here then while you go ahead and do that."

Bob's eyes widened in mock surprise. "Oh! You mean NOW! I thought you meant in a week, after my client is free."

Jonah's expression shifted to cold warning. "Like I said before, boys, the man thinks he's funny. Diego here, he's been training in mixed martial arts for... what... over a year now. And he's got... what, twenty, thirty pounds on you, son. Maybe we let him convince you that you want to go right now. How about that?"

"A *year*?" Bob said. "My goodness! Probably has a belt or two, right?"

"Already got my orange in judo," Diego said. Then he frowned, unsure if he was being mocked. Then he screwed up his features angrily, jabbing a forefinger in Bob's direction. "Mister, you got a real big mouth for someone who's been here nine seconds."

Bob's temptation was to point out that at least he'd still be conscious in nine seconds. But three against one was never a sensible fight, and all three were big men. *Don't start getting cocky now, Bobby. You're getting older, not younger.* "Well now, I don't mean nothing by it, Diego," Bob said. "But as an attorney, I have a responsibility to my client…"

Jonah flexed his biceps, hands ahead of him. He stepped forward until he was looking up at Bob slightly. "Then perhaps we need to teach you what folks think of slimy lawyers," he said, jabbing Bob in the chest with his index finger once, twice… "Perhaps you need to pack up your shit and get on out of here, or else."

His index finger shot out to jab Bob in the chest one more time for emphasis. Bob snatched it with his left hand, grasping it and the middle finger together, twisting them over and then pulling them back, both fingers snapping at the knuckle bone.

"AIEGGH!" Jonah screamed, stumbling sideways, doubling over as he grasped at his broken hand with his free left. "SUM'BITCH!" he bellowed. "AIEGHGH! FUCK! FUUUUCK! DIEGO! FUCK HIM UP!'

Diego stepped into the punch. Bob was expecting it, adrenaline kicking in, violence slowed to a rhythmic pattern he'd seen so many times before as the 'zone' kicked in. He bobbed away, turning a few degrees, the punch whistling by his cheek.

Diego's momentum threw him slightly off balance but

his MMA training kicked in. As he stepped back, he half-turned and threw his elbow towards Bob's face, trying to salvage something. Bob turned his head in time with the move, the elbow barely grazing his cheek as he took a step out of range.

Diego paused, shocked that neither blow had landed.

"I'll give you this," Bob offered. "You're not completely shit. I mean... by pro standards, you're not even the fly that lands on it. But for an amateur..."

Diego's face reddened. He and his friend charged forward. Bob dropped low, driving both fists upward in perfect unison, aiming two inches past his targets, the double groin punch catching both men flush. Diego clasped his knees together and tried to maintain his balance, bellowing loudly as his friend collapsed.

"My... my junk," he moaned.

Bob righted himself.

Jonah's anger was overcoming his pain. He strode towards the older man, reaching into his rear waistband with his unbroken hand. Bob sprinted at him, not giving him time to draw the gun, turning side-on to lock up Jonah's arm as it came clear.

He wrenched downwards, smacking the man's hand against his knee, the gun popping loose even as he head-butted Jonah across the bridge of the nose, the bone snapping.

The pistol bounced to a standstill on the asphalt.

Colt Gold Cup Trophy nine mil. Hmmm. Nice gun.

The ex-jock dropped to one knee. Bob hit him on the side of the chin, just a tap on the mental nerve, enough to turn his legs to rubber.

He collapsed to the ground, stunned.

"Now... in case I haven't made it crystal clear, I'm not going anywhere without my friend. Take that back to whoever sent you."

The three men moaned as they dragged themselves to their feet. Bob picked up the pistol and popped the magazine, tossing it sideways, into the scrub of the adjacent lot. He wiped the pistol down quickly with his shirt, then chucked it in the same direction.

The men began to crawl and stagger towards the truck. Bob rushed up behind Terry and gave him a hard boot to the rear end. "Go on, get out of here!"

Two of them climbed into the cab. Jonah leaned against the door frame, panting, blood streaming from both nostrils. "Broke my fucking hand! This ain't over!" he threatened.

"You might want to rethink that," Bob said. "I like you the least of all. Your parents may have named you Jonah, but come back here, and I'll wail on your ass."

Keep them thinking. Plus, it was a good line, and it would've been a shame to waste it.

Jonah glared at him, one hand trying to stop the blood flow from his nose. He climbed into the cab after his friends and slammed the door. The pickup kicked up gravel as it peeled out.

A few feet away, the office door opened. Mel Feeney peeked out from behind it. "I saw it all through the window. You want me to call the police?"

Bob shook his head, keeping his eyes on the road, wary of a return or shot from the distance. "From what I'm told, I'm not sure how helpful they'll be. Besides, I'm guessing the three of them got the message."

"Uh huh. I saw that. You're one mighty strange example of a lawyer, if you don't mind my saying."

"Yeah... well, I've always figured a good defense starts with self-defense," Bob said. "Something like that."

"Uh huh. Sure. And you just picked all that up at your local YMCA, did you?"

Bob glanced over. "Why, Mr. Feeney, do I detect a note of sarcasm? Isn't that against your local tradition of plain-talking, homespun directness?"

"Uh huh. You could say that. But in return, I'd note that you just kicked the whole hardy living shit out of three large local boys in about one minute flat. I get the sense I'm not the only one massaging the truth a mite. Most lawyers don't hit that hard, I reckon. You a former cop, or athlete or something? Green Berets or some such?"

"Or some such." Bob looked over at his room. "I can't stay here, obviously."

"Ptthh!" Feeney waved a hand at him. "Don't you fret! This is a big city now, but it ain't that big. Everybody here knows me. Ain't none of them coming after me."

"No, but they'll come after me again. What if they torch the place or something?"

"Well then... I get the insurance and get to retire to my little cabin near Merida on the Yucatan, and we're all winners. Except maybe whoever does the torching, after what I just saw."

Bob shook his head. "Look, it's not that simple. I have a history with this kind of thing, a friend in Memphis who—"

Feeney cut him off. "Not up to you," he said grumpily. "My place. You're staying."

"Fine." Bob tried not to sound exasperated. The man was just trying to be hospitable, albeit stubbornly.

"Well then, it's settled," the motel manager said. "Marcus

ain't even here, and I already feel a little better about his prospects..."

"Good!"

"I mean, assuming some feller don't shoot you dead first."

11

TUCSON, ARIZONA

The spider was small and spindly, and it moved with deliberate caution. It skittered across the hardwood kitchen counter a few inches at a time, stopping, waiting to make sure it remained safe, then skittering a few more inches.

Three feet away, Han Binh sat parallel to the counter, tied to a wooden kitchen chair, his eye level just above the counter surface. His hair was dyed black, unconvincingly. He was nearly eighty-five years old, wizened to a stature that belied his fearsome history as a colonel in the Viet Cong.

He watched the spider's approach as beads of sweat traced their way down his forehead and temples.

"Please... sir..." His mouth felt parched. The dry cleaner's building was air conditioned, but he was thirsty nonetheless, unsure of how long he had been unconscious. He'd opened the shop, he'd stepped into the back room, where the most profitable—and illegal—part of his trade took place.

And then the lights had gone out.

The spider skittered towards him. His eyes widened. "Sir... I implore you..."

"Shut up." The man whose attention he was trying to reach was across the room, rifling through the metal gun cabinet in the corner.

As if sensing Han's predicament, the spider raised one leg aloft... then resumed its crawl, more slowly but steadily, in his direction.

"Sir... I implore you. There is a spider..."

The man looked over the shoulder of his leather jacket. He was ugly, Han thought, in a unique sort of way. His nose had been broken numerous times, and was crooked, with a bump in the bridge. One eyelid was partially covered, replaced by scar tissue from a bad burn. A blade-thin scar traced the man's neck in a half-circle, just below his Adam's apple. His left earlobe had been sheared half off. His dirty blonde hair was shaved at the bottom, parted in the middle.

"Shut up or I'll just kill you now," he hissed.

Han tried to place the accent. He sounded like the Dutch pederast who'd stayed in the family hotel in Hanoi when Han was a little boy.

His captor glanced briefly at the counter. "It's just a bloody spider, you coward. If that worries you, you are going to have a very uncomfortable few hours before I kill you."

He went back to searching the cabinet.

Han's eyes flitted back to the arachnid. "He is quite close to me now. This spider..."

"It is *tiny*!" the other man blustered. "In South Africa, we have spiders so big they could cover your face while you sleep and suffocate you! Yissus!"

The elderly man felt his breath shortening, panic beginning to set in. "But sir—"

"I told you—"

"But sir, this spider is very dangerous. I know it is small... but it is a brown recluse. Its bite causes flesh to necrotize, to blacken and die. It... would be most unpleasant if it..." He froze. The spider was just inches away now, forelegs reaching over the edge of the counter, the tip of each just about brushing the arc of his ear.

A fingerless-gloved hand slammed down upon the counter and the creature, smashing it to bits. The stocky South African shook away the debris, then scraped the palm of his glove on the edge of the counter, extracting the last of it. "You think that's dangerous and unpleasant..."

"Yeah," Han said wearily. "I know, you are much more. But... I do not have any idea who you are."

"I'm Van Kamp."

Was that supposed to mean something? Han shook his head blearily. "Okay. You're Dutch and still a complete stranger to me."

Van Kamp scoffed. "Dutch! Hah! Some black market dealer you are!"

"Because I don't know you?"

"Not true, surely. I am the world's greatest living assassin," Van Kamp said matter-of-factly.

"Doubtful," Han said.

Van Kamp leaned on the counter, perplexed. "Eh? Why? Who's better?"

Han shrugged as much as his wrist bonds would allow. "Someone nobody knows. From your appearance, it is clear you have had many conflicts, some that perhaps did not go as you would have liked."

"Yeah? So? I'm still standing, aren't I, kak kop? My

contract completion rate remains one hundred percent. What the devil are you blathering about?"

"The best is someone so good you never knew they were there. And I imagine there are quite a few men who fit that description. They would probably consider you... uncouth."

Van Kamp crossed his beefy forearms and stared at his captive, nodding. Then he smiled broadly. "Yeah... they don't count."

"And why is that?"

"Because they're not warriors. They're cowards, vermin who hide in the shadows. But me? I wear who I am proudly. I have nothing to hide. I am known and feared. Probably no more so than by the man I seek. He owes me. Most just fear what I'll do to them. But he and I have history."

Han wiggled his head from side to side. "Eh... I am not so sure. He must have you spooked pretty good, or you wouldn't be tearing this place up, looking for... what, exactly?"

"I suppose if I just ask you about a client, you won't tell me."

"Of course. The forgery business somewhat relies on discretion."

"Good. So, I am not wrong to search. I figure you made this man papers in the last month, at most. But I also figure little ferrets like you, Han... well, you'd keep copies for leverage, correct? You'd keep something to hold over your customers in case they became dangerous."

"It's a theory," Han said, which seemed better than admitting he was right.

"And I suppose since you are an ancient, decrepit piece of detritus, you would keep hard copies rather than digital. I noticed your drafting table. You do most of your work by hand."

"Yes... well, you have your art form, I have mine," Han said. But the man was dangerously accurate, he decided. "If you're going to tear the place apart and kill me, what do you need me for now?"

Van Kamp took a few paces and stopped so that he was standing over the old man. "I thought we might be able to speed up the process by you telling me where and what to look for. It's the only way to make sure it ends quickly."

"What? What ends quickly?"

"The pain I'm going to introduce to your life." Van Kamp bent at the waist, hands propped on his thighs, like a school mistress lecturing a small child. "You see, I know who you really are, Han Binh. I know what a brutal, nasty fellow you were in the war, running that POW camp. Someone admirable once, really, a man who knew no limits in seeking power. And now... now, look at you. A washed-up actor running a dry cleaner's."

"Life takes its turns," Han said with a practiced sigh. "But I did two episodes of *Simon and Simon*, and two of *The Fall Guy*. That's something."

"Well, you won't have to worry about your legacy much longer. I'm going to torture you, Han," Van Kamp leered, "and I'm going to greatly enjoy myself doing it. I'm going to introduce pain to every part of your body. I will leave the teeth and the testes to last, of course, as their excruciating nerve agony is the sweetest ecstasy to me. And before I'm done, you're going to help me find Bob Singleton. I know he was here, Han. I know you helped him, because you are the only man in the southwest qualified to forge papers to the exacting standards he would demand. And when I am done, I will kill you."

Han was sure he knew who Van Kamp meant. He'd only

had one high-rolling client in four months, and he'd had a set of Nevada ID made up in the name of Bob MacMillan. "I have no idea who you're talking about."

Van Kamp smiled again, though it was barely a grim line; a man unaccustomed to good humor. "Well, that is just fine, my decrepit friend. Just fine. I have killed so many men in so many countries, I've just about lost track..."

"Oh... I doubt that," Han offered wearily. "I imagine you're the type who keeps a firm count. Probably trophies, too."

The smile disappeared. "And you won't be added to the tally, as no one is paying me for you," the South African said. "Typically, I would use my necklace, you see." He reached down and lifted it out of his t-shirt for Han to see. "It's titanium, very strong. The locket on the end was my mother's. She made me hard, like her, beat me daily like a dog. One day, when I got tired of her discipline, I strangled her with the chain it was on, a platinum rope thing one of her male clients bought her. She was an expensive whore, my mother, but she died squealing like a pig. I throttled the life out of her. I think she would have approved, had it been anyone else."

"Charming."

"That chain did not survive the act in question, so I got one made to replace it, one strong enough to throttle a thousand throats. But I save it for paying jobs. You? You're just a little bit of fun, a healthy scream or two to start my week. Right? Now... I suppose for the sake of posterity, we should do this correctly. I'll start with the fingernails."

He reached into his coat pocket and withdrew a hypodermic needle. He took off the red plastic cap and held it up to the light, flicking the syringe to ensure it was free of air bubbles. "This has a particularly irritating form of botulinum toxin in it. I'll slide the needle into the nerves under each of your fingernails, and it will exacerbate the pain a thousand-fold."

He took a deep breath, as if drinking in the majesty of it all. "Are you ready, old man?" Van Kamp crouched and began to insert the needle into the quick of Han's forefinger.

The pain was agonizing and Han felt his entire body tense to rigidity, the sensation so awful he couldn't even scream, the sound trapped in his chest. "CUH... CUH... CUH..." he repeated, unable to form a word.

His torturer looked up at him, wide-eyed with a mix of joy and wonder, as if giddy with happiness, his monstrousness overcome by a child-like glee. "YES! YES! That's how it starts! A little bit of shock protecting you from the worst of it! Soon, you will scream, old man. You will scream like you have never screamed before. And then you'll tell me what I want. But... hopefully not too quickly. By the time I'm done, Han Binh, you're going to wish that spider had bitten you. Because suffocating to death would be sweet sorrow compared to the short time you have left."

The needle pushed in further and Han let out a terrified shriek. Van Kamp smiled broadly this time, as if feeling something inside. Not pity, or guilt, or any recognizable human emotion, just an animal's excitement at the imminent death of prey.

"And then, after six months of him running, I can add Bob Singleton to my tally properly."

Han prayed that his screams might be heard outside. But the place had cinder-block walls. He knew it was in vain; he knew he could scream until his lungs collapsed, and no one would hear.

12

BAKERSFIELD, CALIFORNIA

Bob slept fitfully. He'd spent a half-hour before bunking down to set up a crude alarm: a trip line using some of Mr. Feeney's fishing line, connected to bottles that would shatter when pulled off the window shelf in his motel room.

Not that he expected an immediate return. If the goons worked for Merry Michelsen, the meth dealer Sharmila had mentioned, they'd be trying to figure out how a lawyer handled them so easily, and how far they could push things.

He woke just past dawn, as was his habit, and spent a half-hour with his 5BX workout routine, concluding with five minutes of high-speed, high knee-lift jogging on the spot, his bare feet barely touching the carpet at pace, a fine sweat developing on his brow.

The decades-old workout system had long been abandoned by its inventors, the Canadian Armed Forces, for the brutal toll it could take on joints and its general rigor. But it allowed him to ram intensive exercise into a half hour reliably, and it had worked for two decades, keeping him trim and some of his muscle tone intact even after nearly ten years of mostly sleeping rough.

He showered and checked the news for any sign he was wanted; he didn't expect the officers in Nevada to track him there, and any description probably included his beard. Losing it made him that much harder to pick out of a crowd. But he had to be careful, he knew. Marcus was depending on him.

At least for a few more hours.

Sharmila had been surprised when he suggested they needed a second lawyer to handle the Monday bail hearing, while he investigated. But it saved Nurse Dawn some trouble; Sharmila called her attorney cousin from San Francisco.

They were supposed to meet around eight at the clinic downtown that also served as her HMO's headquarters. Instead, Sharmila called just after seven in the morning. "Feel up for a drive?"

SHARMILA DROVE them across the city and into Oildale. The change was obvious and immediate, downtown replaced by mostly residential blocks, the homes smaller and less expensive, the big backyards and pools disappearing.

It's hardly an inner-city ghetto, Bob thought. *But rich, it ain't.*

They passed a trailer park. "Is that..." Bob began to say.

"Nope," Sharmila said, keeping her eyes on the road. "Oildale has a few."

The lot was off East Petrol Road and Wesley Lane. They pulled up along its edge and parked. "Well... this is it," she said. "If you follow the western edge of the property north, you'll see it hits a stake in the ground eventually. It's sort of a dot from more than an acre away, but..."

Bob opened the car window. He could hear the sound of engines whining. "Is that...?"

"The racetrack. It's just a few blocks northwest of here."

He surveyed the potential trailer park site. "Doesn't look like much." He sniffed. "Smells... sulfurous."

"Natural gas being processed near Barstow. They add a chemical called mercaptan to it so that it's detectable. Then the excess—like everything within three hundred miles—ends up drifting into our valley."

Bob nodded. "Show me Michelsen's trailer park."

She put the car back into gear and rolled past the empty lot. Just south of its entrance, the road led into a vast field of mobile homes, all permanently set on blocks. People milled around, talking in what passed for front yards, kids playing.

"Doesn't feel that bleak. Sure smells it, though." He nodded towards the mountains. "That haze—it looked like it was hanging over downtown when I arrived."

She nodded. "The dust collects other pollutants as well. Pretty normal these days, with so much of the county's topsoil disturbed. There's a lot going on here, a lot of money and productivity. Not a lot of worry about the effects on any of these folks, really."

Behind them, Bob heard the squeal of dusty brake pads. He checked his six. A moment later, an older dark blue Dodge truck with a Confederate flag on the door rolled slowly past their vehicle.

Through the passenger window, a stone-faced man with a short brown crewcut watched them, his eyes dark, a half cigarette clamped between his lips, smoke billowing. He raised one hand and flapped his fingers in a downward motion, a blunt little half-wave.

"Recognize him?" Bob asked.

"I do. That's Tommy Kopec. Famous local trouble. Tommy Clobber to his friends and the many frightened souls he's beaten down over the years. He's made the news a few times."

"Charming."

"His twin brother Vern was probably driving."

"Michelsen's men?"

"That would be my guess, or they wouldn't be near the place. Vern's famously slow. He beat a murder charge last year. The paper said he was caught in the middle of removing some guy's kidneys."

"Excuse me?" That was a new one.

"In less-than-sanitary conditions," Sharmila noted.

"And they both harassed Hap for months?"

"Uh huh. Hard to tell them apart, except Vern's got a big scar above his left eye," she said forlornly, like they were in the last place she wanted to be. "Dad didn't tell me at first, but the pressure in the last two months really got to him. Gangsters rolling by his place, miming shooting him through the car window, using their fingers as guns, that sort of thing. Stunting, the police called it. Bottles thrown at his front door, windows shattered, his tires slashed."

"Frightening."

"They showed up at my place as well, when he came over for Sunday supper," Sharmila said. "My husband came out with his double-barrel twelve-gauge, let them know what would happen if there was a return visit."

Nice to know the hardy pioneer spirit extends to both sides,

Bob thought wryly. *Nobody deserves to be terrorized by people like this.*

"And did Tommy Clobber and his brother ever show?"

"They came by the clinic one day. One of our clients recognized his former meth dealer and knows him to be supplied by Michelsen."

"And the police..."

"The police had little interest."

"To be fair," Bob said, "that isn't much they can work with. They'd be tough to individually identify, tough to make the argument it was a deliberate threat without a stated rationale, tough to even pick them up for questioning on that."

Sharmila frowned. "I know."

"Sorry... I just thought—"

"It's not like we're all yokels, Bob. I don't need everything explained to me."

"Yeah. Sorry about that."

"It's fine. I know you're just trying to help. And most of the police here have been nothing but good to us."

Bob gestured to the empty land stretching out from the town. "So your dad's idea was to stop this from going ahead?"

"If he could. He figured as sheriff, he could make a strong law enforcement-supported argument that any new affordable housing should be proper homes, built at cost, sold to the new owner through a combination of sweat equity in building them and low-interest or no-interest loans."

"Because nice neighborhoods don't attract drug dealers, they deter them."

"Pretty much, yeah. And initially, he thought he'd get some help from the local business community. About a quarter of the undeveloped land was owned by Jenkins Mechanical."

"Marcus's employer on his job placement?" Bob said. "That's darn coincidental."

"Possibly just that, however," Sharmila proposed. "For such a big city, Bakersfield can be awful small sometimes. And Oildale never won any awards for sophistication."

"They didn't take his ideas seriously?"

"He said they did, said he spoke with Dick Jenkins personally and he seemed enthused."

"I sense a 'but'..."

"You got that right," Sharmila said.

The locals were looking their way now, wondering why someone was hanging around the periphery watching them.

"Then last week, when he had his business community meetings, he called me. Said he'd just met with Jenkins and was steaming mad. I tried to get some detail out of him but he said he'd tell me more after he got home."

"And..."

"And he never made it. He was shot about a block away from their offices."

At the edge of the lot, near the trailer park, a child had wandered in their direction, curious. He was blond and deeply tanned, with a mullet, in cutoff jean shorts and a baseball shirt, maybe seven or eight years old and barefoot. He got within about twenty feet before tentatively holding up a hand, like he was in class.

"Can we help you, son?" Sharmila asked.

He wandered closer. He looked sheepish, blushing. "You were here with Dr. Hap?"

"I was, about a month ago."

"I heard about that," he said. "He come up and visit us. I'm... real sorry he's dead."

"You liked him?" Bob asked.

The boy nodded. "He... He was nice to me and my sister. That's Zadie. I mean... my sister. She's got comic bronchitis."

"Chronic bronchitis," Sharmila whispered.

"So he helped you guys out?"

"And he gave me twenty dollars. He..." The boy frowned. "He said he owed it to my pa, but not to tell him 'cos pa would feel bad."

"Ah," Bob nodded knowingly.

The boy frowned again. "My father's dead. Died when I was little." He looked down grimly. "My mom said he was just trying to help. He was nice, Dr. Hap." Then he looked up at them nervously. "I'm sorry. I..." He lowered his gaze again and shuffled off quickly.

Bob looked over at Sharmila. She bore a bleak expression, like someone watching a friend drive away for the last time. "There are stories about Dad like that all over the county," she said. "In the end, all those grateful souls, all those friends, his family... none of us saved him."

13

They were halfway to downtown when the truck reappeared, pulling out of an alley and falling in behind Sharmila's ten-year-old BMW. Bob spotted it in the rearview mirror, watching as its back end fishtailed slightly, rubber peeling out onto the road.

"We have a problem," he said calmly.

Sharmila took her eyes off traffic for a moment and checked their six. "Is that...?"

"Our Dixie-loving twins? The odds are solid." He gestured to the side of the road. "The gas station up ahead, on the corner of Nineteenth. Get us there quick, buy us a second of lead time. When we reach it, swing into the parking lot, hit the brakes and bail out."

"Why?" Sharmila demanded. "What are you going to do?"

"If they were after you, they could have done so at any time, long before I got here, after they first swung by your house. That was for your pa. They came after me at the motel. This is probably an extension of that."

"And you're... what, just going to lead them away?" Sharmila said. "That's crazy."

"Why?"

"Because there's at least two of them and one of you. I'm going to call the police." She took out her phone.

"Put it away," Bob said. "I can't involve them right now."

"Why? I mean, it's not like I'd even trust them to show but—"

"Because I'm not really an attorney, but I'm registered as my friend's counsel of record. If they dig, they'll arrest me on a false impersonation charge. Anyway, no time to argue. The station's right here."

"You're not a lawyer..." Sharmila began to say, bewildered.

"Long story. I needed to make sure he was okay and it was the only way to see him."

She swung the car into the Mobil lot, pulling over immediately, adjacent to the road and sidewalk. Sharmila clambered out quickly. Bob slid over to the driver's seat. He checked the rearview mirror.

The truck swung into the gas station lot at speed.

He threw the BMW into drive and stepped on the gas, spinning the tires slightly, a shudder as it found traction and shot ahead. He ignored the curb and sidewalk, driving onto Nineteenth Street, the car thudding, bouncing and shaking as the tires found asphalt again.

The truck's wheels squealed as it slid out onto the road behind him. It had a big engine, based on its acceleration, Bob realized. He wasn't going to beat it for speed.

He checked the rear view. The truck surged forward, filling up the mirror until it slammed into the car's rear end, the BMW jerking forward and bouncing, Bob's head narrowly avoiding the steering wheel.

The truck veered slightly to the right, then shot forward again, this time crashing into the back right corner of the BMW. Bob swung the wheel to the right to counter any slide.

Traffic on Nineteenth Steet was heavy, Bob realized, as he swerved into the other lane and around the red sports car ahead of him. They wanted him off the busy road, away from prying eyes.

That means they're serious. They want to finish this now, where they can use weapons, not worry too much about witnesses.

Ahead, to his right, an empty lot sat awaiting redevelopment.

That'll do.

He threw the wheel over to the right again, bouncing over the curb and skidding into the cracked, overgrown parking area.

If the last thing they wanted was witnesses, it made sense to guarantee some, Bob figured. He slammed on the brakes, the lot gritty, the compact sedan sliding forward to a stop.

He climbed out of the car, checking the bulge at the small of his back, where his FN's speed holster was clipped to his belt.

The truck jumped the curb aggressively, flying over it, crashing to the surface on the other side. The driver slammed on the brakes, the truck sliding in a semi-circle before coming to rest fifteen feet away.

They climbed out.

Sharmila hadn't been wrong. The Kopec twins were identical, both well over six feet, both... *Attractiveness-chal-*

lenged? Bob wondered. *What's the polite term these days for uglier than a rotten pumpkin?*

They approached at a lazy pace. Tommy was smiling while his brother Vern—the scar exactly where Sharmila had noted, above his eye—looked blankly dour.

Flat effect. He'd seen it on the face of his late Team Seven teammate Edson Krug when he didn't know he was being watched, a complete absence of expression or feeling, as if empty inside.

Tommy, on the hand, was grinning gregariously. "I take it you'd be Mr. Richmond, the lawyer from Los Angeles."

"Well, boys… I don't generally accept clients who try to get my attention by running me off the road, but if you want to give my assistant a call next week…"

"Heh! You're a funny man!" He looked at his brother. "See, V? He's a funny man. That's what we heard."

"Funny," Vern droned.

"Yeah… I get that a lot here. You people all think I should open a Comedy Barn or something." Bob gestured beyond them. "Lots of traffic on Nineteenth Street today, boys. Must be a thousand witnesses going by, cameras on the stores. Terrible spot for a business meeting."

"Uh. Well, we know who you are, Mr. Funny Man," Tommy drawled. "But you don't know who we—"

"You're the Kopec twins. You're hitters for Merry Michelsen."

Tommy frowned. "How'd you—"

"You're probably less anonymous than you think, despite your careful disguises. Not that it matters to me either way."

"Yeah?" Vernon asked, crossing his arms defiantly. "Why's that?"

"Because I'm not about to get into a fight with two yokels

who are stronger than me and have a nasty history of causing trouble. You really think every cop here is as dirty as your buddy Jeb Fowler? You figure no one's going to speak up if you shoot someone on Nineteenth Street in broad daylight, or start beating some dude up?"

He leaned against the BMW casually and crossed his arms, relaxed. "No, I'm just going to stand here until the two of you fuck off back to whatever one-room, podunk, no-running-water hovel you crawled out of. I mean... shouldn't you be off somewhere, helping your momma birth some more babies?"

Vern's eyes flashed anger, his face contorting into a half-snarl. He strode forward. But his brother's arm came up, blocking his path. "Hold on there, brother. Don't let him jerk you around. He's looking to set you off for a reason."

"Ah," Bob said with a knowing nod. "You must the brain cell of the operation."

Tommy's smile disappeared, his scowl equaling his sibling's. "I figure you want Vern here to throw the first punch so's you can argue we assaulted you later on. But..." He looked around. "...Like you said, not a great spot for it."

"Plus, I can see two enormous quivering cowards from a mile away, so I knew you'd turn chicken if confronted," Bob said. *Wind them up, see how long it takes them to—*

He hadn't finished the thought when Vern snapped, pushing his brother aside and charging forward, trying to wrap Bob up in his gigantic arms.

Bob timed the flat-palm strike carefully, slamming it squarely into the bridge of his attacker's nose, the bone snapping. Vern stumbled, falling forward, Bob skittering aside as he crashed into the door of the sedan.

He fell to all fours. "Broge my dose..." he muttered. He

looked around quickly to find his brother, watering eyes obscuring his vision, blood streaming from both nostrils. "HE BROGE MY FUGGI DOSE!' he bellowed.

Vern scrambled to his feet, turning, both fists clenched, blood and snot continuing to stream out over his lips and chin.

Tommy shuffled forward a few steps and blocked his brother once more.

"Yeah, but like your brother said, Vern... you attacked me. Pretty sure that antique store across the road's going to have a camera out front, so this is assault by you, and self-defense by me."

Bob rebalanced his weight between both feet, anticipating reprisal.

But instead, Tommy stared at him coolly. "Think you're pretty smart, don't you, mister? Getting him all worked up like that. But I can wait. I can wait until you're sleeping. Or one of our friends can visit you. Or maybe I can go by your lady friend's place... Yeah. You think we didn't know she bailed out a ways back, at the gas station? You throw a nice punch... That karate or something?"

"Something like that."

"Uh huh. Well... you'd best be careful round these parts. Fists won't do much good against a bullet. Bullet wins every time."

"Which is why if someone brings a gun to a fist fight, I'll shoot first," Bob said, "and worry about the cameras later."

Tommy's eyes narrowed. His gaze was penetrating, like a scientist studying a lab specimen. He crossed his arms, showing off his biceps. "Who are you, mister? Ain't never seen a lawyer get into scraps. Not and win them, no how."

"I'm just a big old boy scout," Bob said. "You know the

motto, right, Tommy? 'Be prepared'. Does your boss know you're running guys off the road? I imagine an enormous tub of crap like that would want a lower profile, what with all the meth and misery and such."

The thug sucked on his tongue a little. "Yeah... smart guy. They don't last too long around here."

"I had that near-immediate impression," Bob said. "Like everyone smart left town."

"Huh." Tommy nodded a few times. "Trying to goad me like Vern. He can go off real hot sometimes... Don't argue it, brother. You know it's true. Me? I like to keep things smooth and simple." He glanced back across the road, as if wistfully hoping any security cameras might have disappeared. "But we'll settle this soon enough."

He took a few steps sideways and grabbed his brother under an armpit, pulling him in the opposite direction. "Come on, Vern. Let's leave Mr. Richmond to think about what he's getting hisself into, whether he'd be a mite happier driving back to Los Angeles."

He led his brother back to the truck. Vern climbed in as Tommy rounded it to the driver's side. "Big city. You never know when someone's going to be cleaning a rifle or shotgun, and it just goes off, kills some poor sucker across the road dead as dirt, 'for he even knew what hit him."

That's how bullets work, idiot. "Okay then," Bob said, offering them a cupped half-wave. "Bye-bye now."

He waited until the truck had pulled away from the lot before heading back to the car. He inspected the back end. The rear bumper was hanging low, dented. It beat the alternative, he figured, but Sharmila wasn't going to be happy.

He needed to call her, see if she was okay.

Then he needed to see a man about an oil company.

14

Bob parked the BMW down the block from Sharmila's clinic. As he walked back, he saw the young physician standing in front of the clinic doors, her arms crossed.

"You don't look happy," he said.

"Bob... I know you haven't been in town long, but Bakersfield... she's a tough city, a real working-class place. Those attitudes are pretty common whether it's rich or poor we're talking about. People don't tend to give up easily. Life here was never easy, so they don't take it as such."

"It is what it is," he said.

"I appreciate you're dead-set on helping your friend and finding out what happened to my father. I sure as certain am. But if you get killed as well, I don't know if my conscience could rightly handle that. And I'm darn sure..." She gazed past him. "...That my car can't take any more rough stuff. This isn't your fight, not for real."

She was a good soul, Bob figured. For all the city's problems, fully half the people he'd met there seemed as nice as anywhere else. *Doesn't matter where you go, there's always good and bad. At least this time, you're working with the good ones.* "The thing is... it is my fight," he said. "Marcus is like family to me. I'm not going anywhere as long as he's behind bars."

She peered at him curiously. "How did the two of you end up becoming so close, anyhow? He's an inner-city kid."

"He's really not. He's from the suburbs. People just jump to conclusions. He's smart. He's a sweet guy. He helped me when..." Bob lost himself in the thought for a moment, struck by the reality of where he was versus where he'd been. "...when I was basically garbage to everyone else."

That disturbed her. "I'm sorry that happened to you."

"It's okay. It's a work in progress. I'm a work in progress," Bob said. "Anyway, his guardian is probably the best person I know, and she asked me for help. Even if I didn't know him, I'd be here if she needed me. At the park... you mentioned your dad met with the people at Jenkins Mechanical."

"Sure."

"Then we need to talk to Richard Jenkins," Bob said. "He might be bankrolling this whole thing if he has a land stake. We need to see how he reacts to some tough questions."

Sharmila didn't seem to buy that. "Have you ever met the professor? No, you wouldn't have."

"Eh?"

"You'll see. I'll give his assistant a call, see if he's available today."

15

Professor Richard Jenkins owned a ranch five miles southeast of town, which Bob figured was par for the course—although Sharmila had been cryptic about it.

She'd just snorted when Bob asked what kind of guy Jenkins was. "You'll have to meet him. He's... well, you can judge for yourself."

But a ranch was about what he figured he could expect from a steely, tough engineer, the kind of place to do man stuff, while feeling manly and reflecting on his manhood. The Team would have loved it.

He guided the Buick past a traditional wood ranch gate, a sign on chain loops hanging off it. "TEREDO" had been branded into it. A dirt-track driveway crossed a half-acre, past cacti, scrubby, straw-like grass, and a rock garden fronted by an old wagon wheel. Beyond them was a ranch house in white plaster, with an orange clay tile roof.

He pulled the Buick up in front of it. The red front door was adorned with a calf's skull, horns intact. "Okay, before we go in," he asked Sharmila, "can you tell me what you found so funny about me thinking he's a cowboy type? The place sure looks the part."

"He's... more of a Western enthusiast," she said. "Trust me, nobody's going to mistake Professor Jenkins for John Wayne."

A younger male housekeeper in a white shirt and black slacks answered the door on the second knock.

"Please, come in."

They ambled past him. The front door opened directly into a living room area with low-slung chairs and a bell-shaped fireplace. The off-white walls were decorated with Western art, old oils of cowboys and Indians battling eternally, a brass statue of a cowboy on a wild, bucking bronc on a table by one wall. "The professor is expecting you," he said, closing the door. "If you would follow me, please..."

He led them through the lounge to a long, tiled corridor at the back of the room. It took them past the adjacent kitchen and two more rooms, doors closed. They reached the back door. He held it open as they walked out onto a rear-facing wooden deck painted grey.

Professor Jenkins was sitting in a rattan armchair, smoking a pipe, reading a stapled document. He was a small man, his mix of brown trousers and a blue-yellow-green wool sport coat like something from a fifties' movie about teachers. He had half glasses, his brown hair flecked with white, the creases and crow's feet betraying a man in his seventies.

He looked up from his document as they approached. "Ah! You're here. Good, good," he said, his English accent clipped and formal. "I suppose you both must be having a rather difficult time of it. I was exceedingly distraught to hear about your father, Sharmila. He was a good man. Please... join me, won't you?" He gestured to the rattan three-seater across from him.

Where the heck am I? Bob thought. If Bakersfield was lacking, it wasn't in diversity. *Sharmila's so normal I could've plucked her out of any city in California. But the gangsters were straight-up Ozarks, and this dude is like an extra from a Benedict Cumberbatch movie.*

"Your accent seems oddly familiar," Bob said.

"I'm English," the professor said.

"I know. It was a joke. Sorry, it's been a hectic few days, and my sense of humor is coasting on dry. I've worked with some English guys."

"Oh? As a lawyer?"

"When I was in the military."

"Ah. And how did that go?"

"It was a period in my life," he said, keeping noncommittal.

Jenkins smiled affably, but Bob got the sense he was being studied. There was a gaze there, not immediately detectable, but enough to say some assessment was going on. "My father served in the Royal Navy," the elderly engineer said. "Not for long, but enough to see a bit of the world. It was a rite of passage for many, I suppose."

They were interrupted by the housekeeper. "May I offer your guests something to drink, Professor?"

Jenkins turned back to Bob. "Do you like tea, Mr. Richmond? Tea, please, Carlos, milk and sugar on the side, there's a stout fellow."

He waited until his helper had left. "Now, Mr. Richmond, how may I help? I understand from your message it's about Hap's meeting with us?"

"He was parked close by when he was killed."

Jenkins looked solemn. "He'd been to see us less than an hour earlier. I must say—and I've told this to the police already—he was extremely upset. He stormed into my office and... well... it was frightful, really, Ms. Singh. I'm sorry, but it was not pleasant."

"When he really believed in something, he took it very seriously," she said. "He was passionate, no doubt."

"He was ranting that I was personally responsible for people getting addicted to methamphetamine in Oildale, that people like me were why the county is, and I quote, 'going to hell in a handbasket'. That I was 'encouraging addiction'."

"He must have told you why," Bob suggested.

"He claimed I was hiring goons to harass him over an affordable housing deal. 'You're not going to scare me off, Richard!'—things like that. And I can absolutely assure you that that is not the case."

"I assume you told him that."

"I did. He said he didn't believe me, and he'd have proof soon enough. I asked him what he could mean, as I was genuinely confused, but he seemed so certain. He insisted I knew what he was talking about. And then..." He paused, as if puzzled.

"Then?" Sharmila prompted.

"Then he said 'it's all going to come out.' And then he stormed off. I was quite perplexed." Jenkins reached into his shirt pocket and retrieved a fold-out metal pipe cleaner. He scraped the contents of the completed bowl into the ashtray next to his chair, then folded it up and returned the cleaner to his pocket.

"All? He didn't..."

"Explain? No! Not at all."

"Was anyone else present for this?"

He shook his head. "But my office door is always open, even though I'm rarely in it. I'm quite certain everyone could hear him."

"And... how many people could that realistically be?" Bob asked.

"Well, my office is adjacent to a research laboratory and there are usually, oh... six or seven people in there working. Then there's our chief executive, my financial right-hand man, Parker Baird. He'd likely have been in his office next door. His assistant, Greg, would probably have been with him. And then there's my secretary, Ms. Lopez. So... possibly ten people, along with anyone who might have been visiting... I'm sorry... why is this relevant?"

"Well, let me put it to you this way, Professor," Bob said. "Do you believe he was killed by Marcus for his wallet?"

The professor looked taken aback. "Ridiculous! I mean... one can't claim to know everyone, but I think I'd have had at least some sense if the lad were a sociopathic opportunist. Marcus is a lovely boy."

Carlos returned with their tea. He set a cup and saucer in front of each. "There's milk in the small pot," he said before departing.

"Then that leaves one option: someone framing him," Bob continued, "because the police claim he was carrying the murder weapon. The only reason to frame him is to cover up the real motive and killer. And Hap had just finished telling you—and apparently an entire office floor full of people—that he had information coming, dangerous information."

The realization caught. "You think someone at Jenkins killed him."

"Or had him killed." Bob studied the man's pupils, the creases around his eyes, the muscles around his mouth. Most liars weren't smooth, but even the good ones often had a tell: a tiny smirk, flittering pupils, flaring nostrils. Something they repeated unconsciously.

But if Jenkins was responsible, he displayed no outward sign.

"I can't believe that!" he said. "We're a house of science, a gathering of the curious. I can't believe any of our men would be involved in anything so perverse, no more than I can believe Marcus would shoot someone. No, Mr. Richmond. That doesn't make sense. And... why!? Because Dr. Singh didn't approve of a trailer park being built? That's ludicrous."

It had been Bob's experience that most people weren't very good at hiding who they really were, despite many thinking duplicity second nature to the people they most disliked. Professor Jenkins was probably a lot of interesting things, but he'd met butterflies more ruthless.

"If not them," he asked, "who? Who hated Hap Singh enough to look for a patsy, other than Merry Michelsen?"

"Merry what?' Jenkins said.

"Michelsen," Sharmila said. "The drug dealer. He runs one of the parks, uses it as a base of operations."

The professor frowned. "I don't think I've ever heard of him."

"You run in different circles," Bob said. "Dr. Singh was concerned he would branch out to your new development, I guess. That or some other rationale."

"Why other?" Sharmila interrupted. "Maybe interfering with his business was enough."

"No, I don't think so," Bob said. "You've seen the type of men Michelsen employs, their methods. But the police claimed they have security footage from the alley, and no one enters or leaves it before Hap or after Marcus. Just Hap's car, and a few minutes later, Marcus on foot. Even if one of his men pulled the trigger, they'd need help pulling off something that clever."

The professor frowned. "I'm afraid I've not been much help, Mr. Richmond. I haven't paid much attention to the housing plan, I admit. It's not my forte, as it were. But rest assured, if there is anything that I can think of that might help, I will make it known promptly," he said. He looked at Bob's cup and saucer. "More tea?"

PROFESSOR JENKINS WAITED until they'd left before heading into his study and picking up his landline handset. He used speed dial to call a number.

It was answered on one ring. "Richard."

"Parker."

"Aren't you off today?"

"I just had a visit from a lawyer named—"

"Bob Richmond?"

"Yes, that's the one, tall and gangly. He had Sharmila Singh with him."

"You're kidding. They don't think this has anything to do with us, do they?" the CEO asked. "Because of... you know, your argument with—"

"I'm *aware* of the appearance," Jenkins interrupted. "Good gracious, that's why I'm calling! What are we going to do about this, exactly? We can't have this young woman walking about thinking Jenkins Mechanical was involved."

"Now... be patient, Richard..."

"I *am* being patient! But my patience is running thin. People want answers. Bob Richmond wants answers. And I increasingly suspect we are going to see a lot of him."

"Look, I'm sure I can handle this," Baird said. "It's just a distraction, a bunch of noise. Don't let it take you away from your work."

"How? How will you handle it exactly?"

"Well, I'm sure I can talk to Mr. Richmond, get him to calm down," Baird said. "He'll realize we were just looking to help the community house the poor and—"

"He already knows that. But the mere fact Hap was in our offices just seconds before he was killed looks, as you might imagine, rather peculiar. We need to fix this properly, Parker, figure out exactly what our exposure in this thing is."

"Leave it with me," Baird said. "And enjoy the rest of your day off, okay?"

"Yes, all right. But—"

But the other man had already hung up.

Jenkins stared at the phone. Then he set it down on the cradle, irritated. Surviving in Bakersfield's business community—not just surviving, but thriving—had taken him forty years of blood, sweat and tears.

Now everything seemed to be going sideways.

16

The professor's good intentions weren't going to resolve anything, but he'd given them a lead, Bob knew. Whoever killed Singh might have heard them argue in Jenkins's office.

So far, that potential list only had two solid names on it: Parker Baird, his CEO, and Baird's assistant, a man named Greg.

He dropped Sharmila off downtown before driving back to the Jenkins building.

The parking lot was small and almost full, just two spaces near the doors reserved for visitors, one of them full. He didn't have an appointment, instead asking the downstairs receptionist to call up to Baird and see if he was available.

Thirty seconds later, Baird trotted down the short, central flight of stairs in the modern building's lobby. He was thin and moved adroitly. His suit was well cut, his blonde hair still thick despite him being middle-aged.

"Mr. Richmond!" He approached with his hand

outstretched. "I'm so glad to meet you, although not in such terrible circumstances, of course. You drove up from LA, I understand?"

"I did," Bob lied.

"Real estate law normally, isn't it?" Baird said. "Richard said you'd stopped by his place. I admit, I had my assistant look you up."

"It's the modern way," Bob said. "Do you have a few minutes to talk, or..."

"Regretfully, no. I have a string of appointments. But if there's anything I can help with relatively quickly, while I've got you here."

He was smooth, Bob thought. In Team Seven, part of his training for overseas placements had been in diplomacy, messaging, use of language. Baird's 'while I've got you here' was calculated, to send a message that he was on his side.

"I understand you were upstairs when Mr. Singh dropped by to visit your boss," Bob said. "He said you were next door and would have heard the argument."

"I did, yes, although I wasn't actively attempting to listen in," Baird said. "He was pretty loud."

"You have some history with him, I understand," Bob lied again. One of the most useful tools he'd had when in the field was the presumption of knowledge. Tell someone—or obliquely hint—that you already know something, and they'll confirm it's true by talking about it.

"Not... extensive," Baird said. "A little over a year ago, one of the subsidiaries Richard founded was interested in exploring for natural gas northeast of Oildale."

"Where the trailer park development is planned?"

"That's right. Natural gas would have required fracking,

which the state won't allow in most circumstances. So we pivoted."

"I understand he was upset about the decision to go with more trailers rather than proper housing. He had concerns about public health."

"I believe that's true, yes. But we were being practical. It would be a near-non-profit venture for us, and we needed to keep costs down."

"Your assistant..." Bob mentioned.

"Greg Thomas?" Baird looked mildly curious. "What about him?"

"He was there when the argument took place as well?"

"He was." Baird smirked slightly at the notion. "Mr. Richmond, Greg is... not a complicated person. He does my errands. He has no role in the business per se, and I can't see him having any involvement with Mr. Singh."

"He's here?"

"He stepped out on some personal business, I believe."

"And Marcus? Where was he when the argument took place? No one's mentioned that yet."

He looked down at his dress shoes momentarily. "He was out of the office, picking up Richard's dinner, I believe." His tone was less pleased, almost annoyed.

"So... for him to be involved in any way can't have anything to do with why Singh was there, then." Bob stared at the man, looking for cracks. "Because he didn't hear that argument."

Baird sighed. "Mr. Richmond, look... I appreciate you have a job to do. But I think you might be overcomplicating all of this. I liked Marcus, I really did. But my understanding is that he had the weapon that killed Mr. Singh on him, and his wallet."

Bob studied the man's face as he asked the question. "And how did you feel about that?"

Baird shrugged. "What am I supposed to think? The truth is that I hardly know the boy. He's from a big city, Chicago, that has a lot of crime, and clearly he is not from an affluent background."

"He's poor... so he'd rob your boss and kill him?" Bob said. "Is that what you're suggesting?"

Baird's expression shifted, nervousness creeping in. "Clearly, it is not my intention to suggest... It's just that the circumstances—"

"Yeah. Yeah, I get that."

Baird abruptly checked his watch. "The time is... getting away from me a little. I really do have to take a conference call in just a few minutes."

Bob could tell he was being blown off. "Okay. It was good of you to meet, sir," he said. He nodded back towards the doors. "I'll head out... but I may need to talk to you again. Is that okay? You know... without the formality of scheduling depositions, that sort of official thing?"

"Absolutely," Baird said. But his head shake was definitely askew, circling between yes and no as if he couldn't quite decide. "Just call my secretary and we'll set something up. Good day, counsellor."

He turned and headed for the stairs.

"JUST... one other thing," Bob called out.

Baird stopped. "Yes?"

"Merry Michelsen. Tell me about him."

Baird peered at him, motionless for a few seconds. Then he said, "I'm... not sure I know the name. Seems vaguely familiar."

"Not a problem," Bob said. "Thought I'd ask."

"It was good speaking with you, Mr. Richmond." Baird turned and headed up the stairs.

Bob exited through the front doors. The last question had been telling. Baird had just stared him, not like a man searching for why a name is familiar, but with a penetrating gaze, like he'd wanted to know why the question was even being asked.

As he turned left to head to the parking lot, a man bumped him, their shoulders clashing, both men staggering slightly.

"Sorry," Bob said.

"Watch where you're going, champ," the other man muttered.

Bob looked back as the man grabbed the front-door handle. "Excuse me? You bumped me."

The man had straw hair, eyes pale blue, pink skin that looked like it didn't think much of the sun. "Nice try, pal. Watch yourself," he said. The man pulled the door open.

Before it could swing closed, Bob said, "You wouldn't be Greg Thomas, would you?"

He paused, holding the door open. "And now who would be asking that?"

Bob held out his hand to shake. "Bob Richmond, Marcus Pell's legal representative. You have a minute to talk?"

Thomas ignored the hand and sucked on his tongue, sizing him up. "Uh huh. Don't really know him. I mean, I know he's an intern here, but... Can't help you. Now..." he nodded towards the doors, "you got anything else to ask? I need to get back to work."

"I'm good," Bob said, lowering the hand.

"Fine," Thomas said, disappearing through the open door.

Bob made a mental note to work up information on Baird's assistant. He had a menacing vibe.

His boss hadn't been much more reassuring. As smooth as he was, Bob's presence had made Parker Baird nervous, a man who doubtless spent any number of hours around other people's lawyers.

That bore investigation, too.

17

The American bully XL had been baited for hours, poked, prodded with needles, starved since the day prior.

The jet-black oversized Staffordshire terrier clone paced its tiny cage like a lion that had treed its foe. The cage had 'DEMON' pasted onto it with masking tape.

Merry loved dog fighting. He'd been bankrolling Demon, even though he didn't own the dog—or much of anything, technically.

His associate, Javier, owned Betsy, the dog across the ring.

Demon shuffled in place, unable to even turn around, just waiting for the gate to come up. Its lips were drawn back over glistening canines, the snarl near constant.

Across the pit, Javier's dog was in a similarly foul mood.

The farm was a smallholding, just a few acres with a barn, grazing land and a hog corral. Technically it wasn't Merry's, either, but belonged to the Kopec twins. He'd had a lawyer tie up most of his assets as a corporate entity, in case he ever had to go down for a stretch, and others transferred to associates for a dollar, putting the onus on them.

That way, nothing could be seized as proceeds of crime. Or some such thing. He was never quite sure what the lawyers were yammering about it.

Dog fighting, comparatively, was simple; the sheer viciousness of it, the abandon. It was like the rules faded away when he was at the fights. It even made it worth driving out into the county for the afternoon, leaving his business worries behind.

Or that was how it was supposed to be.

"What do you think, boss? He sure looks mean."

He looked over at Terry, his underling, then leaned back in the director's chair that had been provided especially for him. In Bakersfield's criminal circles, Merry was increasingly top dog.

"You sound like you might want to put some money down yourself, Terry. Is that what I'm hearing?"

"Well..." Terry looked a little nervous, as Merry was not known for his outgoing nature. "Well, maybe. I just might at that."

"I wouldn't want you to miss out," Merry said. "I wouldn't want you to be so concentratin' on your chores and responsibilities and such that you'd miss this titanic engagement."

"Yeah..." Terry said, worry creeping into his tone.

"I wouldn't want you to go on and lose your focus on what's important... you know, the way you did last night, when that lawyer handed the three of you your asses."

Terry studied his boots. "Yes, boss. I'm sorry."

"Now... you figure that's anywhere near good enough, Terry? 'I'm sorry'? After I ask you to do one simple god-dang thing..."

"It weren't like that, boss, honest. He surprised us."

"He..." Merry whipped off his sunglasses, then used the back of his hand to wipe the sweat from his brow. "He *surprised* you? A real-estate attorney from Los Angeles got the drop on all three of you, did he?"

He took a deep, cleansing breath. It kept him from losing his temper, pulling his pistol and shooting Terry in the face.

Then he put his sunglasses back on.

The two dog trainers were hunkered by the mouths of their cages, waiting to let their fighters loose.

"AH!" Merry said loudly, directing the attention his way. "KENNY! Kenny... maybe just let our boy into the ring first. Let Demon out to get some air. Javier, keep Betsy behind bars for just a minute."

The two dog owners looked puzzled, but knew better than to argue with Michelsen. The gate came up and Demon charged into the ring, snarling, driven to madness. He prowled around, staring at the other cage, ignoring the bystanders.

"Now, Terry, I'm thinking if you want to show us all how sorry you are, you can prove to me that you still know how to handle yourself in a fight. Demon here looks like he's itching to prove himself, too. So now... why don't you go on and climb on in the ring there, minus your piece, of course. Can't have you shooting a defenseless creature, even it is smarter than you."

Terry turned white. He looked over his shoulder at the dog, its fangs glistening, a look of sheer hatred in its eye. "Bu...but, boss... he'll rip me to pieces."

Merry beckoned him closer with a crooked finger. "If you don't get in that pit and show me you've still got a set of balls for that dog to potentially remove, I'll make you drop your britches right here and take 'em myself with my knife, save ol' Demon there the trouble."

"But, boss…"

Merry reached down and undid the snap button on the sheath holding his hunting knife. "Uh huh?"

Terry hung his head. He reached down and took his gun out, handing it to Javier.

He wandered over to the raised sides of the pit and looked over them. Demon began to growl.

Merry leaned over and whispered to Javier. "Pull it off him as soon as it sets to, okay? Can't spare the body right now, so we don't want it killing him or nothing."

Of course, Terry wasn't the only one who'd failed him. But he was the weakest and most disposable. Jonah was his most loyal soldier, while Diego was the best fighter. And the Kopec twins wouldn't take kindly to being lectured, let alone get into a dog pit. They had courage and self-respect, he figured, or at the least were just about scary enough to not piss off.

But Terry had always been slightly chickenshit. He'd make a fine example for the rest of them.

"I… I can't…" Terry whined. "He'll be right on me, Merry, please…"

Merry's eyes narrowed. "Are you *begging*, Terry Perrine? Am I watching a grown-ass man or a sickly child?! GO ON, GET IN THERE!' he bellowed.

Terry was a fit man, big and strong. But he'd seen Demon fight before, Merry figured, which explained his trepidation. "Just vault the damn wall!" he barked. "Sure, he'll take a piece or two out of you but we ain't going to let you suffer long."

The other man looked around at his fellow henchmen.

To a man, they looked away or refused to meet his gaze. His shoulders slumped, reality setting in. He took two steps back then ran for the edge of the fence, using his left hand to vault it, landing in the pit four feet below.

Demon reacted without pause, covering the fifteen feet in a few bounds, leaping at him. Terry instinctively threw up an arm, trying to jam it past the beast's mouth, to lock up its bite as it tried to pin him down and finish him, a look of utter madness in its eye.

A fang sank deep into the meat of his forearm and Terry screamed.

Merry felt a warm, welcoming sensation at the noise. He inhaled deeply, like a lost traveler seeing a friendly horizon.

Life sure was good, he thought, as Terry continued to scream.

He noticed his men weren't watching the carnage ahead of them, and were instead looking obliquely his way, as if waiting for something.

"FINE. Fine, you bunch of pussies. Kenny, noose the dog. Someone help that idiot out, get his wounds looked at. But he pays the bill himself, you hear!"

Behind them, he heard the sound of tires on gravel. He looked over his shoulder. A police squad car was pulling up in front of Tommy's ranch house.

Merry rose from his chair. "Excuse me a minute, fellers, while I attend to some executive business."

He wandered over as Officer Jeb Fowler climbed out of the cab.

"Jebediah," Merry said. "Your partner too good to visit us?"

"Well now, clearly he thinks so," Fowler said. "But you

know how Witty is. He's real sensitive about appearances and such. And it's Sunday. Lord's day and all."

That was a puzzler, Merry figured. "Jesus ain't looking out for him. Everyone in Kern County knows you two are crooked as shit. And I say that with love, Officer Jeb."

Fowler grimaced a little. "Don't sound too much like it. Yeah, we smooth the playing field on your behalf a little, but we do our jobs, too. Just ticketed some guy for being fifteen over in a school zone, just this morning. That's protecting the community, right there. And Witty... he ain't nothing but my boy, you know that."

"Well sure, Jebediah, sure," Merry said. "Now... you've gone and arrested that Chicago boy and everything in that regard is fine and dandy, 'cept for his lawyer, 'course. He's being a mite difficult."

Merry waited for him to respond then realized Fowler was looking past him, horrified.

He turned just enough to see them dragging Terry away from the dog pit. "Oh... that. That's just a little tough love, is all. Don't you worry about that. Anyhow... we need you to deal with this Bob Richmond feller."

Fowler peered at him. "You mean... you want me to kill him."

Merry shrugged. "I just want him permanently gone. I believe our financially appreciative friend's got some business for you, too. I don't really care how you go on about it. How, I ain't concerned."

"I told you last winter after the thing with the illegals..."

"I know. I know what you said, Officer Jeb, I sure do. But times and circumstances change. Time to dig another hole."

"You said if I took care of them for you, you'd forgive my debt..."

"Speaking of digging holes, and all. Yeah, I did. I forgave the financial portion. Didn't make you play Operation, didn't make you spin the Sig. But that don't mean you don't owe me still... it just means you don't owe me money. Favors? Well, given how many you already done me, and how much evidence I have of me paying you, I'd say we're pretty much darn near stuck with each other at this point. I'd say you'd do best to keep me happy, large and in charge as they say."

"Merry... Witty ain't up for that sort of thing. He knows it happens sometimes, but... dang, you know what his nerves are like. Even taking your money, a little payola, is enough to shake him. With the illegals, I had to leave him a mile off, go pick him up once they was buried."

"Get him involved proper, so's his hands are good and dirty, like the rest of us. Tell him he needs to keep the money happy. And right now, happy is if someone takes that bigmouthed lawyer out into the desert somewhere and introduces him to a new home, preferably about six feet under the ground. Am I making myself clear, Officer Jeb?"

Fowler crossed his arms defiantly. "Push too hard, Merry, maybe you'll leave me in a desperate situation. You'll want to think real long and hard about that. If I'm willing to solve this for you, in the fashion intended, then you best know darn well I'm more than happy to pay you and yours a visit one day."

Merry placed a hand over his heart. "Why, Jebediah Fowler! I am hurt you'd say something like that. How long we known each other? Twenty-five years, near enough. Since grade school."

"Uh huh," Fowler said. "And you've been troublesome since you were knee high. You ever wonder why you didn't have no friends in school, why the other kids picked on you for your weight? You ever think maybe it's because you're sonuvabitch to everybody? That enter your thinking, Merry? That's why I don't trust you. Because I KNOW you."

"My hand to God, Officer Jeb... you deal with this little problem, we are all clear. You don't owe me nothing. I'll even tell the boys you've got a line of credit with them again if you want to do some wagering. That sound fair to you?"

The idea of having free money to gamble with clearly appealed to the undersized policeman, a gleam appearing in his eye. "Well now... that might be all right, I guess."

"'Course," Merry said. Fowler was as hopelessly addicted to gambling as his customers were to crystal. Given a little rope, he'd be thousands in debt again by Christmas.

Jeb could raise the specter of their youth, but most of those people had disappeared since high school, made nothing of themselves while he ran Bakersfield's trade. Merry didn't worry about them any more than they ever worried about him. "'Course it's all right. All you're doing is disposing of some trash... keeping our fair city clean."

18

Bob felt self-conscious. Both Mel Feeney and Sharmila Singh had offered to take him out for dinner, show him the town a little.

He'd countered with an offer to use the meal as a strategy session, to go over what they'd learned so far and plan their next move.

Mr. Feeney had taken that suggestion with a look that flickered between pity and concern. "Or, you know... we could just have a nice meal and listen to some nice music," he'd suggested.

So they'd taken his truck, and picked up Sharmila along the way. "We're going to take you for a taste of local culture," Feeney had said.

Then they'd pulled up outside a massive pink, Western revival-style building on Buck Owens Boulevard, next to the arching "Bakersfield" sign that greeted people rolling into town. It was complete with square wooden pillars, balconies and stained-glass windows. The wood clapboard siding had been decorated with Western storefront motifs and signs reading "Trading Post", "General Store", "Saloon," and "Dry Goods."

Then Bob saw a larger sign. "We're having dinner at... a hotel?" Bob said.

"Nope," Feeney countered. "That's the inn next door. This here is Buck Owens's place."

The Crystal Lounge was the biggest saloon Bob had ever seen, an old-fashioned Western bar, thousands of square feet of floor space, a big theatre-style stage with a red-velvet-and-gold curtain, a second-floor balcony fronted by wooden bannisters that wrapped around it all. They were barely through the front doors when the band picked up again, the volume rising above the crowd, a pedal steel guitar kicking in as they began a rendition of "Move it on over."

Their table was the furthest from the stage. A waitress offered to get them drinks. Feeney ordered a beer, Sharmila a coffee.

"Water," Bob said, forcing a smile. They were clearly trying to be sociable, nice to someone they thought was doing a good thing. But Bob had given up being sociable after Tucson.

Eva. He hadn't thought about his friend in months. He didn't want to revisit the lasting image of her dying from gunshot wounds, unaccountably happy, a quick and meaningful death so much better to her than fighting cancer, but the sense of her loss immediate and numbing.

The waitress brought along menus. He checked his six, then looked for the exits, anyone positioned near them.

Sharmila put a hand on top of his for a moment, a reassuring pat. "Relax, okay? We've got things to worry about, but nobody here is on the clock or a threat."

He felt a flush of shame, that she could be so courageous

in the face of her father's death as to try and make him more comfortable, more accepted.

When his fiancée, Maggie, had died in a car crash, storming out after an argument he could've prevented, Bob learned to avoid the places they'd gone, the club near his old dive where they'd danced to live blues, the market, the restaurants in Chicago's West Loop.

As he'd moved further away from people, away from the world of pain and suffering, time had passed, too. After a decade, avoiding his grief had become second nature. He didn't want to see her make the same mistake. To see her forget how to live.

And maybe she already knows that. Maybe that's why she's trying for normalcy. Even when you're being awkward... you make it about you, Bobby. Just give them this, and try to relax.

The dance floor ahead of the stage filled up, folks two-stepping together, cowboy hats bobbing, skirts spinning, as the band extolled "A Working Man Ain't Working Out for Me," the pedal steel going into an extended solo.

"So... does he play this place himself?" Bob asked.

Feeney looked a little taken aback. "Who? Buck?! He's been dead going on twenty years now!"

"Sorry. Now I feel a little foolish."

"It's okay. I take it you're not a big country and western fan, though, as he's sort of royalty."

"Yeah... not much of it in my neck of the woods. More a blues and jazz guy, I guess. A little rock."

"Lots of parallels," Feeney said. "Lots of similarities. Blues is working-class music from black folks. Country is working class music from white folks. But lots of slide—or pedal steel to us—lots of tales of working, and drinking, and love gone wrong."

Sharmila seemed less impressed. "If you grow up here," she said, "you're fully versed in Buck and Merle by the time you're in grade school."

"Is that why you didn't bring the family?" Feeney said. "Lots of big tables. Could've come."

"I've told my husband Ajay that I don't want him or them involved in any of this. But speaking of families..." She turned Bob's way.

"Hmmm?"

"Bob... who *are* you exactly? I mean, not to be rude or anything, but until the Kopec brothers decided to chase us, I thought you were a real estate attorney from Malibu."

"Good question," Bob said. "I'm... a friend of Marcus's. I was headed to Seattle to talk to a psychiatric specialist about some... issues. I tried a guy in Vegas, but that didn't go so well."

"You didn't like his answers, you said. On your way to Seattle for a second opinion."

"Something like that. Anyway, all that stuff—my baggage—it's in the past. I was... between jobs for a while, fighting stuff out," he said.

"Fighting stuff?" She looked puzzled.

He grimaced. "Figuring. Slip of the tongue. I'd... drifted away from people."

It sounded better than "being a drunk who slept rough."

"Ah. That... No, wait... that tells me nothing whatsoever. You're from Chicago originally, like the police said of Marcus?"

"Marcus isn't even from Chicago, not really. He grew up in Hickory Hills, a suburb forty minutes out of town. I'm from the U.P., a Yooper."

"The 'you pee'?" she asked.

"Upper Peninsula of Michigan, the bit that stretches into Canada, sort of. You ever heard of Marquette University?"

"I think so. I'm not big on sports but it's familiar."

"Good school," Feeney said. "So... you're a country boy... sort of."

"That neck of the woods, though in my family's case it was very much the actual woods. My background is pretty... rustic, I guess you'd say. If you want good cell phone service, you don't go to the U.P."

The questions were becoming uncomfortable. If they learned personal details about him, maybe they'd become closer. Then they'd be another pair to worry about constantly, two more people to protect. "Maybe we should discuss what we do tomorrow."

Sharmila sighed and leaned back, placing her fork on the edge of the plate. "Okay, Bob."

"We're just being friendly," Feeney offered.

"Of course," Bob said. "I'm just... I try to keep focused on whatever's operational in the moment."

Feeney smiled wryly at that. Bob got the sense he was disappointed.

Sharmila took the hint and changed the subject. "Where do we stand after your meeting with Baird?"

"Not sure. He's a friendly sort for a CEO. In my experience, they're usually a little more ruthless. I have to assume it's a front, his work voice, so to speak."

"But he couldn't help?"

"I got the sense he wanted me to accept that Marcus did it. He seemed quite confident in the local law enforcement."

"Then we know he was lying," she said. "Nobody who's lived here any length of time would make a statement like that."

"But he's also just a corporate front man. It's Jenkins's company, and Jenkins is the one trying to paint himself as on our side, on Marcus's side. He seems the more likely."

"I have a hard time believing that," Sharmila said.

Mr. Feeney nodded in unison. "Not Dick Jenkins. He's a good soul. I mean, I've heard some crazy ideas in my time, but that one takes it. The man is a softie."

It seemed unlikely at best that Merry Michelsen would act alone, go after the housing project's detractors just to improve his customer base, Bob figured. He was, by all accounts, already the biggest meth dealer in the valley. "It's possible he's paying Michelsen's men to harass us. He wants the existing narrative to stick."

"I'm sorry, but I can't see it," Sharmila said. "Jenkins has a sterling reputation in Southern California as an engineering innovator, but also as a kind and considerate man. He pays his employees well, he gives to charity. He ain't behind this."

She was being naïve, Bob thought. Plenty of men seemed outwardly chivalrous and generous, covering up monstrous intentions. He'd learned that trusting the wrong people could be fatal.

Feeney leaned in a little and lowered his voice, to save Bob any embarrassment. "Son... listen to her on this. Dick Jenkins ain't no killer. I don't mean to insult, but that's just foolish."

Too trusting, Bob thought. *You're both too trusting.*

But he changed tack anyway, rather than argue.

"We need to figure out the meth tie-in either way," Bob said. "It's one thing to use a dealer's muscle if you're a crook. This is a project right on Merry Michelsen's doorstep. In every other respect, it doesn't fit Jenkins's profile, or Baird's. So why there and why work with him?

Why partner with Merry if all you're doing is building a trailer park?"

"Just... take your own advice," Sharmila cautioned. "Be careful, and watch your back. People here put on simple airs, but they're not simple people. Whoever's behind this has money, police influence, and all the time in the world."

"And that's not Dick Jenkins," Feeney grumbled. "Dang. You sure can tell you ain't local."

"But whoever it is," Sharmila said, cutting Bob off before he could argue the point, "you need to keep your head down. There are a whole lot of bodies in that desert out there, you can be sure of that."

Their waitress sashayed back to the table. "Are you all ready to order? We've got a special on just about the best darn chicken-fried steak you ever ate."

19

"What do you mean by 'not available'?" Bob tried to keep his tone even and civil.

He'd been waiting at police headquarters for nearly two hours, passed off from one clerk to another. Yelling at police civilian employees wasn't going to win him any brownie points.

So he'd been relieved when Sgt. Gayle Dyche appeared at the front booking counter.

For about a minute.

"He's not available, just what it means," Dyche said. "He's not even here anymore. They moved him to Lerdo, our remand facility, two days ago."

"So I'll go there." He hadn't talked to Marcus in three days. The kid had to be nervous as hell, surrounded by would-be criminals.

"You can't," Dyche said.

"My client has rights…"

"Your client (a) has a bail hearing this afternoon, so you

can see him then, and (b) is not allowed visitors. Not in pre-trial."

"But I'm one of his representatives."

"And there's a procedure. He has to formally request access for you, not the other way around. That's the rule at Lerdo."

"So... I can't even check on him."

Dyche shrugged. "It is what it is. I noticed on his file that he has a different lawyer representing him later today."

"Anuvab Kumar," Bob said. There seemed no percentage in mentioning Kumar was Sharmila's cousin, and that she was actively helping Marcus, a man accused of killing her father.

"Well, then... he's going to get help from somebody today," Dyche said. "Maybe your attitude when you first showed up prompted him to look elsewhere, Mr. Richmond. Perhaps there's a lesson in that."

"Maybe," Bob said. He turned to head for the door, then caught himself and turned back to the veteran officer from halfway across the atrium. "If anything happens to him..."

"Nothing's going to happen to him, other than facing his charges," Dyche said wearily. "Have a nice day, Mr. Richmond."

Bob shoved the heavy front doors open aggressively, one bouncing off the adjacent wall. He'd worry about Marcus until he knew better, he supposed. But he had things to do, including hitting the library to read up on Jenkins Mechanical.

He's a smart kid. He'll keep his head down, stay out of trouble. Just... lean into that notion.

. . .

THE LINEUP at the Lerdo Jail lunch counter was twenty-men long, stretching back to the corridor outside the cafeteria. Lawrence Cresswell used his height advantage to glance over those ahead of him.

He half-turned to face Marcus Pell, in the lineup behind him. "Good news! We're having shit today, with a side of soft white shit, and some steamed shit for vegetables."

Marcus couldn't help but smile. He'd only been in Lerdo for a day and the first night had been disturbing, trying to bury his head under his pillow to shut out the screams and wails. A little dry humor went a long way.

"You think we can get shitty seconds?"

"Nah, barely enough shit to go around," Lawrence said. Then the big, bald meth addict shook his head. "Man... you know there are legal limits on how poor the food they serve us can be, right? I'm not sure who the inspector is, but that dude has family in government, would be my guess."

"I guess." Marcus kept his back to the counter so that he could keep his eyes on the room and the inmates lined up behind him. The dining hall's long rectangular tables were mostly full, orange jump-suited inmates seated with their free arms ahead of their trays, to protect their meagre diets from theft.

They had thirty minutes to eat, three times per day, along with an hour in the yard for exercise. There was no other free time outside cells, which Lawrence told him wasn't the case at penitentiaries. Convicted criminals got way more freedom than those awaiting trial.

Sharing a cell with Lawrence had been good fortune, but he didn't take the big man's protection for granted. They barely knew each other. He checked out his new friend in his periphery, Lawrence chatting with one of the staff as if they went back a while.

Marcus turned his attention back to the dining hall, the shotgun-bearing guards at either exit. *I can't end up in a place like this. I just can't.*

He clocked movement to his right, a shortish orange blur as someone strode up the side of the line. It was Horton, one of the guys in the cell nearest theirs. He'd been arguing with Lawrence the night before.

He slowed as he approached, then reached into a slit cut into the jumpsuit. The shiv he withdrew was short, a cardboard-and-tape handle with a polished, needle-thin blade, probably crafted out of scrap in the workshop. Horton looked up at Lawrence, who was still talking to staff, facing the wrong way. He drew back the shiv.

"NO!" Marcus jumped forward, hammering down on the man's forearm with a fist, the shiv knocked out of his hand. The blade clattered on the cement floor as Lawrence turned to see what was happening.

The burly giant looked down at it, as did his attacker. Then they looked at each other. Horton had turned white. Lawrence's cinderblock fist shot out with surprising speed, catching the smaller man's jaw. Horton crumpled to the ground.

Inmates stood en masse to see what was going on, murmurs of a fight growing.

A whistle sounded, then another, shrill, piercing. The correctional officers continued to blow them even as they approached. "SETTLE DOWN! NOW!" one yelled.

The crowd cleared as they neared. Lawrence stepped menacingly towards the prone Horton.

"Lawrie, leave it!" Marcus advised, grabbing the other man by the shoulder of his shirt and tugging on it.

Lawrence turned his way, his expression rageful, eyes dark. But instead of attacking, he took a deep breath, his features scrunched as he tried to ward off his desire to beat on his attacker.

"Inmate, step away!" the guard cautioned.

Lawrence held up both hands in a show of placation and stepped back.

"Saw the whole thing," the second guard said as he joined his colleague. "Inmate Horton, on the ground, attempted to stab the big fella. Big fella cold-cocked him."

"Like he said," Lawrence offered, his hands still up. He lowered them slowly.

The first guard stooped to help Horton up, gripping him tightly by an upper arm. "Don't get any stupid ideas because of this," he warned Lawrence. "He'll be dealt with by the proper channels."

His partner picked up the shiv.

"Wouldn't dream of it," Lawrence said as they led Horton away.

The room began to return to normal, inmates turning back to the lunch queue, the dining room ruckus resuming.

"That could have gone worse," Marcus said.

Lawrence looked at him, his eyes shining a little. "Yeah. Man... you saved me. You didn't have to do that."

"I mean... yeah, of course I did."

"You're going to have to keep your head down," Lawrence said. "Robbie's got a brother in here, and his cell mate is quite the piece of shit, too. That's why it was a big deal. Because they're going to be gunning for you too, now."

"But… I didn't do anything anyone wouldn't—"

"And that's lesson number one," Lawrence muttered, leaning in so he could keep his voice low. "Never forget where we are."

20

The Kern County Library had archives going back decades, and its files on Professor Richard Jenkins's various ventures added up to dozens of articles and photos.

Bob kept himself to recent years, getting help from a young assistant librarian. The more recent newspapers she brought up via an internet portal incurred a charge per file accessed, which seemed disappointing.

Didn't this all use to be free? Bob thought as he thumbed through it at a research table.

Most of it was run-of-the-mill stuff: year-end results in the business section, a string of sports section pieces on Jenkins Racing and its many IndyCar, endurance and stock car wins over the years.

But it didn't tell him what he really wanted to know... which was why they had a fuel truck fueling up a Nitro Funny Car at a track in Pahrump when that track didn't feature Nitro Funny Car races.

Maybe it was just PR, like the guy at the track suggested.

Maybe you're angry that Marcus's supposed benefactors may have set him up.

A guy walking past his table nodded politely on eye contact. Then he noticed the glossy photos of Jenkins's award-winning mid-nineties IndyCar Team. "Doing a magazine piece on Dick Jenkins or something?" he said curiously.

"Something like that," Bob said.

"Great man, great guy. Big man in this town."

"So I've heard."

"Paid for my brother's rehab when he was working over at their shop. Didn't have to do that."

"True."

The man could sense Bob's reticence towards a conversation. "Well, good luck to you," he said.

"Same."

The race fan wandered off. Bob furrowed his brow. He hadn't met anyone yet who thought Dick Jenkins was much less than a saint. Maybe Sharmila and Mel Feeney were onto something when they said his involvement wasn't possible.

THE FOUR BLOCKS back to the car were pleasant, the day unseasonably cool and overcast, temperatures in the seventies.

It felt almost like work, or a job, anyway. He'd missed his routines from Tucson, even contemplated getting another driving job. But that was for later, when he'd figured himself out and freed Marcus.

He was still a block away when he realized the police cruiser idling ahead was right next to the Buick.

That doesn't bode well.

If the police had helped to set up Marcus, it stood to

reason they wouldn't mind slowing down anyone helping the kid, Bob knew. He wondered how far they'd go.

The cruiser pulled away.

He didn't see the 'boot' locking his rear wheel and axle until he was almost at the old beater.

There was a ticket on the windshield. 'Parked beyond time allotted' was scrawled on it, along with a two-hundred-dollar fine.

Bob gazed over at the curb. Just ahead of his car, a small sign said 'loading zone, no parking beyond thirty minutes.'

"Goddamnit," he groused. Bob looked down at the ticket again. At the very bottom, in red ballpoint, the issuer had scrawled "Have a nice day!" along with the signature "J. Fowler."

Did he actually follow me around just to give me a ticket?

Jeb Fowler wasn't much of a physical specimen, but Bob had seen a little mad dog in the man's eye.

Yeah. Yeah, I'm guessing he would.

21

Sharmila gripped her coffee nervously. She wasn't expecting much out of the meeting, but she figured she had an 'in', and that meant she had to try.

The coffee shop door jingled. Officer David Czernowitz entered, Stetson in hand. He was dressed in civvies and had a nervous expression.

Does he still have a crush on me? She hadn't encouraged him at all in high school, breaking off their nascent friendship ostensibly because he was friends with Jeb Fowler, a bully. But in reality, it was that he just wasn't very bright.

He hadn't gotten mad or anything, unlike Jeb, who'd slapped his girlfriend around and only given her a reprieve when her family moved out of town. Witty was nice to everyone back then.

And now he arrests them.

He made his way past the other raised tables.

"Sharm," he said with a nod. "Can I sit?"

"I invited you, David. Of course." She'd never called him

his nickname, at least not to his face. It was just cruel, even if he never really saw it that way.

He sat down. "I suppose you want to talk about your pops."

She nodded. "I don't want to waste your time—"

"That's okay, Sharm. We're friends. I mean, it's been a long time—"

"It has, and I just want to stick to business, David, if that's okay with you?"

"Okay. I mean, I understand, I guess."

"You signed off on Jeb's report."

He stared at the tabletop. "Uh huh. Yeah. I mean, yes. I did." His right hand drifted to his left wrist, fidgeting with his watch strap.

"So you saw him take the gun off the boy?"

"I... I mean, if Jeb says that's how it went down, then that's what happened."

She'd never quite understood that, his fealty to a skinny little menace like Jeb Fowler. She fixed him with a stare. "David, what is it with him, anyhow? He stood up for you once when you were getting beat up—"

"He's my friend. Always had my back," Czernowitz insisted.

"David, we were kids. That was more than twenty years ago. And I figure maybe that's the last time he did anything nice for you."

The police officer shook his head gently. "No, ma'am, that is not the case. Got me this job. Got our old captain to sign off on me, even with my dyslexia. Jeb... Jeb looks out for me," he said.

I need to get under his skin, at least a little. Get him to admit who Jeb is. "Everyone knows he's got you mixed up in his crooked business, David. The same crooked business that got your former captain fired, and a few others. He has to be running out of friends at the department, with some of what I've heard."

Czernowitz looked away sharply, as if studying the counter clerk. *He can't even hold my gaze*, Sharmila thought.

"Jeb's got plenty of friends. And he never hurt nobody what didn't deserve it. We're on the right side, that's what he says. The side of law and order." He nodded brusquely, affirming what he knew had to be true. "Ain't hurting no one good, no one people ever worried about."

"Eventually, he's going to hook you in too deep," she said.

Czernowitz frowned. He returned his attention to her. "Well... I'm a gosh-darn grown-ass man, Sharmila, and you know what? We ain't in high school no more. And I'll make my own darn decisions, thank you very much."

She glared at him.

His expression shifted quickly, obvious regret and surprise setting in. "Oh geez... I mean... I know you just lost your father and all..." he said. "I'm sorry, Sharm, I didn't mean nothing by that."

"It's okay, David," she said. He hadn't changed much since high school, she decided. There was still a sweet guy under there. Sweet, and dopey, and far too willing to trust Jeb Fowler.

"I... I can't really drink coffee after three, or I don't sleep no good," Czernowitz said. "Maybe I should go."

"Think about what I said, David, please."

"Okay, Sharmila." He rose and put his hands in the pockets of his jeans, as if suddenly conscious of their presence, his body language awkward. "If you need to talk about the case, you can call me whenever."

"I will. Take care, David."

He gave her a nod and strode towards the door, each stride a little off, anxiety in every step.

22

Sharmila had a steely grimace when she met Bob by the clinic. "You look irritated."

"I had to walk here. They booted my car. Parked illegally."

"Let me guess..."

"One and the same," he said. "Which is funny, because he told me he had the day off. It's almost like he decided to follow me around town or something."

They ambled silently over to her car, then climbed in. "We should go to the cops, tell them what we know so far," she said. "At least then maybe we have some official people on our side."

"If we talk to the wrong person, what we know will quickly become useless," Bob said. "And right now, all we have is the framework of a conspiracy. Your father wanted to run for sheriff and didn't like the new trailer park. Merry Michelsen didn't like your father. That's all we've got. It's not enough. Did you eat yet? I'm starving."

"I'm having dinner with my family. I'd ask you to join us,

but like I said, I'm trying to keep all of this out of our home," she explained.

"Understood," he said. "I need to find a new place to stay."

"What's wrong with the motel?"

"They know I'm there," Bob said. "Mel is a nice old guy. I don't want him to get hurt, but he's stubborn. So... I'm going to skip out on him. I paid him a week in advance, figuring this would all take at least that long to figure out, so he gets three extra days' cash out of it."

"Or, you could just leave him to make his own decisions..."

"No! No, I can't," Bob said. "Sorry... I didn't mean to sound harsh. I've been through this before. People who deal with bad people, they know the risks involved. Joe Public always underestimates it when they're close to those involved. People close to me have been hurt too many times."

She slowed the car to stop at a light. "So... this isn't a one-off event for you, then? I guess that explains the subterfuge about being a lawyer. You've had 'friends' in trouble before."

"Basically... yeah. I mean, you can stress 'friends' like I'm an employee or something, but that's not what this is about. Marcus is a friend, a close one."

"I'm just frustrated," Sharmila admitted. She was silent for a moment, then added, "You haven't asked yet."

"About..."

"Marcus. His bail hearing was this afternoon."

Bob hung his head for a moment. "With everything else, I put it out of my mind. Your cousin—"

"Tried for bail, but we knew that wasn't going to happen. As Marcus is not from here and has no local assets, he is considered a considerable flight risk." She pulled the car into the motel parking lot. "So what do we do next?"

"I know both you and Mel are sure Jenkins isn't involved. But even if that's true, he might have useful information he hasn't given us yet, some explanation for the heat from Michelsen, maybe. He'd have to be a cooler customer than he lets on if he's genuinely responsible. I'll see if he wilts under a little pressure."

"Pressure?" She sounded skeptical.

"Hey... I'll play nice," Bob said. "Promise."

Mel Feeney appeared at his office door as Bob climbed out of Sharmila's BMW.

"Evening," he said. He had his pipe in his free hand. "How did your case go today, counsellor?"

"Yeah... about that. I think I need to move, Mr. Feeney. I know what you said the other day, but I can't help feeling they'll be back here sooner rather than later."

"And go where?"

"I don't know yet. Probably a holiday rental off Airbnb, something like that. Whatever I can find."

Feeney shrugged. "Well, I can't force you to stay. It's your life. Just know that this city is still small enough that, if they want to find you, they're going to find you. You have to be out doing things, I expect?"

"Sure. They've found me already."

"All they need to do is watch Lerdo, then follow you after you next get in to see your client. Moving... well, seems a mite wasteful of your time. Besides, you shouldn't be worrying about me. I'm eight doors down from you and barely know you. They have no reason to bother me, on top of me having been here for years."

He had a point, Bob thought. "Okay, I'll buy that argument. It's not like you're involved in Marcus's problems. But…"

"But? I make my own decisions, friend Bob. I'm not involved and I'm eight doors away. If you wish to leave, I ain't stopping you. But I'm not going to agree with you, no sir. I'll listen civilly, but that don't mean I have to endorse your every opinion."

Bob felt torn. He had a point, and he was going to be hurt if, after all that, his only customer took off on him. "Okay then," he said. "I'll stay."

"Lord sake's, ain't I fortunate," Feeney said dryly.

Bob crouched at his room door and checked the single hair he'd pasted across the gap between it and the frame. It was still in place.

23

LAS VEGAS, NEVADA

The tea was warm enough to finish. Dr. Michael Strong gulped it back. There was nothing worse, he'd long decided, than lukewarm or cold tea with milk, that sour mix of tannic acid and dairy.

He put the cup down on the saucer, which rested on a delicately carved oak side table next to his wingback chair. "Are you sure we can't get you anything?" he asked his patient.

The man on the chaise longue sofa was the last patient of the day. It was nearly six-thirty, and despite priding himself on his professionalism, Strong wanted to go home.

Mr. Smith was sitting up, as many patients chose to do. He'd crossed one leg over the other and had a self-satisfied expression. "No, that's quite all right, thank you," he said.

He was a ghastly looking individual, Strong thought. That in and of itself was not uncommon; it would have been the height of unprofessionalism, for example, to tell his Friday regular, Mrs. Anderton, that she looked as if a truck had backed over her repeatedly. But it wouldn't have been untrue.

He chastised himself. *Annie would be ashamed of you, dude.* His wife and two-year-old daughter, Alice, were the reward at the end of long days, the people he cared for most, far beyond any patient.

Still... even by some of his past clients, Smith was rough. He was missing an earlobe, he had a scar that looked suspiciously like someone once tried to cut his throat, and burn tissue gathered over his left eyelid.

Strong smiled professionally. "Your accent... I'm having trouble placing it."

"South Africa."

"Ah." Smith hadn't offered much. Usually new clients barely had time to sit down before they began unloading personal details. But he was stoic by comparison, barely saying a word as Strong readied for their session.

"Now... my assistant who did your pre-session interview indicates you'd like to discuss Post Traumatic Stress Disorder."

"That's why I booked with you, doctor. It's supposed to be your specialty, and... well..."

For a moment, his new client looked too sheepish to continue. "And... Go ahead, John. This is a safe space."

"Well, I understand you specialize in people with difficult backgrounds. You've counselled some mobsters, former mercenaries."

It was true, but Strong didn't want to brag. "Well... it's mostly that we have a PTSD specialty and we're in Las Vegas, where many people from those backgrounds tend to wind up." *See? Annie would be proud. You can show some humility after all,* he told himself. "Is there a reason that's appealing? Your own background, perhaps?"

"Not... quite." Van Kamp leaned forward on the sofa and rubbed his hands as if considering a weighty reality. "You see, I believe you may have helped a man I'm looking for. And while I could probably benefit greatly in your eyes from some kind of intervention, I have no real desire to be anyone but who I already am. So... I don't really need your medical help, as fine as I'm sure it is."

Strong felt a surge of irritation. *What is this guy playing at?* "Mr. Smith..."

"Made that up," his new client said. "It's Van Kamp. You might have guessed that from my paying cash..."

"I see." Strong began to rise from his chair. "Sir, if you're not here for care, I'm going to have to ask you to leave..."

"Oh... you don't want me to do that, mate, believe me."

"Sir, if I have to call security..."

"I'll have to hurt them. And it still won't get you the antidote."

"What?" Strong asked blankly.

"The antidote. To the deadly neurotoxin I slipped into your tea while you were gabbing with your assistant and making me wait."

Strong felt his stomach flip. "What?" he managed meekly.

"I put a neurotoxin—I'm sure a smart fellow like you knows exactly what that is—into your tea. If I don't give you the antidote, your lungs will cease to function in about..." He checked his watch. "...nine minutes, given that you wasted nearly ten minutes making me wait. But that's on you, kak kop. And if you're wondering... yes, I do kill people for a living."

Strong felt his body heat rising, a flop sweat coming on. *Would that be right?* he wondered. *Am I feeling it already? Maybe he's lying. No one would...*

But he'd heard mob clients and gangsters admit to far worse. He reached into his pocket and whipped out his phone.

"Won't do you any good, mate. Best response average here is about seven minutes. Even if you're that lucky, you'll be dead before they have you in the ambulance. Or..."

Strong put the phone away. "Or...?"

Van Kamp took the second small vial out of his pocket and placed it on the arm of the sofa. "Or you give me the information I want and I'll give you this vial. You do want an antidote, I take it? You're not feeling like dying today, eh?"

"No." The color had drained from his face. He felt numb.

"My information is that you processed a payment from a Bob MacMillan less than a week ago. He, like me, was careful enough to pay with cash. But your assistant printed a receipt for him using your accounting service software, and it used his name and given address. That address, I was not surprised to discover, is false, and led me to the Bally Casino, which was fun but unproductive. Now... you may start feeling some tightness in your chest right about now."

Strong took a sharp breath in through his nose. *Is that...?* He felt a slight congestion. "I... can't give out a patient's information..."

"Oh... that's all right. Just give me his file."

"I... I'd have to print off my notes..."

"Then I'd get moving. You have..." He checked his watch, "... seven minutes now. So not even enough time for the ambulance to get here."

Strong got up and took two paces to his desk. He hit a

line on the phone. "Jenny, please print off my patient report for Robert MacMillan and bring it in as soon as possible. Now! Please. Time waits for no man."

"Yes, sir. Do you need anything else?" she replied.

Van Kamp shook his head gently but said nothing.

"No, that's it."

Strong hoped the police would get there quickly. "Time waits for no man" was their panic code, a sign she needed to get help for an out-of-control client. "Do you need anything else" was her confirmation she understood.

"She better get a move on," Van Kamp said. "If this doesn't work, you see, I'll have to work on her. And that will be much more unpleasant."

"Why are you doing this?" Strong asked, though he realized it was probably a pointless question. Whether Van Kamp had clear purpose or was just psychopathic, the situation wasn't going to change.

The South African shrugged. "It's my job. You heal people, I kill them. Not complicated."

"And you want to kill Bob MacMillan? Why?"

"You know who he is. You treated him."

"Briefly."

"Why briefly?"

Strong felt uncomfortable. He'd been a psychiatrist for more than two decades and patient privacy was sacrosanct to him. "I can't talk about my clients..."

Van Kamp rolled his eyes. "Believe me, mate, he's not half as worried about you as you are him. Go on, spill your guts."

"Really, I can't..."

Van Kamp sighed loudly, exasperated. He reached into his coat pocket and took out his Sig Sauer ACP 45 pistol. He laid it on his lap. "We can really speed this up if you're going to be difficult."

"He didn't want to accept that he has PTSD and possibly ADHD," Strong said, almost too quickly. "He said he had to think about what that meant, and his life and where it's going. He wanted a second opinion."

Van Kamp's expression shifted visibly at that, from a sort of tired, blank stare to annoyed. "Bloody coward," he spat. "I can't believe this guy…"

Asking 'why' came naturally to Strong. "Because…"

"Because he was the best, or at least by reputation one of them."

"The best…"

"At killing people. Did he convince you somehow that he wasn't a killer, Doc? Because anyone in the trade prior to ten years ago knows how wrong you'd be about that. He's a bloody legend; or, depending on which country you're from, a nightmare."

"He told me about his past… working for people he no longer trusted. Hurting people he didn't want to hurt." *Where was that report!? Hurry up, you silly girl!*

Van Kamp rolled his eyes, mortified. "You must be joking! He's developed *a conscience!?*" He shook his head. "Revolting! A man of his expertise and he hates who he is? What a bloody cliché!"

Strong's tongue had begun to feel slightly fat. *He wasn't lying. He's dosed me with something.* "That antidote…"

Van Kamp held up the vial and shook it a little. "The vial's almost full. Plenty to go around… if your assistant isn't doing something stupid, like calling the police. I'll be gone before they get here, but she'll be as dead as you."

A surge of panic struck the psychiatrist again. "I see."

The door opened and his assistant entered. She had a paper file in one hand and a worried expression. "Thank you, Jenny. That... other call you were going to make for me... We need to cancel that."

"You mean..."

"Yes, immediately. Quickly now!" he urged.

She nodded and turned, then scurried out of the room.

"Very clever, Doc. You had a trigger word and she's called them already, I'd guess. She better hope they don't get here before I leave."

Strong leaned forward and handed him the file. "This is all I have."

It was thick, perhaps a quarter of an inch. "You got all of this from him in a few weeks?"

"He's... a complicated man." MacMillan's case had been fascinating. Now Strong could only wish he'd never heard of him.

"Good, good." Van Kamp rose. "Here." He tossed the glass vial to Strong. It pirouetted, turning end over end as it flew through the air.

Strong snatched at it. He bobbled it twice, the glass vial dropping, heading towards the hardwood coffee table. Strong snatched at it again, his fingers grasping glass, a wave of relief spreading across his face.

Van Kamp walked to the door. "Now, if I were you, I'd get yourself to a hospital, mate, see if they can figure out what I gave you."

Strong stared at him. "What?!"

"Yeah, well, they can't give you an antidote if you don't know what the poison is. You should have bargained for that instead of the vial."

"But... but you said..."

"I never lie, mate. I said I'd give you the vial, and I said you need an antidote or you'll die. I never said the vial was the antidote."

Strong's heart was pumping now, pounding in his chest as fear began to set in. It had become hard to swallow.

"You... Fuck..."

"Now I'm going to go have a word with your lady up front, yeah? Problem is she's seen my face. I noticed you had active security, so she's going to show me how I access the recording. Then, I'm going to kill her, too. But she doesn't have anything I need and I'm not getting paid, so I'll make it quick."

"You... Gahk!" Strong grabbed at his own throat out of reflex, tilting his head back, the sensation of swallowing his own tongue settling in. "Please..." he managed. "I have a family... a daughter..."

Van Kamp's shoulders barely registered a shrug. "Eh. Not my problem, mate. But... nice meeting you, I suppose. In the end, I guess making me wait got you ten more minutes alive, so... not a bad decision in the end. The rest? Well... you can't win them all."

He left through the door he'd used to enter.

Strong tried to whip out his phone. Halfway from his pocket, he lost all sensation in his right arm and hand, the phone falling to the floor beside his chair.

From the lobby, he heard Jenny shriek. He tried to move, to rise so that he could help her. But his legs wouldn't work. Nothing would.

He felt his breathing labor. He wanted to look around, call out for help, scream, fight for his life.

But it had already been taken from him.

24

BAKERSFIELD, CALIFORNIA

Bob wiled away the remainder of the evening with a book, a thriller about the environment that was badly out of date but engagingly written.

He slept soundly.

But before the alarm clock could wake him at six thirty the next morning, a fist pounded on the door three times.

He got up and pulled on his jeans from the day before.

Bob checked the window from behind the curtain.

Officers Jeb Fowler and David Czernowitz were both in full uniform.

After retrieving his blue golf shirt from the day prior and putting it on, he fished his wallet out of his jacket pocket and took out the needle-thin set of lockpicks. He gripped them in his left hand, between his ring and middle fingers.

He opened the door.

"Mr. Richmond, as you are already aware, I am Officer Fowler of the Bakersfield Police Department, and this my partner, Officer Czernowitz. We have a warrant for your arrest, sir. We've received a complaint that we believe to be accurate that you did on the nineteenth of September unlawfully assault Mr. Vernon James Kopec of Bakersfield. I am going to restrain you now. Please turn around and place your hands behind your back."

On cue, his partner's hand drifted to just above his holster.

Bob sighed deeply and turned around. He held his hands together in fists, holding the lockpick tightly. "You know darn well this is bullshit," he said. "There are stores and traffic cams along Nineteenth Street. This won't stick, and I'll be out by tomorrow... Wednesday at the latest."

"You have the right to remain silent," Fowler intoned. He slapped the cuffs on Bob's wrists and closed them. His partner began to pat Bob down. "Anything you say can and will be used against you in a court of law. You have the right to an attorney. If you cannot afford an attorney, one will be provided for you. Do you understand the rights I have just read to you? With these rights in mind, do you wish to speak to me?"

"He's clean," Czernowitz said.

"Officer Fowler," Bob asked, "does anyone *ever* wish to speak with you?"

"Hardy har har. That's what I heard about you—"

"I'm a funny man. Yeah, so people keep reminding me. I think your friend Tommy Kopec said the same thing."

Czernowitz closed the room door behind them as they led him to the squad car. As he ducked to climb onto the back seat, Fowler put light pressure on his head to make sure it remained below the roofline. They slammed the door behind him. It locked automatically.

The two officers climbed into the front, separated from the back by a cage. "Let's take ourselves a little drive, Mr.

Richmond," Fowler said. "See if we can't spend some time together, work out what's what."

The cruiser immediately turned south onto Elm Street, the traffic light in the early hours.

"Where are we going?" Bob demanded.

"Shut it!" Fowler barked.

"Police headquarters are the other way," Bob said. "I've been there, as you're well aware."

"Yeah... well, you don't get a say in how we do things," Fowler said. "So shut it! We'll get where we're going."

Czernowitz looked over his shoulder. The words dripped out almost gently. "You'd best not make things worse on yourself."

He turned around again.

Bob kept an eye out the window.

After ten minutes, it was clear they were heading out of the city.

This isn't going to end well.

The trick to freeing himself from cuffs, he knew, was to be quiet about it.

Flexibility and practice will allow someone to pull their knees to their chest, extend at the shoulder joints and swing their cuffed hands under their buttocks and shoes, so that they're ahead of the body.

Doing it without one of these idiots hearing, on the other hand...

Bob moved slowly and deliberately, first sliding his cuffed hands under his backside, then pushing forward with them and his chest simultaneously. His shoulders burned, the left socket near dislocating, a sudden stabbing sensation telling him he was in trouble. *This was easier when I was younger.*

A last push forced his hands past his buttocks. He leaned back, lifting his knees to his chest as he slid his hands up his legs, just about getting them clear...

The lockpicks tumbled from his hand, onto the cruiser floor.

Shit.

His rustling was too loud, he knew. Fowler peered into the rearview mirror, then whirled in place, eyes off the road completely for long enough to see Bob's hands ahead of him.

"Sum'bitch!" Fowler declared. "He's trying to pull a fast one, Witty! Keep your eyes on him!"

Czernowitz drew his service weapon and trained it on Bob, through the cage. "He got his hands from back to front. How'd he do that?"

"Flexible joints," Bob muttered. He figured his shoulder was going to hurt for a week.

Fowler glanced quickly at his partner. "Put that dang thing away! Use your backup, dumb ass!"

It left little doubt they didn't plan on processing him, Bob figured. Any time a service weapon is fired, it has to be reported, every round accounted for. But they didn't want anyone looking into this arrest.

"Sorry, weren't thinking," Czernowitz muttered. He holstered the Glock and drew a Sig Sauer P238 from his ankle holster, using his thumb to flick off the safety. He trained it on their passenger. "You just relax, there, sport. You stay quiet, answer our questions, I'm betting everything'll be just fine."

Fowler giggled. "Yeah... I don't think Mr. Richmond is quite as dumb as some of our local meth heads, Witty. I suspect he knows this ain't a friendly tour of the county."

"You're really going to murder an innocent man?" Bob proposed.

"Murder?!" Czernowitz scoffed. "It ain't like that."

He sounded genuine, Bob thought. "Is that what he told you? That you're just putting a scare into me? That you'd just lay the boots to me for a while? Give me a shitkicking?"

Fowler sniffed at that. "Well now, that's a dirty word, right there."

"Shitkicking?"

"Murder! No one forced you to come up to our town, start sticking your beak into everyone's business. Someone kills someone else for no good reason, sure, that's wrong, I'll give you that. But you come into someone else's yard and start shitting on their daisies, son, well... you gone and brought that on yourself, way I figure it. That's just self-defense."

Czernowitz looked puzzled. "Yeah... self-defense," he repeated nervously.

"For a law enforcement officer, that's a pretty darn generous interpretation," Bob said. "It sounds more like you're trying to justify it for your partner here so he doesn't start getting all guilty, think about doing the right thing."

Czernowitz shook his head. "Mister, if you're thinking of turning me on Jeb, you got me all wrong."

"Witty knows what lawyers are all about, how you're basically one step off Satan himself," Fowler said. "Ain't that right, Witty? We talked about you types to no end, what we'd like to do with the lot of you. I'll give you a clue: it involves forty-caliber bullets and a big, dark hole."

"That right, Officer?" Bob asked Czernowitz.

He glanced quickly at his friend, long enough to see Fowler paying attention, waiting for his answer. "Hell, I'd volunteer to shoot a low-life defense attorney, you bet," Czernowitz said boldly. "You ask the average officer, he's playing by the book, like Jeb says. But we talk. We talk about what we'd do if we could make the whole system work. But nobody does nothing. Well... this ain't nothing."

"What is he blathering about?" Bob asked.

"I think what Witty intends to express is that you trying to get this boy off for killing our local medical hero, Dr. Singh... well, that ain't sitting well with nobody."

"So... you're taking me out of town. For... a chat?" Bob proposed. He snuck a peek out the window. They'd gone ten miles already, he guessed. "I figure maybe it's a little more than that."

"And what happens if we let you go?" Fowler said. "You go on out next week, get some other guy off what don't deserve it, and some poor individual gets raped or murdered by them. Dealing with you is a blessing to society. Pest control."

"Pest control!" Czernowitz repeated overzealously, like the prospect was a little exciting. "That's what you said, right, Jeb? Damn lawyers."

The venom rang true. *He hates defense attorneys. But he wasn't up for whatever Fowler's got planned, not initially. That's something I can work with.* Bob chuckled loudly. "Well... I hate to disappoint you, Officer Czernowitz..."

"What?"

"I'm not a lawyer."

'Whuh?" He looked confused. He glanced sideways at Fowler. "Jeb...?"

"It's true," Bob said. "I think your partner already knows this, because I wasn't in court with my alleged client yesterday. Sharmila Singh's cousin, Anuvab Kumar, an actual lawyer, handled his case. And your partner was there."

Fowler nodded thoughtfully. "Yeah... I did suspect that to be the case, so I looked up Mr. Bob Richmond, attorney at law, after the bail hearing. Took some digging to find a picture from the state bar association. He's at least ten years older and quite a bit heavier than you, Bob, or whatever your name is."

"Sum'bitch!" Czernowitz exclaimed. "He's an impostor!"

"Not really," Bob said. "I just used fake ID to get in and see an old friend and borrowed someone's name to legitimize it. Things... snowballed."

"Huh." Czernowitz pushed his hat back. "Well, don't that beat all." He looked unsure, Bob thought, as if the new information had thrown a wrench into his expectations.

Fowler turned off the highway, onto a dirt trail. They were at least fifteen minutes out of the city, Bob figured. The Ford Crown Vic rumbled along the dirt track, the shocks cushioning each rut, dust partly clouding the view through the rear side windows.

"You ... sure we should be doing this now, Jeb?" Czernowitz asked his partner, his voice quiet.

"What's eating you? Spill it," Fowler demanded.

"Well... he ain't a scum-sucking lawyer, for one thing. You said this was a win, that we was taking a problem off the streets. But he ain't a lawyer, just some loser whose talked his way into the station."

Fowler shot him an angry look. "He's still trying to take us down and embarrass the department, ain't he? Embarrass our brother officers?"

"Well, yeah, but..."

"But what? But what, Witty? And pay heed: think before

you speak. You know darn well you ain't smart enough to make these decisions, that I always done the thinking for us. Got you a job, got you a badge. Don't start trying to play genius now, when there's careers on the line. We leave this guy out there, he kicks over more rocks, maybe finds something on our friend..."

"That would be Merry Michelsen, I take it," Bob interrupted.

"SHUT IT!" Fowler barked. "You shut your god-dang mouth or I'll draw on you while you're cuffed, I do truly swear to God!"

After two more minutes of silence, the tension in the car had built. Fowler yanked the wheel to the right, taking the sedan off the trail, into the desert dirt southwest of the city. "No derricks means no visitors any time soon," he said.

Two hundred bumpy yards in, he stopped the car.

"They could still maybe see us from the road," Czernowitz noted quietly.

"Shut it, Witty, god-dang it! Just... shut it! What did I just say about letting me do the thinking? You are a god-dang high school dropout who never read more than an Archie comic in your god-dang life! Let me keep us safe, like I always do. Is that okay with you?"

Czernowitz nodded. "Didn't drop out by choice," he muttered sullenly. "Had to help Momma make the bills."

"Okay. Whatever! Just help me get this sum'bitch out of the back."

The dust around them had settled. Bob looked to his right. About twenty-five feet from the car was a two-by-six rectangular hole in the ground.

"Yeah, you see right," Fowler sneered as he got out of the car. "Took me near an hour last night and it's still not deep enough. You've got some digging to do, son." He shook his head and sighed. "Fat bastard better be god-dang grateful, is all I can say."

He slammed the car door as his partner joined him. Both men drew their service weapons. They opened the rear right passenger door. "Come on, Mr. Bob Whoever-You-Are. Get on out of there. Don't kick now, or make a fuss, or it'll be long and painful from multiple shots. Come nice, it'll be clean and quick."

"Clean and..." Czernowitz repeated, the words hollow. "Jeb, you sure this..."

"Like I said, he's dangerous. It ain't enough to just talk, Witty. Sometimes, to do right, we've got to get our hands dirty. Just... get hold of him there."

They pulled him from the car, Czernowitz's strength surprising Bob, his collar grasped firmly. He tumbled to the dirt. They waited as he righted himself and rose to his feet.

Czernowitz stared wordlessly at the hole. He began to raise a hand to point at it.

"Yeah, it's a god-dang grave," Fowler said. "Man... You need to sack up, Witty! This is what we talked about. Righting wrongs, taking care of problems for real!"

"He means me," Bob said dryly.

"I tell you what. I'm sort of glad you tried to escape with that there handcuff trick," Fowler said. "I was going to have to uncuff you so you can carry your friend, and now you can just do it wrists together."

"My friend?" Bob said.

"Jeb... what're you saying there?" Czernowitz asked.

"Yeah... about that." Fowler reached into his pocket and took out his wallet. He took out a wad of cash and handed it to his partner. "Here, this is your cut."

Czernowitz frowned, unsure. Then he took the cash. "That looks like a lot for the widows and orphans' fund." He lowered his voice, unaccustomed to discussing corruption in front of strangers. "It's usually less than two G's in a month!" he hissed. "This looks like more than ten grand!"

"Uh huh, twelve-point-five, more precise," Fowler said. He wandered in a wide circle past them to the trunk, keeping Bob out of range. He unlocked it, opened the lid, then stepped back five paces. "Go on then." He waggled the pistol in the trunk's direction, then took another deep breath. Bob couldn't tell if it was to relieve tension or irritation at all the questions.

Bob walked around the trunk. The wind gusted, dust and dirt blowing across their boots.

Fowler was clever enough to keep out of reach. But eventually, he knew, there would be an opening.

He looked into the trunk.

There was a long-handled spade. Under it, Professor Richard Jenkins was bent at the waist, his arms tucked behind him, a spasmodic, twisted pose that Bob figured would have hurt like hell, had two gunshot wounds to the back of his skull not removed any chance of feeling anything.

His eyes were open, the light gone from them.

Well... there goes my lead suspect. Damn.

Sorry, professor. I had you wrong.

"Let's get going," Fowler said, gesturing with his head towards the unmarked grave. He took the shovel out of the trunk. "Go on, pick him up."

25

Bob reached into the trunk. "It's kind of hard with my wrists together. Youse guys have guns. I'm not going anywhere. Would you just undo the cuffs for a minute?"

"Uh-uh. Nice try. But I hear you're a slippery one. I heard about your little set-to with Vernon Kopec, and another with Jonah Kepler," Fowler said. "Vern said you sucker-punched him, which I can believe..."

"Vern's highly creative. He charged at me, as I'm sure those aforementioned cameras would've told you."

"Cameras? Man, those take court orders, time. A request being filed. And you did break the man's nose."

"Uh huh. And if I knock down a third redneck with a letter 'K' name, I get a matching set. Apropos to the mood around here, I'd say."

Fowler waved his Glock at the body. "Hardy har. See, ignorant statements like that is why you're in the shit now, Mr. Clever. Go on, now, slip them long arms under his torso. Witty, help him lift the body out, okay?"

Czernowitz walked over tentatively. He peeked into the trunk. "Oh my..." he said. He appeared dazed, off balance, taking an awkward step backwards, his pallor turning white. "Dang..."

"Weren't expecting that, were you?" Bob muttered. "Your partner's gone off the deep end, Officer Czernowitz." *He probably hates that nickname.* "You let him do this and you know you're crossing a line between good and bad. You think this is a one-off? Let him do it once and this becomes what you *do*."

Czernowitz froze, staring at the professor. Then he shot a glance at Fowler. "Dang... a lawyer was one thing. But I didn't sign up for this, Jeb..."

"Witty, god-dang! Now, how long we been friends? Since grade school," Fowler demanded. "And ain't I always been there, watching your back? When the other boys picked on you, who was there to set you straight when you come up crying and such? Who got them to all lay off you? Who helped you get your job with the god-danged department!?"

"Well... yeah, Jeb, but... Professor Jenkins!? I mean... he didn't ever hurt nobody."

"He planned to!" Fowler insisted. "He was putting all sorts of heat on Baird about the land. He was sticking his nose where it don't belong when he's supposed to be retired and out of the picture. Eventually, he'd go public."

Czernowitz looked deeply uncertain. But he positioned the body over Bob's outstretched arms nonetheless. "Go on, lift and turn. I'll get the weight on the other side."

Bob did as commanded, the two men facing each other, spreading Jenkins' dead weight across their arms like a makeshift stretcher.

Even then, he was heavy as hell, Bob figured. Dead

weight is dead weight, and Jenkins had to weigh at least a hundred and fifty pounds.

They carted him twenty-five feet to the hole in short steps. Bob alternated his view from their route to Czernowitz's empty eyes and half-dazed expression. The doubt was building, he figured. It had to be.

Bob looked down. "This hole is only a half-foot deep. You couldn't bury a dead beaver in it."

"Uh huh," Fowler said. "That's why you got a shovel, smart man. Just... set him beside it there and get digging."

The two men lay Jenkins' body in the dirt. Bob held up his wrists. "Again... I'll give myself all kinds of credit for getting hard work done, Officers, but..."

Fowler looked annoyed. He clearly hadn't considered that Bob needed two hands to use a shovel. He took a few steps back, so that he was a solid ten feet from both men. "Witty, undo his cuffs... Ah! Do up the clip on your holster first. Don't want him trying to grab your weapon or nothing. There we go."

Czernowitz removed the handcuffs then scurried backwards, out of range.

"Well, don't act like he's a gol-dang tiger, Witty!" Fowler chastised. "Dang, son! He's just a troublemaker!"

"He's a troublemaker who kicked Vern Kopec's butt. I ain't taking no chances," Czernowitz said. "'Sides, you don't get to make fun, Jeb, not after getting me in this mess with you. Dang! I mean..."

"Don't get lippy with me, Witty!" Fowler commanded as he jabbed his forefinger in the other man's direction.

Czernowitz glanced down at the professor, his expression morose, like a child watching a grandparent's funeral.

"Drink it in, Czernowitz," Bob suggested. "One day, he'll have someone trying to bury you in a hole in the desert."

"YOU BE QUIET NOW!" Fowler snapped. "You be quiet, or this'll be a lot quicker and uglier for you."

"You're going to kill me twice?" Bob said. "The trouble with leading a man to his own grave, fellas, is that he has no other options, and a man without options has no reason to give a shit. Maybe I don't want to dig a hole. Maybe I figure I'd be better off charging you; either way, I'm dead, but in my version... you dig the hole."

"Huh." Fowler strolled until he was behind Bob, but still out of reach. "Go on and pick that there shovel up and I'll let you know how that concept sits."

Bob sighed and did as requested. Halfway through bending down, Fowler skittered forward and pistol-whipped him, slamming the butt of the gun into his temple from behind.

Bob collapsed to one knee, a jolt of pain shooting through his brain.

Damn it. He fought wooziness, remnants of concussions past.

"Thar! That's what I think of your suggestion," Fowler said. "Let me give you a little hint that a big northern city fella like yourself should have had down by now: it hurts a whole lot more when I use the other end. Now get digging!"

Clearly, he's never been shot, Bob thought. It entirely depended on where, and how, and by what. But he did as he was told, rising to his feet and moving to the edge of the grave.

He looked down at Jenkins as he shoveled the first pile of dirt out of the hole.

You deserved a damn sight better, I figure.

"Now maybe that'll get you thinking right. I know what you got to be doing, which is weighing all this, figuring out the angles," Fowler said. "You're thinking, 'this is going to take a while, and eventually, they won't be paying attention.' But remember, Bob—or whatever your name is..."

"It's Bob. Really."

"Well, you remember, Bob, that we picked you up on a legit charge. Even if you escaped, even if you killed us both doing it, you're a wanted man. They'll just figure you dug this hole to put all three of us in it. So you're stuck, Mr. Clever. You're up shit creek and there ain't no paddle... or even a boat, I'll tell you what."

Bob glanced back at him angrily, the point irritating him. Then he noticed Czernowitz's empty, broken expression. He was staring ahead blindly, into a distant place, his mind somewhere else, as if there was nothing left but to contemplate loss. The professor's death had shaken the other officer who clearly still saw himself as on the side of the angels.

That's something I can work with. He really does not want to be here.

Patience, Bobby.

This could take a while.

26

The ground was hard, baked by the sun to a resilient crust. It took Bob nearly an hour to get two feet deep, a pile of dry, pale dirt building slowly.

The two officers wandered back to the cruiser, sitting on the edge of the front and back seats with the door open and engine on, cooling themselves and the rest of the desert with its air conditioning.

It was quiet, aside from the wind and the sound of shovel on dirt, the only company an occasional squawk from a buzzard.

Bob stood up straight and leaned on the shovel. It had to be above a hundred degrees, and he'd soaked through his shirt in minutes. He stretched, trying to loosen his joints. The bum knee hadn't started to ache yet, which was a plus.

"You ain't done yet," Fowler said.

Bob looked over. The little man was waggling his gun, directing him back to work.

"It's strenuous. I'm tired. If you actually want me to

finish, you're going to have to give me an occasional break, or it'll be dark when I'm done."

Fowler checked his watch. "Past noon. We've got all day, don't we, Witty? Assuming you didn't make no dumb plans or nothing."

"I remembered what you told me, Jeb," Czernowitz replied brusquely. "No need to be so dang rude about it, not after everything you done already."

He's just bristling now, Bob thought, *every time Fowler takes a shot at him*. "He calls you 'dumb' a lot, doesn't he, Officer Czernowitz? Doesn't seem respectful. Still, I bet you did better on the entry exam than he did."

"Hah!" Fowler interrupted before his friend could answer. "Shows how much you know. Witty ain't no Bill Gates or nothing."

Between Jenkins and the constant haranguing, Czernowitz was becoming irritated. "Matter of fact, I do believe I was five points higher, Jeb."

Fowler shot him a dead-eyed stare. "You what now?"

"I asked Captain De Jong 'fore he was fired. He said I was five points better."

"Did not!" Fowler muttered. "Don't you go lying to me about police business, Witty! You know dang well you never done nothing right without my help."

Bob intervened. "He said..."

"Now just SHUT IT!" Fowler barked at Bob. He turned back to his partner. "Don't you see what he's trying to do, getting us fightin', like we was kids in class? He don't know you or respect you, Witty."

"Yeah... about that," Bob said. "I bet it sucks that he keeps calling you 'Witty' all the time."

Czernowitz's brow furrowed in puzzlement. He stared

back at Bob with something bordering on disappointment. "Why? My name is Czernowitz."

"Witty?" Bob said. "As in, he thinks you're anything but."

The officer looked at his partner, befuddled. "What's he mean, Jeb?"

"He don't know what he means."

"I mean the word," Bob explained. "Witty, as in funny and smart."

"I know'd that," Czernowitz insisted. "I know'd was what it meant. That... that ain't right! That ain't right, is it? You ain't being sarcastic or nothing?"

"No, brother, it is not right, no, sir!" Fowler said. "You're just smart enough for you. That's all you need to be, like I always told you." He raised his pistol and levelled it at Bob. "Now, you've had your break and your tongue's doing all the work. Time to put your back into it again. Go on, climb on in there."

Bob turned and climbed back into the hole. He resumed digging. After another hour, it was nearly four feet deep, his shoulder muscles aching. "That enough?"

The two men rose and wandered to within ten feet. Czernowitz looked away almost as quickly as his glance. Fowler stood on his toes to get an idea of the hole's depth. "Yeah, I reckon that'll do it. Go on, then, roll the professor in."

Bob climbed out. He rounded the hole and crouched by the professor. He rolled him over. It would only take one more shove to get him into the grave, he knew. He heaved the body onto its side, slipping his hand inside the professor's coat and into his top shirt pocket.

Got it. He palmed the pipe cleaner then finished the maneuver, Jenkins' body sliding into the hole in a woosh of dusty dirt.

"Fit just about right," Fowler said.

"Yeah... about that," Bob said. "The professor's under six feet tall. I'd say five-seven, maybe five-eight in generous heels."

"So?"

"So I'm six-four. The way I see it, you barely have an inch clearance under his heels, and he's bent up a little."

Czernowitz frowned. "You started the hole too small, Jeb," he said. "He's right. He ain't going to fit in that."

He sounded almost hopeful, Bob thought.

"So we bend him up a little," Fowler said.

"Jeb..."

"Oh sure," Bob said dryly. "It'll be really easy for the two of you to 'shape' my two-hundred-pound torso into a two-foot-wide hole... assuming you can even get me in there."

"Dang," Fowler said. He pushed his hat back with his free hand and rubbed his chin with the other, staring at the hole like it might provide an answer."

"I mean, you could just have me kneel in front of it, like they do in war zones," Bob suggested. "But they make sure it's a deep pit, no adjustments needed, so the bodies can just fall in with others. You two? Well, you'll have to climb into the hole, stand on the professor's corpse and move me... all preferably without leaving any DNA, and no room to spare."

Fowler snarled a little as he spoke. "You knew the god-dang hole was too small, but you just kept digging, didn't say nothing!" He waved his gun at the hole. "Maybe you pick up that shovel, get back to work, make it deeper and longer."

Bob picked up the long-handled shovel and leaned on it. "Sure, deeper, too. Like... maybe deep enough for three bodies."

"Maybe," Fowler said. "Maybe you keep pissing me off, I'll have you digging until nightfall."

"Three bodies deep would be convenient," Bob said. "Then he can shoot you, too, Officer Czernowitz, take back that twelve and a half grand he just stuck in your pocket. It's not like he respects or really likes you."

Fowler raised his gun and stepped forward angrily. "GO ON! Keep talking bullshit, son, see how quick I put a bullet in that fat head of yours!"

"Jeb wouldn't do that," Czernowitz said. "Jeb looks out for me."

"Sure… like when he told you about the professor beforehand, so you'd have a choice about being implicated in a murder. Oh, that's right… he didn't. Didn't even bother. He calls you dumb all the time, but let me ask: you ever take any tests for him back in high school?"

"SHUT UP!" Fowler barked. "Shut your goddamned mouth!"

Bob ignored him. Fowler needed this to go as planned. But his partner's doubt was massing. They'd learned about duos like Fowler and Czernowitz in CIA behavioral training, that sociopaths preferred to find a mentally weak person to do their day-to-day bidding.

"I used to do his math tests for him," Czernowitz said. "But that's because Jeb's got the math dyslexia, like I got with words."

"That's not how dyslexia works," Bob lied. "It affects the order of words, not numbers. He just wanted you to do his homework."

Fowler leaped forward, showing more quickness than Bob would've assumed, the pistol clouting him again around the temple.

Bob staggered sideways.

The officer skipped back almost as quickly, out of range. "YOU WANT THIS TO GET A LOT MORE PAINFUL?" Fowler yelled. "Because if you do, we can shoot you a few times, bury you alive, let you bleed out."

"Yeah?" Bob said, rubbing his bleeding temple with his right hand, his left still on the shovel handle. "And who's going to do the work, shoveling all that dirt back on top of us? Oh... yeah. That's right. Let me guess: that's the kind of thing he gets you to do for him, too, right, Officer Czernowitz?"

"He don't make me—"

"Shut up, Witty!" Fowler's anger was growing. "He's trying to trick you! You don't listen to a god-damned word he says! You feel me, brother?"

There was something in his tone, the tension of the day's changing circumstances, that struck his partner in the moment. Czernowitz looked uneasy, shuffling in place slightly, his view of his relationship to his bully friend sitting in a new light. He wandered over to the hole and looked in.

"The professor..."

"You got to trust me, Witty..."

"Yeah. Yeah, I know, Jeb, but... He seemed like a nice feller, is all."

"Yup," Bob interjected. "And now he's fucking dead, because your 'friend' Jeb murdered him. Now he's going to have you bury him, so you're implicated as well."

"God DANG, mister!" Fowler barked, turning back to Bob. "I am just about done with you."

"Go on, get digging," Bob said. "You're next, Czernowitz... Maybe not today, but..."

Fowler lost his temper. He strode the ten feet, pistol

raised to prevent Bob from reacting. He pressed the tip of the barrel to Bob's temple.

"I figure, hole's too small or not, we'll make it work. That means your time is done, smart mouth."

By the edge, Czernowitz was staring into the grave again, his gaze bleak. "That right? You want me to do all the shoveling, Jeb?" he said. "You want me to bury the professor?"

Fowler took a deep breath, trying to compose himself, ward off another outburst, his eyes flitting between them, his body language nervous. "Witty, we both know you're bigger and stronger. Take you half the damn time, and one of us still has to keep watch."

"Watch?" Bob muttered. "From what?" He gestured around them. "Nothing for miles but sagebrush and coyotes."

"Yeah," Czernowitz agreed, a small nod. "From what?" He glanced at the hole again. Then at his friend, as if weighing things. "Maybe you can do it, Jeb..."

Fowler took a few steps back, then turned to his friend, closing the gap between them. "Witty... I ain't doing nothing but running the god-dang show, making the smart decisions for both of us, like I always do!" He pounded on his own chest with his free hand. He tried to soften his tone. "He's making it sound real bad, but they'll fill up most of the hole. Won't take you more than twenty minutes."

His partner glowered at that. It was anger, Bob recognized, years of doing a bully's bidding because losing his protection would feel worse.

"Plus, when you're shoveling in that dirt for him," Bob said, "you'll helpfully be right next to the grave. That way, if he decides he wants that twelve and a half grand back, well... no heavy lifting for little Jeb."

Czernowitz turned quickly to stare Fowler down.

Now that look, I know, Bob thought. *That look is pure suspicion.*

Fowler stared back warily. "What? WHAT!? You ain't listening to this bullshit!?"

"Ain't bullshit!" Czernowitz said. "Ain't bullshit, not at all! He got a lot right. You did make me take your tests for you. You didn't tell me about the professor. Why'd you *do* that, Jeb?" His tone was pained, frustration growing. "You always tell me we do the wrong thing sometimes, but it's for the right reasons. But the professor... that don't feel right. And you always call me dumb, like he said. It's 'you're so stupid, Witty. You're so dumb!'"

"He's trying to divide us!" Fowler blared. "Trying to confuse you because you're a little touched in the head! Don't pay him no goddamned mind, Witty, goddamn it, you simple motherfucker!"

Bob saw Czernowitz's eyes widen, a sense of outrage setting in, years of being the butt of the other man's shots coming home to roost.

Bingo.

Czernowitz's hand drifted towards his holster.

"Now, Witty... don't you do nothing stup—"

"DON'T YOU FUCKING CALL ME STUPID!" Czernowitz roared. "I been taking that shit from you for too goddamned long, Jeb Fowler!"

He twitched, ever so slightly.

Fowler's hand shot upwards, raising the gun to chest height, even as Czernowitz pulled his piece, a fraction too late. The Glock spat fire, the shot catching the bigger man chest-high.

Czernowitz went over backwards, his body thudding to the ground.

Bob was swinging the shovel before Fowler could finish turning towards him, stepping into it, letting the four-foot handle slide through his palms so that the tool was at full extension. The spade head caught Fowler in the shoulder as he turned, the Glock flying from his grasp.

It pirouetted through the air, bounced twice on the dirt, and came to rest.

Fowler regained his balance.

Both men saw it land. They had the same thought, glancing at each other, then diving for the pistol, scrambling across the hard-pack dirt to get to it first.

27

Bob tried to scramble over top of the smaller man, but Fowler's right hand reached the pistol first.

Bob's fist came down on it. The pipe cleaner plunged into the tender flesh, between the ligaments. Fowler shrieked, twisting under the bigger man's weight and throwing a hard elbow. It caught Bob above the eye, and he fell sideways.

Fowler scrambled out from under him, his other hand grasping the pistol. He made it to his feet and turned as he rose, raising the pistol and training it on Bob.

He looked down at his right hand, the pipe cleaner's short metal spike still protruding from it. "FUCK!" he bellowed. "GOD DAMN!" Fowler leaned down and used his teeth to pull on the cleaner. It slid out, accompanied by a quiet 'squelch' of torn flesh.

He spat out the pipe cleaner. "Sum'bitch." Fowler's face was bright red, contorted with anger and grief. "Sum'bitch hurts! You... you made me shoot Witty... you... you dirty motherfucker!"

"Oh, please... don't pretend you gave a shit," Bob said.

"Witty was dumber than fruit punch, mister. But he was mine! Mine to do what I want and have as a friend, whenever I needed him. And you fucking killed him, sure as you pulled the trigger!" He raised the pistol, aiming down the iron sight. "I should have shot you before we even came out here. That old bastard Feeney too."

Get him mad, make him jerk that trigger, give yourself a chance to reach him when he fires wide. "Here's your chance, you scrawny, braindead, inbred hillbilly motherfucker! Show me what you've got!"

Fowler's finger drew back the trigger smoothly, training kicking in... the shot ringing out before he could complete the action, the hole appearing in his forehead in that split-second before the gun's retort.

His grip gave slightly, the pistol hanging from his index finger by its trigger guard, his expression confused. "I-I-I..." He tried to say something, but the bullet had damaged something in his brain, the words not coming out properly, blood running freely from the hole. He dropped to his knees. "I-I-I..." he muttered, his head jerking sideways with each sound.

Fowler pitched face-first to the ground and stopped moving.

Bob turned around.

Czernowitz had managed to raise his torso, get onto one side. His pistol was in his right hand. "Pre... Pretty good shot, I guess," he managed. His eyes narrowed as he peered, dazed, at Bob. He turned the pistol towards him.

Bob walked over. "You going to shoot me?" he asked as he closed the twenty-foot gap.

Czernowitz's eyelids fluttered, his strength abandoning

him again, gun hand dropping to the dirt. "Guess... guess not. I think... I think I need an ambulance."

Bob reached down calmly and took the pistol. "You were going to kill me, stick me in a hole. Why shouldn't I just leave you here to bleed out? They probably wouldn't find you until your bones are picked clean."

Czernowitz's head bobbed slightly as he tried to think. "I can... I can tell them... about the professor. I can tell them what Jeb did. I figure, if I don't, they'll blame you for sure."

Now... that's a good point, Bob had to concede. "And you'll confess to setting up Marcus Pell for Hap Singh's murder."

Czernowitz peered at him, confused. "Wah?"

"The boy! My friend. The car in the alley near Jenkins Mechanical!"

Czernowitz shook his head gently. "Didn't do it," he said.

"What?!"

"I didn't do shit, mister. I ain't lying."

"Your partner... Go over the scene again. Quickly. The gun..."

"Jeb leaned in the car. He..." Czernowitz paused, confused. "He reached in first, dropped something."

"He dropped the gun in the car, then claimed he found it there. His report said he found it in Marcus's pocket."

The prone officer nodded. "Kept an old Walther that was clean as a backup piece. Same as the gun they seized."

"He planted the piece." Was it enough to get Marcus sprung? *Probably.* "Why? Who ordered him to set up my friend?"

"I... I don't know, for real. He... He said he was just making sure. Making sure we get the right guy."

"Cut the shit!"

"I... I ain't lying. You... you want me to lie?" He slumped back, panting slightly, the effort of sitting up too much.

"No. No, I don't want you to lie." Bob sighed. *Goddamn it. He was going to murder me twenty minutes ago, but now he decides to play it straight!?* A motive would've cemented the notion of a setup. "Stay still. I'm going to take a look."

He crouched beside Czernowitz. The entry wound was fleshy. Blood pooled around the hole near his left armpit. *Turned slightly at the last second to raise his piece, probably saved him.* He reached around the officer's back and found the exit wound. "Got you really clean, missed your lung. You're lucky. Is there a first aid kit..."

"Lower door... panel on the driver's side," Czernowitz managed.

"Stay put." Bob headed back towards the car. He needed to get the man patched up enough to stem any more bleeding. Then he needed Sharmila's help. If anyone knew where they could stash a wounded cop witness, it would be a local doctor.

28

Sharmila stared through the observation window at the man in the addiction treatment center bed. A saline drip, sedatives and painkillers were hooked up to his arm, clear plastic tubing leading back to a chrome pole his intravenous bags were hanging from.

He slept, head elevated, his chest wrapped in wide white bandages.

She'd known Czernowitz on and off for half her life. He'd never really grown up. Everyone knew that.

She turned back to the waiting area chairs, outside the room. Bob had his head in his hands, massaging his cheeks as if trying to stay awake, even though it was just past four in the afternoon. His shirt was soaked through with sweat, dirt streaks up and down his forearms.

"You look exhausted," she said.

"Yeah." His expression was bleak. He'd told her what happened, the two hours of digging in the blistering heat, the fight with Fowler.

"This wasn't your fault," she said. "And it changes everything, of course. Witty can put Merry Michelsen away for bribery. And beyond that, once he ties Fowler to Michelsen, Fowler's credibility goes out the window in your friend's arrest."

"That's why he's here," Bob said.

"Because otherwise, you'd have left him to die in the middle of nowhere?" she said sardonically. "Sure."

He looked up sharply. "Don't assume you know me well enough to discount it. He tried to kill me and bury me in a hole in the desert. His homicidal stupidity and general positive intentions notwithstanding, that kind of behavior tends to piss a man off."

Sharmila realized she needed to weigh her words more carefully around Bob. Whoever he really was, there was anger simmering just beneath the surface. If it blew before she had answers, her father's killer could disappear into the extensive annals of dubious local murder cases, the truth fading away with them.

"I picked up your stuff from the motel, like you asked."

"Thank you," Bob said.

"They're going to find his cruiser in Bakersfield because of its beacon," she said. "Then they'll know something happened to him. One of the first places they'll look is local hospitals, in case he had a knock and is incapacitated. But eventually, once they think it's been long enough to assume foul play, they'll try the smaller clinics."

"I thought you said this wouldn't be a problem, keeping him under wraps while I figure this all out?"

"It's not," she said. "Not immediately. A private addiction center isn't going to be high on their list. But the longer this stretches on, the more nervous my administrator friend will get. She's a big 'true crime' podcast fan, so this is exciting for her. But her job is at stake, her career. Mine too. And you're wanted for assault. And you have a client..."

"Your cousin has a client."

"...who is also your friend, and now can't see you."

Bob hadn't thought about that. "Shit, Marcus."

"The actual reason you came here in the first place," she reminded him. "I'll have Anuvab talk to him, tell him you're okay. At least that way he won't be worrying."

"I get that there are other people to consider," Bob said, "like your administrator friend. But the plus side is that we're ahead of the game now. We know Baird was involved somehow. We know he's got friends on the police."

"I had a thought on that," she said. "I did some reading from the local newspaper archive. When the initial fracking permit was rejected for Jenkins's quarter lot—before they pivoted to housing—it had already gone through the local level, the county board of supervisors, and gotten the okay. Despite the fact that most folks expected it to reject the plan outright."

"Then why didn't it go ahead?"

"Because the Energy Management Division—that's the state board that overviews drilling approvals—said there was no point asking for a permit, that it considered that area of the valley's oil and gas profile overdeveloped already."

"The professor mentioned that; he said the state never approves those sorts of projects anymore. So... it wasn't the local politicians who shut it down, not really."

"Technically, they withdrew their permission before any permit was issued. So technically, it was. But everyone knew they'd initially given it a thumbs-up, by a 3-2 vote."

"So... Baird had political supporters," Bob said. "He

wouldn't have the two who voted against it in his back pocket. And the other three..."

"Two of them are arch-libertarians who sit on the board to dissuade over-regulation. They rubber stamp anything they see."

"And the third?"

"The third?" She frowned. "Gerry Tucker. He's sort of a local educational hero. That's not going to a warmly received notion, that an assistant high school principal is in bed with a developer."

"Maybe he isn't," Bob said. "Maybe he genuinely believed it was in the county's best interests. There's really only one way to find out."

She nodded. "Okay. Okay then. But... I talk to him first, Bob. Gerry's an open book, or seems it to most local folks. I just can't see him being on the bad side of this."

DISTRICT FOUR SUPERVISOR Gerald Tucker's office was above a picture framing store in a strip mall off Brimhall Road.

Sharmila had never visited before, but as she climbed the stairs, it struck her that the place fit his reputation: unassuming, unglamorous.

He'd helped put two generations of kids through schools in Bakersfield and Oildale before being drafted in to represent the mostly affluent district on the non-partisan board.

A middle-aged receptionist greeted her as she entered the office. "Gerry will be just a few minutes, Ms. Singh, if you'd like to have a seat," she said.

A moment later, a broad-shouldered giant of a man in a grey two-piece suit appeared. "Ms. Singh?" He held out his hand to shake as she rose, then clasped both their hands with his left. "I was so very sorry to hear about your father," he said. "We worked together several times over the years; he was a good man. Please... let's talk in my office."

He led her across the room to the back corner. The office was large but plain and functional. "Grab a seat there. Do you need a coffee?" Before she could answer, he sat on the corner of the desk and hit a line on his phone. "Ms. Joyner, if you could bring us a fresh pot of coffee..."

"I'll be right in."

He released the button before giving Sharmila his full attention. "Okay. Can't hustle without my caffeine," he admitted ruefully.

"I think that's most of us," she said. "Supervisor... you may have heard I have problems with the police version of things on my father's death."

"It's been a topic of conversation, sure," he said. "But... you know, it's just people talking."

The door opened and Ms. Joyner entered with a small tray, two cups and a tiny carafe. "I'll leave you to it," she said.

He waited until the door closed. "She's a pistol, Ms. Joyner. I don't think I'd get anything done without her."

He poured them each a cup. Sharmila accepted it and perched the saucer on her lap.

"I'm looking into some of the projects that drew my father's attention."

"His opposition to the new trailer parks. It goes without saying, I hope, that he had my support on that one. Probably wouldn't have mattered, as we need housing badly right now in the county. But we needed something longer term, real chances at homes for people."

"That's nice to hear," Sharmila said. She took a sip of coffee and weighed his eager demeanor. He was either so practiced at politeness that nothing true came through or he was genuine, she thought. He had to be. "I was thinking more about one of the other cases that came up, the fracking application."

He nodded sagely, thinking back. "Oh yeah, sure. That wasn't going to happen, not on my watch."

"But... you voted for it."

He seemed slightly amused, Sharmila thought. "Because it was a dead vote, a non-starter. There was no risk. But it kept a few people whose support I needed happy, for my worker safety initiative."

"So it was purely political. Worker safety?"

"I'm working with my District 5 peers to try and improve labor conditions for undocumented workers, potentially through safety-related zoning requirements for new agricultural projects."

"That seems worthy. And the housing proposal? That's still Jenkins, technically, isn't it?"

"I believe so," he said. "They have some silent partners, and when you add in the adjacent lots, we're talking close to twenty-five hundred new units. That's a lot of homes."

"And a lot of concentrated poverty," she said. "They'll all end up as overpriced rentals."

He sighed. "Possibly, yes. Your father felt so. Filing papers to run for sheriff was shrewd on his part. He could've asked for enough restrictive covenants on the project to have sunk the whole thing, I imagine, or at least delay the heck out of it."

"And he'd have had jurisdiction to try and keep people like Merry Michelsen out," she said. "A motive for murder."

"Perhaps," Tucker said. "Mind you, it almost wasn't going to happen anyhow, whether your father got involved or not."

That's new. Sharmila felt her pulse race. *That's something new.* "Why?"

"The county had the same poverty trap concerns, concentrations of crime and violence, and what have you. But then Jenkins up and promised to offer twenty full-time jobs for residents who could do labor and needed work."

"Professor Jenkins said that?"

"Well... I'm using the term in the corporate sense, as most here do, but I think he knew about it. I mean... I assume he did. His CEO, Parker Baird, was leading the negotiations. Said he could get other investors to offer the same. He figured he could create a hundred new positions easily."

"Did he say where? How? Because I haven't heard anything about Jenkins expanding."

Tucker nodded slowly. "I believe so. He owns a cheese factory under a subsidiary. It's not even ten minutes away, which means they'd be able to get to work easily even without transportation. It looked like one hell of a deal. I can get you the address. I understand they make a fine cheddar. They've got a little shop up front, real quaint."

"A cheese factory?"

Tucker raised both palms to ward off her concern. "Now, I know what you're thinking: a factory, a trailer park full of meth heads a few miles away, some of them maybe working there..."

"Doesn't that seem a little suspicious?" she said.

"Now... Parker Baird is a respected businessman. And besides, just to be careful, I had one of our boys do some checking. Making methamphetamine requires certain precursor chemicals, most notably pseudoephedrine. Our investigator's a former local vice guy and had seen plenty of cook houses, so he knew what to look for. Inspected their stocks, checked their inventories and purchase orders."

"Nothing?"

"Nothing. Our boy was real thorough, checked their incomings and outgoings, even had someone go in looking for work who knew the business. They had a whole lot of cheese in stock… but no sign of crystal meth, no cook tables. It sure seemed legit to us. He wound up leaving with a wheel of gouda."

OUTSIDE THE BUILDING, Bob stayed low in the passenger seat of her BMW, his eyes behind a pair of sunglasses, a "San Jose Earthquakes" ballcap on his head.

"Did you get all that?" Sharmila's voice was clear through the phone's external speaker.

"I did. Are you done?"

"I'll be there in a minute."

He'd had her keep the line open on her phone, tucked into the side pocket of her purse. It wasn't that he lacked faith in her ability to ask a question. He had training in spotting relevant details others missed, changes in cadence, potential lies or white lies.

Tucker had struck him as sincere, but in the context of someone who plays the same character all the time. Was he really that nice and genial? Was anyone? Probably not.

She opened the driver's side door and climbed in. "Okay. So how did we do?"

"We have something to follow up."

"The subsidiary business. The cheese factory."

Bob nodded. "I've had run-ins with any number of

jagoffs over the years. I've never met one yet who was going out of his way to create work for the poor."

"So it's hiding something. Maybe that was what my father had figured out."

"It has to be," Bob said. "From what Tucker was saying, the housing battle was somewhat lost already. But your father figured out the one position—sheriff—that could intervene without politics getting in the way. He'd have been all over Merry and Baird."

"So they killed him," Sharmila said bleakly.

"I need to check this place out. Even if not meth, I think we can make a safe bet that whatever that factory is producing, it sure ain't just cheese."

29

Merry Michelsen scratched at the pale red stain on his UCLA sweatshirt and lamented that it wasn't ever going away. "Dang McDonald's. Should buy me a new one," he muttered.

But it wouldn't be the real deal. He'd bought it at the start of year three, just before the money ran out. *And damn you for that, too, Daddy.*

Of course, losing his degree had its benefits, too. It had motivated him to turn his sideline selling a little weed and coke into a real career.

He sat in the office at the back of the warehouse along Gilmore Avenue and watched through the picture window as the lab techs worked. The bigger room was filled with equipment, giant drums and flasks, a machine that looked like a vertical cement mixer, tables loaded with Bunsen burners, rows of glass flasks and tubing.

It was all Greek to him. Merry had learned to "shake and bake"—mix methamphetamine precursor chemicals in a soda bottle, then turn them into crystal by cooking them.

That was simple enough for anyone to pick up, at least until they blew their arms off accidentally.

But the veritable field of equipment between the office and the front part of the building might as well have been making chocolate, or snow tires, for all he understood.

Across the factory floor, he saw one of the double doors open. Greg Thomas paced quickly around one side of the collected machinery, joining him a minute later.

"Well?" Merry said. "What do you think?"

Thomas scowled. Baird's assistant had a collarless leather jacket on, blue jeans. Merry realized he'd dragged him away from a day off.

"What do I think? I designed this. I knew exactly what to expect."

"And? We flipped the switch this morning, so to speak. Everything look okay?"

Thomas's exasperation came through. "I told you, if it isn't, the explosion could level the block. I noticed on my way here that that hasn't happened."

Merry held up both palms. "Now, partner... I apologize if you think I'm wasting your time..."

"You are."

"But more than that, I figured you'd want to see the dream coming to fruition. I know we ain't never going to need to be here, but this is a big day."

"*Your* dream, Merry. Your plan. I'm just the guy who knows how to synthesize methylamine. In the meantime, I told you quite clearly that I don't want to be around this stuff. This is not a stable, safe process, and if your people fuck up—"

"They know they'll probably die. So... they won't fuck up. They aren't allowed to use—anything—and my men pay close attention to what they're doing. Other than going outside to smoke, they never have to leave the premises. We give them a cot upstairs, a lockbox for their stuff, and there's a decent normal kitchen, too. This is just straight money back to their families south of the border."

Merry walked over and put an arm around the smaller man's shoulders. "Now, come on, brother, cheer up! You act like I ain't about to make you incredibly stinkin' rich! But between your know-how and my contacts, we're going to be supplying this to half the labs in California *and* Mexico."

"It's a product," Thomas said wearily. "Nothing more."

"It's a product that makes damn fine crystal, is what it is. Like I said... a cooker's dream. Meth producers from here to Juarez are going to beg us for it. And best of all, the only controlled ingredients don't come off our books. Average fellers like us, we can't buy Nitro Funny Car fuel at Walmart. But Jenkins Racing has an inexhaustible supply."

"You'd best keep in mind the risks we're all taking," Thomas groused.

"Uh huh, uh huh... And you'd do well to remember that without my help in school, you ain't in that fancy job at Jenkins. You ain't hobnobbing with Parker Baird and the like."

Thomas just shook his head.

"What? What now!?" Merry asked. "Does every god-dang thing I say upset you?" The truth was, he'd always found Greg handsome, smart and strong. He'd never said it to him, never would. But he sure did like having him around.

"You're never going to let me off the hook, are you?"

"Oh, now, come on, brother! I told you, we split this right down the middle. This ain't no drive-by shakedown!" Merry says. "This is capitalism in full flight. And the real risk is with the meth producers, not us suppliers. This ain't smuggling Sudafed tabs across the border. In a couple of years, you're going to have so much money—"

"And then you'll stop holding that stupid test over my head?"

Merry held up a hand in protest. "Man... I do not even know how to talk to you when you're in this kind of place emotionally."

Blackmailing him in college by getting him test results had put Thomas in Merry's pocket. But he liked to think eventually Greg would come around, see him as a guy who got things done and created success. Maybe even eventually find him attractive, someone he would want to spend more time with.

Everybody wants love, Merry figured. *Maybe he just don't know it yet.*

30

Bob watched the back of the shop and factory on Gilmore Avenue from behind the wheel of Sharmila's BMW.

It was a quiet sort of place, red brick and thick glass inset windows, surrounded by eight-foot chain-link fencing topped with razor wire. A sign in the lot read 'The Big Cheese.'

Two wooden picnic tables sat by the path to the back door A handful of workers were gathered at them, smoking cigarettes.

The razor wire seemed a bit extreme for a place selling dairy. *Maybe they have a history, robberies and such. That Parmesan doesn't come cheap.*

Merry Michelsen had gone in fifteen minutes earlier, parking a few spots ahead of where the BMW now sat, then walking around the building to its commercial entrance. Bob had followed him from the trailer park after a two-hour stakeout.

Sharmila had been called home for an emergency. Her

four-year-old son had heard about his grandfather's violent death in a radio report, and was having a panic attack.

Poor kid. He'll be dealing with that for a long time.

Bob got his mind back on the job. Michelsen's parking decision had been interesting in and of itself. Instead of trying to negotiate the cheese shop's postage-stamp parking lot, he'd gone directly down the side street, to the spot behind it. That suggested familiarity.

He'd been in there for at least a quarter-hour. *He's there on business, nothing less.*

He peered past the smoking workers. In the back corner of the yard, close to the building, were a pair of diesel generators, the type used as emergency backup in developing nations, each just a little bigger than the picnic tables, like squat, oversized pill capsules.

They were both running, tiny rectangular orange lights illuminated, each vibrating slightly.

Now that's odd. Why would a cheese factory be running a pair of diesel generators at a little after three in the afternoon? The county supervisor was adamant the place wasn't up to anything. But the generators weren't saving them money, that was for sure.

But it might lower their draw from the power grid, Bob figured. *What are they trying to hide?*

He rolled down the window and craned his neck out for a moment. Usually, a drug operation would have guards who had nice wheels, at the least. He looked down the row of cars, past Michelsen's Lexus.

Bingo. A Cadillac Escalade, tinted windows, and beyond it, a green Audi. *That's some serious bills for cheese factory workers.*

He ducked back into the car and raised the window.

Okay. My bet has to be methamphetamine. But...

That doesn't work, if Gerry Tucker was right. They know exactly what to look for, the precursors, the system. They're not taking in inventory that would work or help cover their intentions. And they've been inspected, probably without notice. Hiding cook tables, burners.

So what are they making, and how?

It took another five minutes for anyone to make an appearance. The backdoor opened.

A man's head flashed briefly into view, a blur of platinum blond hair, his considerable figure filling the doorway for a moment.

Michelsen.

A figure shoved past him, through the doorway. The door closed behind him.

The man who'd bumped him at Jenkins.

Greg Thomas.

Thomas looked both ways a little self-consciously as he made his way across the yard. At the gate, he waited a moment, presumably for someone to buzz the lock from inside.

He crossed to a Range Rover, two cars ahead of the BMW. A minute later, it pulled out of the spot.

Bob waited until he was fifty yards ahead before pulling out to tail him. He kept his distance, letting his speed drift up and down slightly, allowing other cars space to move between them.

He's heading back home.

Bob waited until Thomas had pulled into the driveway of the bungalow in Riviera/Westchester, a modest neighborhood west of downtown. Once the assistant had gone inside, he took out his phone and called Nicky Velasco.

. . .

Nicky answered after the second callback ring, as per convention. "Alpha! It's been a while. I was starting to think someone had punched your ticket."

"Nope, still breathing."

"Good. You owe me a pair of grade-A, first-class favors, and I aim to eventually cash in."

"Ah... so not genuine concern about my health, then." Nicky could be as callous as people come sometimes, even if he generally sided with the angels.

"It is what it is," Nicky said. "If I didn't pick up, would your first question be 'what happened to Nick'? Or would it be 'how do I solve this problem without Nick?' I hate to bring our relationship back to the jarring reality of it, Alpha, but I kind of suspect it would be the latter."

He was right, Bob knew. *I'm being a hypocrite.* "Apologies. But whether you believe it or not, I would worry about you, Nicky. I did when you were in the Team, and I do now. Not often, I'll admit, because in this business, people are out of sight, out of mind."

"That's life in general, Alph—" He caught himself. "Boss."

"Or even just 'Bob' works," he suggested. "I'm not your boss. I never really was; that was Eddie Stone's job. I just led the Team, and the Team is long gone. Or, our version is, anyway."

"Important distinction," Nicky said. "From the scuttlebutt, the modern version is plenty busy. They were in Chechnya, last I heard."

"Chechnya?! What the hell are they..." Then Bob caught

himself. "Never mind. I don't want to know. That was a different life."

"And is in no way related to whatever weird compulsion has you travelling across the country like a particularly dangerous hobo. Sure."

"Look... I need a workup on someone. Can it be quick?"

"Depends on the someone."

Bob gave him Thomas's address and work details.

"Eh... seems like a fairly normal job for someone of my stupendous talents. I'll get back to you this evening, I expect."

"Appreciated. If you get the time, I have a puzzler."

"Shoot."

"Why would a cheese factory owned by a car engine designer be involved somehow in the meth business? And we're looking for an answer other than 'cooking meth', as they've been scrutinized. No sign of pseudoephedrine, no cook tables, wrong equipment, an actual product in their own cheeses. So it has to be something else."

"Eh... I'll poke around," Nicky said. "Keep your head down, Alpha... Bob."

"Will do, Nicky. Follow your own advice, okay?" If there was one truism about Nicky, it was that he'd never been as serious or cautious as the job required.

31

The family bed and breakfast on Dracena Street wasn't ideal. But motels and hotels were out, given the heightened police interest. After being greeted by the owner and told the front door locked after 11 p.m., Bob went up to his room and closed the door.

It was a simple setup: a twin bed, a small TV, a USB charging station on the bedside table. There was a shared bathroom down the hall.

He opened his soft-sided case and retrieved the separate burner, reserved for talking with Dawn Ellis in Chicago. It had been five days since Marcus's arrest, and she would be worrying, he knew.

"*Really!?*" she exclaimed on answering.

"No 'Hi, Bob, great to hear from you,' or anything..."

"*Really?* Five days without so much as a hint at what's going on, without knowing if Marcus is safe, and you're chastising me for not being Ms. Sweetness and Light!?"

"I could be wrong," Bob said, "but I detect mild irritation."

"*Not* appropriate!" she insisted. "No jokes, please! Not at this juncture. Now, spill! Tell me what's going on before I worry myself to a nub."

"Well... they denied his bail, which we expected." Bob knew he had to choose his words carefully. Dawn had a big heart, but that also made her prone to worrying more than was productive. "I'm making headway. Progress, I guess."

"At what, exactly?"

"Figure out who actually killed Hardeep Singh. Figuring out why they're pinning it on Marcus. It's... a different sort of city, Bakersfield. It has its own tensions."

She was silent for a moment. "I'm not sure I like the sound of that," she said. "You're staying out of trouble, correct?"

"Well... I haven't told anyone important to f—"

"Don't you dare!" Dawn insisted. "Don't make a joke of swearing and blaspheming just to get under my skin, because you know you're just trying to distract me from asking questions! And I know that means you're worried."

She was so intuitive and empathetic it could be frustrating, Bob thought. It was probably what made her a great nurse, but it made putting anything past her almost impossible.

"Look... you know that when there's big money involved and I'm keeping my head down, it's for reasons," he said. "But the important thing to keep in mind is that he's safe in custody. The police are involved—some police are involved, anyhow—and if they don't keep their fall guy safe, and he doesn't get convicted, then important local people have to start answering questions."

"About what?"

She'd pry until she got enough detail to involve herself,

he knew. The trick was to not let her browbeat or guilt it out of him. "Money. The usual. The less said the better, really."

"Uh huh," she said, which was Dawn language for 'why don't I believe that?' "And what if I were to take a few days off work..."

"No!" Bob declared. "I mean..." He sighed, exasperated. The truth was, he wanted her there, looking out for them, taking care of them. But he'd never admit it, nor put her in harm's way. "He'll be fine. I promise."

"Uh huh. But he's not the only one in trouble now, is he? I know that tone, mister cool, calm and collected. I heard it in Chicago, I heard it in DC, and I heard it when you called me from New Orleans. You are right up to your neck, without a doubt."

"I'm *handling* it," he said.

"You don't sound like you're handling nothing. You sound like your last fuse is burning short and you're about to blow."

"It's... been a difficult two days. Dawn... you know the rules. As long as they're looking for me..."

"Are they, though?" she wondered. "It's been nearly ten months since you left, and six since you said that gentleman came after you in Memphis. Maybe they've given up."

"Doubtful. What I do know, however, is that a handful of unsavory locals don't really give a damn—"

"Bob..."

"Sorry. They don't really care where someone is from or whose side they're on. They have a deal worth millions, and this guy was threatening it. He had money and some influence, and they still killed him. Compared to that, Marcus and I don't rate much forgiveness."

She sighed. "I know why you don't want me there. I get it.

I get that it's unsafe. But that's also why I feel I'd be of more use..."

"You wouldn't. You'd be in the way," Bob said. He knew it would sting. Dawn was confident and brave, far more than he'd expected from a civilian. But he couldn't allow the risk.

"That's... Okay, perhaps that's true. But it hurts a little to hear you say it, is all."

"I don't mean it like that," Bob said. "I know I think clearer when you're around. I understand that you see things with more... restraint. But I'd worry about you constantly. And if I'm worrying about you, I'm not watching my own back, or looking out for others here who are in real danger. Adding one more person to that list..."

"Even when it's me?"

"Especially when it's you. Because you will get involved. You will try to help. And that's one more person in the firing line... the one I care about."

She sighed deeply again. "Don't much like that term, 'the firing line'."

"It's not that bad, not yet," he said. "I'll try and do better about keeping you in the loop, though. I promise."

"I'll pray for you," she said.

"I know."

AFTER ENDING THE CALL, he stared at the phone for about fifteen seconds, as if it might spring to life and offer him better, less hurtful alternatives. He and Dawn were so different, in so many ways. But the one thing they had in common was giving a damn.

And that's why you don't get to have her in your life.

Because your life is about resistance, the inevitability of violence.

And hers is about making people better.

Bob hung his head. He was too tired to cry, the bone weariness that comes from wave after wave of pressure, wearing a man down like water eroding rock.

Across the room, his other phone rang in his coat pocket. Bob got up and retrieved it.

It was Sharmila's number.

"Hey, what's up?" he answered.

"It's Mr. Feeney," she said. "He's in hospital, and his place is burning down. I'll be outside your door in a couple of minutes."

32

They sat in Sharmila's BMW and watched from thirty yards down the road as the Feeney Motor Lodge burned, orange pillars of flame creeping across the walls and roof, the night sky around the property christened with a halo of light.

On the street ahead of it, a pair of fire trucks were parked at oblique angles, their lights splaying red tones across the asphalt and sidewalk.

"This requires a response," Bob said as he watched the fire crews trying to hook up a second hose to a hydrant, to douse the flames before they could catch the vacant, scrubby lot next door or, wind-aided, jump the road to other businesses.

"I don't think Mr. Feeney would appreciate that sentiment," Sharmila said. "Everyone knows Mel as a stoic sort of feller. He wouldn't want anyone getting hurt."

"I don't think he'd worry too much about the guys who probably did this," Bob said.

"I wasn't talking about them." She glanced sideways from

the driver's seat. "It really doesn't seem to occur to you that you could be the one who gets hurt, does it?"

Bob shrugged. The shrink in Las Vegas had told him he had poor impulse control; not as bad as a career criminal, perhaps, but undeveloped enough to get him into plenty of hot water.

The shrink had told him a lot of things about himself, things he still didn't really want to accept. That had been the point of going to Seattle, getting a second opinion from another expert.

But on the risk? *Maybe he had a point. But...*

"Somebody has to be the guy who wades in," he said.

"Yeah, but..."

"There are always bad guys out there, uncivil, selfish people who need standing up to. Usually, it's not the people we expect who do so. It's not the cops; they come *after* a crime has been committed. They don't prevent it. It's not the politicians or the men with money, because more often than not, the bad guys ultimately work for them."

"That sounds like a pretty broad justification—"

"It's *reality*," he stressed. Then he felt guilty for the harsh tone. "Sorry. But one of the things you learn in the Corps is that there is always—always—an asshole somewhere. And there always have to be good people making a difference. Most people think of military men and women—and law enforcement, for that matter—as a bunch of bullies and thugs. And there's no doubt the combative nature of the job does attract some. But most are there for the right reasons, even when the job is distasteful or wrong. And those good people will (a) never get the credit they deserve, socially, and (b) always wind up in harm's way themselves to make things right for others. It ain't nice, and it ain't right. But it is reality."

"That's a pretty brutal outlook on life."

"It's a realistic outlook on people," Bob insisted. "If I let this go, whoever did this just wins. They may not win long term; they may fuck up or be busted for something else. But they win at ruining Mr. Feeney's life. And all because he rented me and Marcus rooms. And I can't allow that."

"You realize they're just trying to draw you out?" Sharmila warned. "They don't care about an old guy like Mel Feeney. But they know you're wanted by the police. And they know that anything that happens to you they can say was during a citizen's arrest. If you go to them looking for payback, or retribution, or whatever you want to call it, you'll be on their turf, where they have the legal impetus, the built-in excuse of self-defense. They'll try to kill you."

Bob shrugged. "I'm not the one anyone needs to worry about."

MEL FEENEY LOOKED REMARKABLY CHIPPER, Bob figured, for a man with burned feet and a golf-ball-sized lump on the back of his head.

He was sitting up in a hospital bed. Bob could tell that much from the video chat screen on the nine-inch tablet.

Keep the mood light, Bobby. Consider the man's feelings, not your own. It wasn't going to be easy. He'd spent the prior hour vacillating between angered determination and a forlorn sense of, once more, being the problem that brought harm to others.

The older man leaned in slightly towards the screen—or perhaps just drew it closer—and whispered, "There must be ten cops here, minimum. For some reason, they're expecting you to show up."

"Yeah, we sort of figured," Bob said, nodding sideways to the driver's seat and Sharmila. "Sharmila's here too."

Feeney frowned. "My place..."

Bob couldn't hide his bleakness over what had happened. "I'm sorry, sir. Really, I am."

"You tried to warn me, and I didn't listen," Feeney said simply. "But..." He looked side to side to see if he was being observed, then smiled impishly, "...I wasn't lying about the insurance."

"So... you'll be okay?" Bob said.

"Okay? I'm retiring! Heck, I'm worth so much more burned up than operating, I might be able to afford Tahiti, never you mind Merida. Too damn hot there anyhow."

"I know who did this," Bob said.

"We all know who did this, Bob," Feeney said. "I mean, who ordered it, anyhow... Saw Tommy Kopec in a truck out on the street right before someone conked me from behind."

"He and his brother, then," Bob said.

Feeney took on a guarded look. "Now... you don't go doing anything rash, Bob. Merry Michelsen's a bad man, and the Kopecs are crazier than rabid coyotes, only half as kind."

"He's already promised me he's not going after them," Sharmila said. "Right, Bob?"

"Something like that," Bob said, which beat pointing out that he'd technically promised not to kill them. *But there's a lot of room for suffering between alive and dead.*

Feeney seemed less convinced. "Bob, you didn't force me to rent you a room, and you tried to move before something happened. You don't owe me a damn thing," he stressed. "Point of fact, I'll be a little pissed off if you take it as such."

"It's not about owing anyone," Bob said. "It's just about right and wrong. Someone a whole lot smarter than me once said that evil only wins when good men do nothing. I'd say the obvious extension is that 'good men' who do nothing aren't really good men."

"Then I reckon what you really want is me worrying about you," Feeney said. "Because that's all that's going to happen if you charge off somewhere tonight looking for revenge. Good or bad, right or wrong, I'm not in a mood to be worrying."

Bob shook his head gently. "Nobody's ever had to worry about me in the past," he said, though he knew they had, "and nobody needs to worry about me now."

Sharmila leaned into the camera's range. "Besides… we're going to spend the evening thinking about you, not the Kopecs," she told Feeney. "Right, Bob?"

Bob offered Feeney a smile. "You just get better. Okay?"

33

The smell caught up to Jonah Kepler a few feet inside the back door of his house on Lake Street. He'd lived there since childhood, inheriting the bungalow from his mother when she'd died.

She'd been a pious woman and considered her son a terrible failure. She told him so regularly. He'd never told his uncle or cousins, but Jonah felt profound relief when she finally succumbed to cancer.

He wasn't a considerate caretaker. The place was usually a mess, the living room draped in pizza boxes, old beer cans and general slobbery.

But it didn't usually smell strange. That was new, and a familiar reek, something that he knew bothered him but he couldn't place.

He walked through the kitchen and into the living room.

The man sitting on the couch was using chopsticks, slurping fat, wide noodles from a cardboard container. He had his head down, towards the box, and it took the ex-football player a moment to register who it was.

"Fucking Chink food," Jonah muttered. "You not only have the balls to break into my house, you have to bring that shit in here with you. I hate that shit. Had a Chinese place near my uncle's shop, stunk of fish and oil."

Bob slurped back the pad thai, munching a large mouthful before answering. "It's not Chinese, it's Thai," he said. "Shocked—I am shocked that a witless redneck wouldn't know the difference."

Jonah closed the gap between them, standing across the low-slung rectangular coffee table from his unwanted guest. He drew his pistol. "Same shit, different country. Gook food."

Bob put the carton down and pointed at him forcefully with the chopsticks. "See... that right there is why I decided to pay you a visit first, Jonah."

"Because you have a death wish and are stupid enough to think you're faster than a bullet?"

"Nah... because you struck me as the meanest, dumbest of the trio who visited me." Bob stared at the pistol for a moment. "Damn! Do you even know what you're holding?"

Jonah looked befuddled. "It's a Colt 1911. They're pretty fucking common, dude."

"Yeah... but that one has extra-thin sights, suggesting it was made before the First World War. It's probably worth more than that piece of shit jacked-up Chevy you've got outside."

"Eh?"

"Jesus H. So dumb. That, and your home address is still online in the phone book. Who has a listed number these days?" Bob looked around, at the old furniture, the old family photos collecting dust on the wallpapered walls. "I'm guessing you grew up here, got the place from whichever parent lasted longer."

"Yeah. Speaking of stupid, how retarded are *you*, exactly? Half the city is looking for your ass, the Kopecs are trying to flush you out... and you come here? You must be the dumbest motherfucker who ever lived," Jonah said. "You realize I'm legally entitled to shoot you for trespassing? Dang, son!"

Bob nodded. "Oh, sure, absolutely. And from that range—what, six feet away, maybe?—you'd probably even hit me, assuming you've kept that old marvel in shape."

He stood up abruptly.

Jonah extended his arm, nervous tension kicking in, the gun at eye level. "Now, don't do anything stupid, "Bob."

"Perish the thought," Bob said. He nodded past Jonah, towards the door. "As a police officer, I don't think your other guest would appreciate it much."

Jonah turned his head quickly to check the doorway. Bob took a step forward the second his head began to move, the cross-body open-palm strike targeting Jonah's wrist, where the small bones were most vulnerable. The blow stung the younger man, a slap of skin on skin as Bob felt one of the small bones break, the gun tumbling from Jonah's hand to the floor.

"JESUS FUCK!" Jonah bellowed, grasping at his wrist for the split second it took to register what had just happened. He turned back towards Bob in time to see the fist come whistling in, towards his unprotected chin.

JONAH STIRRED FROM UNCONSCIOUSNESS, his right arm jerking involuntarily, as if waking up before the rest of him.

But it didn't move much. Both arms were bound with thick rope to a kitchen chair, with a small length designed to give him some range of motion and prevent him losing circulation. He tried to move his feet, but his legs were tied to the chair's.

He looked around but couldn't see Bob.

"Oh good, you're awake." A hand came down on Jonah's shoulder as Bob leaned in to whisper in his ear. "Now... we're going to do things my way. I guarantee you, it's not going to be nearly as much fun as you seem to have harassing old men and grieving daughters."

"You do anything to me, you're a dead man," Jonah said. "YOU HEAR ME!? YOU HEAR ME!? I'm a fucking NAME in this town!"

"You're a washed-up high school football star in no position to make demands. You're a dime a dozen in this part of the world, Jonah."

Jonah lost his temper, rage building to the point where he thought he might snap the ropes, shaking the chair, bouncing it in place. "MOTHERFUCKER, I'LL FUCKING KILL YOU! FUCK! YOU FUCK!"

Bob walked around him and sat down in the adjacent kitchen chair. "You know what's ironic? Normally, screaming that kind of shit in a neighborhood like this at eleven at night would bring a visit from the cops. But I'm betting you've probably made lots of noise over the years, and you've probably scared your poor neighbors with your erratic criminal behavior. So now, they won't call anyone. If only you'd been a little nicer. Is that ironic? Or is that just, like, Alanis Morrissette-ironic?"

"FUCK YOU, YOU DIRTY SUM'BITCH! I'LL KILL YOU! I'll FUCKING KILL YOU!"

Bob leaned back and crossed his arms. "If I was a smoker, now would be the point where I pop outside and let you tire yourself out, like a toddler who needs to throw a tantrum before his nap. And... pardon me for saying it, but that shit with the head fake, where you actually looked behind you to see if a cop..." He shook his head slowly. "I mean, I highly recommend never repeating anything that embarrassing as an anecdote. I'm personally embarrassed for you."

"Sum'bitch," Jonah mumbled. "Fucking kill you."

"That shit never works with *anyone*," Bob continued. "The police are actively hunting for me, so why would they be here, helping me? I have to tell you, that officially makes you the biggest fool I've ever had to deal with. Plus, it meant I didn't have to throw my noodles at you. I'm enjoying them, and there's more than one meal there, I think." He leaned in a little and softened his voice. "And I am going to deal with you physically, in case you're wondering what comes next. This is going to be a really unpleasant night for you... but how unpleasant depends on how you behave from here on in."

Jonah was still steaming, his head shaking back and forth in small, angry increments. "Then... WHAT?! WHAT THE FUCK! What the fuck do you want, man!?"

"That's simple: I want an address and phone number for Vernon Kopec."

Jonah's expression shifted, anger giving way to momentary amusement. "Heh. This is about the old man, isn't it? He die?"

"Nope. His place burned to the ground, but he's surprisingly okay with it all. Good insurance, apparently."

His captive didn't like that at all. "Dang. Thought he was dead."

"You were there? Good. That's good to know," Bob said.

"It'll prevent any remorse from stopping me doing whatever's necessary to get what I need."

Jonah studied him through lizard eyes, his lids low, his mouth a cruel line. "You're bluffing. Samaritan types—do-good assholes like you—they've got lines they don't cross. You think we don't know that?"

"Possibly," Bob said. He rose and walked behind Jonah again, clapping him on both shoulders like a comrade. "But the question is where that line starts and ends. Is it, for example, north of the point required to prevent me causing you pain? Let's find out!"

Bob grabbed Jonah's head by the back of his hair, slamming the ex-jock's face into the edge of the table in one smooth motion, his nasal bone snapping audibly.

"Eahhh!' Jonah moaned, trying to raise his arms to his face, blood streaming over his lips and chin.

"Now we can do that..." Bob slammed his face into the table once more, "...again." Slam! "And again." Slam! "And again..." Slam!

On the fourth strike, Jonah remained slumped forward, his movement minimal, concussion dazing him.

Bob waited thirty seconds for him to rouse.

"Wah?" Jonah mumbled incoherently.

"Yeah, it's not sophisticated. But when the person on the receiving end is an amoral coward, just good ol'-fashioned pain can be a heck of a motivator," Bob said. He walked across the room and opened a pair of cabinet doors, finding the drinking glasses.

He filled one with water, then walked back over to the table and tossed it into Jonah's face, the sudden cold rousing him.

"What...what happ—" He caught himself midsentence on seeing Bob. "Oh. Yeah."

"And that wasn't even the warmup," Bob said. "That was just because I really, really, really don't like you. Now, you might want to consider helping me. Because you can't breathe through that shattered nose, and if I get impatient, I might just stick a wet sock in your mouth, see how much you dislike the sensation of suffocating. And you can't take many more shots. You look... well... you're not going to be dating any time soon."

"Man... Can't..."

"Or," Bob said, "I could grab that butcher knife you keep in the second drawer and see how many small cuts I can make to your exposed flesh in under five minutes. Then, I'll grab that very old, very rancid bottle of vinegar you have in your fridge—have you even cleaned this place since your mom died? No biggie. A thousand small cuts doused in vinegar have an interesting effect on a man. It's a field torture, so it's pretty darn poor at prompting accuracy. Because the pain is so excruciating, a man will say just about anything to make it stop. Tricks the nervous system, you see, makes it feel almost like your own skin is attacking you, burning you. But if that's what it takes..."

Jonah managed to straighten up in the chair. "You're... you're a sick fuck..."

"No, Jonah!" Bob said, approaching the other man again, sitting on the edge of the table just a foot away. "I'm a disappointed fuck, the kind who worries that his other half doesn't really care about his feelings. And that makes me want to lash out."

He swung the roundhouse right from low to high, feeling

his knuckles crash into Jonah's orbital bone, under his left eye. Something cracked.

Bob shook his hand gently. "Damn. Think that was you, though, not me. I've broken fingers so many times hitting people that I'm not supposed to really use either hand as a fist. But like I said, I really don't like you. You bring something out in me, Jonah, a dark side I don't really like to revisit. And that just makes me madder. So instead of wasting more time, I'm going get the carving knife and some vinegar. And if you're lucky, and scream loudly enough to impress me, then maybe I'll take a break, cut off a few toes and feed them to you."

Even beyond the physical damage, Bob could see Jonah's expression shift, blood draining from his face. "You're crazy, man."

"It's been suggested," Bob said. "But I'm trying to be nicer, Jonah. For one, I'm really trying not to kill people. It's been nearly a year, and while I can't in good conscience say I've gotten through without causing anyone's death, I can say I didn't pull the trigger."

"Pulled... the trigger?" Jonah's eyes widened, the realization finally settling in that he'd met a bigger dog.

"Now... what you have to ask yourself is whether you want to meet the old me, or if, maybe, the version of me you've met so far is just crazy enough to respect and want to help. And when you're done, I'll cut you loose and let you run. But if I see you again in Bakersfield, I will kill you in a fashion so horrible, it'll make you *famous*. They'll talk for years about how someone could do that to another human being. So... what do you say, Jonah? You got an address for me on the Kopec brothers? Or do we go another few rounds, see just how bad this can get for you?"

34

Vern Kopec sat in the wood lawn chair and stretched the long rubber tubing, pulling the slingshot's pocket back as far as he could take it. He had one eye closed as he sighted the trembling, emaciated mutt, fifteen feet away by the old barn.

He let fly, the jagged rock moving so rapidly it embedded in the creature's hind quarters, the puppy yelping, scurrying toward the barn doors, then turning in panic when it realized they were closed.

"Heh heh. Stupid dog," Vern groused. "Couldn't fight none. Can't run none, neither."

His brother sidled up to him, arms crossed. Tommy looked down at his twin, born three minutes earlier but somehow always the younger one in everyone's eyes because of his simple ways. "You having fun, there? Think maybe you could concentrate on keeping lookout?"

Vern reached down beside the chair and retrieved his beer. He took a sip, his face puckering at the warm sourness. "Shee-it! He ain't coming here, brother. No way, no how."

He drained it, then threw the bottle at the dog. It missed, but shattered against the barn, the terrified animal running in the other direction, towards the field beside their property.

"He'll be back. He's a chickenshit, but he still likes food," Vern said. "Can't believe we paid money for him."

"He looked a good'un when he was little," Tommy said. "Thought he was half pit bull. Turned out to be Terry's sharpei what done the deed with a golden retriever."

"I should kill it," Vern said, "save us some feed money. Then get our money back."

"Maybe so, but we got other priorities right now," Tommy said.

Vern scowled. "You ever going to stop telling me what's what?"

"When you don't need my help no more, maybe," Tommy said. "Just... do me a real solid and pick up that long gun there, pay attention to the back road and rear of the property."

Vern sighed and reached down on the chair's other side to retrieve the old Remington Nylon 76 lever-action rifle, setting it across his knees. "Fine," he muttered. "You going to sit out here for any stretch? Or do me and Terry get the shit duty?"

Terry was a mile away, on the other side of the property, watching the road in.

His brother took in a sharp breath of air, as if warding off irritation. "It ain't rocket surgery, brother," Tommy said. "He didn't show at the motel, at least as far as we know from our police friend, and there's only two roads in here."

"Would help if that idjit Jeb hadn't gone and disappeared. Now Jonah don't show neither?"

"Jeb was supposed to pick this Bob feller up, take him somewhere real quiet. Instead, he ain't been seen in over a day. If he'll take out a cop, he ain't worried about paying us a visit. So keep close dang watch, okay, brother?"

"You didn't answer me none."

"I got to go into town, figure out why Jonah didn't drop off Merry's winnings. But I'll be back before four a.m.," Tommy said simply, heading back towards the house. "I'll spot you at four, Javier will spot for Terry, and you fellers can get some shuteye."

"Fine." Vern sighed, though he sure didn't sound fine.

BOB CROUCHED LOW, his gear slung over his back, his FN 5.7 in his right hand. The narrow rows of four-foot potted aloe vera plants in the field next to the Kopecs' ranch provided decent coverage.

He figured they probably leased the land to a commercial grower. The Kopecs were no one's idea of farmers.

That didn't mean he was going to underestimate them. He'd stopped to pick up his gear from the rooming house, much to Sharmila's discontent. She'd argued the risk was too great, then had to admit that Bob wasn't putting anyone else in the line of fire.

Then he'd borrowed her car—which had worried her almost as much—on the promise he wouldn't put it in harm's way either.

Unproductive to worry, he thought, as he crept across the field. The swale of the ground shifted slightly, a rocky ridge in the middle of the field creating a small hummock. *Good spot to take a look.*

He drew the spyglass from his pack and zoomed in on

the buildings, a hundred yards away. He swept his view slowly from left to right, raising and lowering the spyglass slightly each time to account for depth perception, getting a complete picture.

Someone was seated near a ridged pit of some kind—a well?—in a wooden deck chair. He had something across his lap, something long and thin. *A rifle? Could be.*

Guarding the back of the property because of the road? Looks it.

On a ranch surrounded by empty acres?

It was wholly insufficient to cover one angle of approach to a circular perimeter. *But if they're that dumb...* He swung the spyglass to the other side of the property. Initially, he saw nothing. A light was on in the house still, despite it being nearly one in the morning.

He swept the spy glass further right, following where he figured the main driveway lay. After about a hundred yards, a set of legs stepped past the edge of a nearer hill and into view, roughly where the road would be.

Yep, another guard. He had to be nearly a mile away, and even with the glass maxed out and a light standard at the entrance, he was difficult to see. The man had a long gun of some sort slung across his arms, like a bored grunt guard toting an M4.

He swung the glass back to the first man, in the nearer seat by the barn. The Kopecs were only a symptom of bigger problems: their employers, principally Merry Michelsen. But dealing with them would send an important message, maybe prevent more attempts at collateral damage.

I promised I wouldn't kill them. I didn't say I wouldn't hurt them.

Two men walked out of the house, then over to a pickup

truck to its right side. They climbed in and started the motor, the engine throaty and rumbling. A moment later, it backed out of the spot, then headed towards the main driveway, on the ranch's southern perimeter. It disappeared over and down a hill, then appeared a few moments later near the gate.

Bob stashed the spyglass in his pack and withdrew a capped syringe, storing it in his jacket pocket for quick access. He'd had it since an encounter with a torturer in Memphis, a shellfish toxin that in low enough dosage, he theorized, would paralyze a target without killing him. *Just in case.*

He resumed his trek. He crossed the ridge and stayed low, sneaking towards the property patiently. There were still hours until daylight, and no need to rush.

35

Vern Kopec was not an attentive guard. The two men hadn't been gone for more than five minutes before Vern had his phone out, surfing videos online.

It made Bob's life easier. The sound of laughter from the clip was loud enough that he figured Vern wasn't hearing much else. Not the stiff wind, nor the brush rustling, nor the odd car from the road a hundred and fifty yards away, nor the hogs wallowing in mud.

Vern just stared at the bright screen, his face illuminated, mouth agape.

Bob snuck out of cover behind the plants and into the mud and trampled grass near the home and barn. From twenty yards ahead, he heard a crackling sound. "Terry to Vern. You there, Vern?"

Vern reached down beside the chair and picked up an old-fashioned walkie talkie. "Yeah? What you want?"

"Just checking in. I ain't heard from no one in darn near two hours. Tommy just—"

"Tommy ain't here. Went into town."

"Yeah, I know. I saw his truck. When they going to spot us off?"

"Sometime by four."

"Four!?" the tinny speaker squawked back. "Man, I was up at nine this morning, Vern... I got kids."

"Bitch, you think I care about your gol' darn sleeping arrangements? He figures this Bob feller's going to come looking for us, after the fuss at Feeney's. And my brother is smart, Terry. So you best be ready."

"Aw, Vern, come on, son..."

"I ain't your friend, Terry Perrine. You let Merry toss you in the dog pit, get all bit up! I been thinking of shooting me a sad little dog in its ass 'cos of how weak it is, cowering over by the barn, clinging to that one spot of light like its momma's teat. But maybe I should pay you a visit in the meantime."

"Geez! I was just joking, Vern, dang!"

"Yeah? Well, don't be such a joke, then. Mind your business and don't bother me." He released the walkie talkie's side button and dropped it on the grass next to his chair.

Bob resumed his approach. Vern turned his attention back to his videos.

Bob was ten feet from the back of the man's chair when his sole came down on a twig, the 'snap' sound seemingly amplified by the stillness of the late night.

Vern sat up straight, his head pivoting slightly each way as he craned his ears to find the source.

Bob remained still.

Vern's body language slowly relaxed.

From fifteen yards away, the dog began to bark vociferously, its muzzle pointed in Bob's direction.

Damn traitor.

Move quickly, Bobby, before he's up. Bob rose to his haunches, scurrying up to the man, intent on knocking him out with his pistol butt. But Vern was quicker than he'd anticipated, turning and rising in one motion.

Bob raised the FN and squeezed the trigger chest height, aiming center mass from less than five feet away. Vern didn't panic, instead trying to minimize his target aspect, turning side-on just as the gun flared, the shot flashing past him.

The slide on the FN kicked backwards and stuck in place, the next round jamming at the feed ramp.

Vern looked down at himself, shocked not to have been hit. He had a massive bandage across his nose, Bob noticed.

Shit.

I missed from five feet.

"Shit," Bob said out loud. It had been years since a pistol had jammed on him, and he'd never have expected it from the FN. *Power spring went in the mag?*

Vern was already swinging the rifle, barrel gripped like a baseball bat, the stock catching Bob square in the face and jaw, the lights going out in a flash of red to black.

36

Bob woke with a start, bad dreams forgotten in an instant. He was being dragged over rough dirt, his feet elevated, bound together at the ankles, rope serving as both restraint and handle.

His face hurt like hell—a dull throb, as if he'd developed tandem root canals on the upper and lower teeth. His eye socket felt swollen.

Froze in surprise. Must be getting old.

In the movies, operators had no emotional reaction to danger or failure, attacked with robotic intensity, and were never caught up in the moment. But in the real world, Bob knew, anyone could lose focus, especially someone out of the game for so long.

Lost focus. Got clocked.

He tried to raise his head and figure out where he was being taken, but the forward momentum made it difficult. Vern was clearly strong, dragging him like a sack of potatoes with a single arm. His wrists were bound. He pulled against the restraint. It felt soft, flatter and thicker than rope. A *bandana? Something like that. Used all the rope on my ankles, maybe.*

He looked left in time to see Vern drag him past the frame of the open double barn doors. The angry twin yanked him another ten feet before dropping his feet with a thud.

"You awake, there, Mr. Lawyer Man?"

Bob said nothing.

"I figure it don't matter none either way," Vern said. He lifted Bob's feet again. Bob felt the hard, thick metal of the hook being slung between his feet, under both sides of the rope. There was a brief pause, the quiet of the evening interrupted by the clanging rotation of a winch mechanism, the hook being raised towards the ceiling, Bob going with it.

After fifteen seconds, he was hanging upside down, his hands just an inch or so above the ground, blood pooling in his head.

"Now, way I figure it, Mr. Lawyer Man, my brother would be best pleased if I up and killed you right away and didn't fuss. But I remember how you done broke my nose with your sucker punch, and I figure I owe you."

"Creative," Bob mumbled back. His jaw hurt too much to really talk.

"What you mean?" Vern demanded tersely. "What you mean by that? You saying I'm a sissy? That what you mean?"

Jesus Tapdancing Christ... why did I have to miss the dumb one?

"You're a mouthy kinda feller, ain'tcha?" Vern proposed. "Well, let's see what you've got to say about this."

He stepped into the punch from close in, like a boxer trying to knock his opponent's legs out from under him. The meaty fist crashed into Bob's left rib cage, the crack audible, a familiar, stabbing pain shooting through him.

Left sixth again, same as Venezuela. Maybe the seventh, too. Use the pain, push it away and focus on the external, look for a way out of this. He craned his head both ways. The barn seemed nearly empty, other than a workbench near the back corner, a potbelly stove adjacent to it.

Tools on the wall behind us, maybe? Most barns seem to have tools on their walls, Bob figured.

Vern's fist crashed into his right rib cage. "YEAH!" he raged. "YEAH, BITCH! Gonna work you like a heavy bag, bitch!"

Another stab of pain. *Minor this time, though. He's not as strong with his right hand.* His torso was swaying to and fro from the punches. *Work the bandana, get your hands free first.* He pulled both ways against the knot, letting it tighten but seeing how much the material would stretch.

"You enjoying yourself, Lawyer Man?" Vern giggled slightly, a high, tittering sound that seemed perversely out of place. "Sure is fun beating on you like a little bitch."

Smack. The fist crunched into his left side again, the pain shifting again from a radiating throb to a stabbing intensity. *There goes the seventh*, Bob thought. If Kopec kept wailing on him, he knew, his attacker would break his rib cage so comprehensively that his lungs would risk being pierced and he could drown in his own blood.

But it was hard to concentrate. When younger, his adrenaline would have been surging, making it hard to even feel the abuse. Something had clearly changed—his time away, his age—whatever it was, he just felt tired. Exhausted, even.

Can't take it like you used to, Bob.

"You know I could stand here hitting you all night long,

but I figure you deserve something special," Vern said. "So I'm going to go over to the warmer, stick a poker down in the hot coals—she's a wood burner, and she gets real hot inside. Then in about five minutes, when she's got a good red glow to her, I'm going to take that poker and see how you feel about my broken nose then, uh huh."

He's planning to torture me.
Now would be a good time for a joke about disco.
But my damn jaw hurts too much.
...
Snap out of it, Bobby!
Fight back, damn it!

He could hear Kopec opening the front door on the wood stove. Bob yanked at the wrist restraints, pulling his arms apart as far as he could, the rough cloth burning his skin, wrists threatening to break as he yanked them away from one another.

The bandana popped over his knuckles and fell to the ground. He tried to use his core, strengthened by years of sit-ups and crunches, to bend upwards, to reach the hook and rope. But after just a few minutes suspended, his muscles were already weary, fatigued. He slumped back to a hanging position.

"Figure maybe I'll brand my initials over your heart," Vern said from across the room, his back to his captive. "Then maybe I'll heat her up again... before I shove her up your ass."

The syringe. Bob reached for his jeans pocket. He patted at it frantically.

The pocket was empty.

Shit. Must've fallen out. On the way in, or...

He craned his neck around, the swelling in his face

pounding from the extra blood flow. The syringe was nowhere in front of him, or left, or…

He looked to his right. The syringe wasn't on the ground there, either. But twenty feet away, Vern was taking the poker out of the coals. "She's getting there!" he announced with way too much glee. "Gon' give her another minute."

He plunged it back into the open fire, using an old pot warmer with his left hand to push the stove door mostly closed.

Bob tried to lift his head enough to trace their path back to the door. There was no sign of the syringe. He tilted his head back, trying to sway enough to see behind him.

There.

It was less than a foot behind him. He kicked with both feet, trying to get the hook swinging on the rope, his downward weight making it hard to get any momentum.

His fingertips brushed at the syringe, unable to quite reach it.

A metallic squeak of hinges to the right suggested Vern had opened the stove door again. "Thar! She looks fine, just fine."

Bob kicked frantically, the rope sliding slightly on the hook's thick steel curve. He reached back with all his might, fingertips brushing the syringe but going past it, feeling the tiny object shift forward slightly, but unable to grasp it.

"What you doing?" Vern said. "HEY!" Feet dragged dirt as he made his way back over. "You're earning this, son," he said, reaching in with the poker even as Bob tried to swing back again.

His two fingers found the syringe. He pulled it in towards his palm as the hook slung him towards his captor. The poker pressed against the skin on his side, and searing pain flooded his tensed body.

Fight it! He reached up with the syringe, pulling the cap off with his teeth.

"BURN, YOU LIL' BITCH!" Vern leaned in again, skin sizzling as he held the hot iron to Bob's side, Bob reaching up in the same moment, jabbing the hypodermic needle into Vern's thigh.

"SUM'BITCH!" Vern grabbed at the syringe, pulling it out of his leg as he skipped backwards a few feet. "What...? What'd you just do?"

"Let me down... or you'll die never knowing," Bob croaked.

"You dirty sum'bitch..." Vern lurched forward again.

"Ah!" Bob held up one hand, palm out. "I ain't kidding. You... you want an antidote... you better get me down from here, real quick; clock's... clock's ticking."

At least my jaw's not broken. Hurts like hell, though, Bob thought.

"Dirty..." Vern was clearly having trouble overcoming his rage. But his survival instinct was gradually kicking in. He looked down and saw the syringe in the dirt. "You stuck me with something."

He ran over to the hoist button and slammed a palm onto it, lowering Bob to the ground. He unhooked his feet. "Okay. Talk. What you shoot me with?"

Bob ignored the fire in his sides as he rolled up onto his backside. "Feet," he said, nodding to the rope.

"Huh." Vern walked over to the oven and threw the poker down on its cooktop, metal clanging on metal. Then he strode a few feet to his left to the work bench and picked up a pistol. "You try anything funny, I'll shoot you dead."

"Feet," Bob repeated.

Vern crouched down at Bob's feet. He reached down to his own waist and drew a knife from a sheath. He cut through the four coils of rope.

It fell away. He stood up quickly, keeping distance between them. "Talk, or so help me, I'll kill you," Vern said.

"That was shellfish toxin. A former torturer from Laos was going to use it on me. I kept it, but diluted it. His version would've made me suffocate slowly. Paralyze my lungs. The version I gave you... he claimed it works in less than a minute, but like I said, I diluted it."

Vern's expression shifted from angry to deadpan, as if he hadn't quite processed the information. "What you mean, shut d—"

He dropped the pistol.

"Shee-it." He stared down at it. He couldn't hold the arm up, instinctually trying to support it with his left. "Dang." His knees began to buckle and he fell to a half crouch. "You sum... sum..."

He collapsed to the ground stiffly.

Bob raised himself up slowly. His left side had gone numb around his ribs but the burns, higher up, hurt like the devil. Every joint in his body ached.

He stumbled over to Vern. He was laying on one side, but his eyes were flitting about. *He's breathing. He just can't move.*

Bob heard the scratch of a foot in dirt behind him. He ducked low, trying to ignore the pain as he turned, and the shovel swung over his head, the man swinging it staggering to one side from poor balance.

Bob drove his right fist upwards, into the man's groin, punching past the point of contact, trying to drive his knuckles an inch back. It was instinct, but it caught Terry square in the testicles. The other guard dropped the shovel and staggered back a foot, his face turning white, his hands drifting to cover his groin. He dropped to his two knees and vomited.

Bob lurched forward, throwing a hard right cross, his fist meeting Terry's chin side-on, the attacker's legs gone. He collapsed beside the puddle of vomit.

The pistol lay a few feet past Vern. Bob limped over to it cautiously, trying to regulate his breathing by alternating between nose and mouth. The more gently he could breathe, he knew, the less the fractured ribs would hurt.

He retrieved the pistol and made his way back over to Terry Perrine, who was waking up. He looked up at Bob through haggard eyes. "My nuts. I... I think you crushed my nuts."

Bob looked him over. The guard had a bandage wrapped around his left forearm and bicep. A square adhesive bandage covered much of his right collarbone, another covering half of his right forearm. "What... what the hell happened to you?" Bob asked, trying not to wince.

Terry was panting slightly from the pain. "Warding off the dog. Merry's dog. Made me..." He looked at the dirt, humiliated. "Made me get in the dog pit."

"He made you..." Bob squinted at him. "Are you serious?"

"Yeah."

"And he's a friend of yours?"

Terry stared at the dirt again, ashamed. "Yeah. I mean... Nah, not really. He's my boss."

"You're scared shitless of him."

Terry nodded vigorously.

Bob nodded toward Vern. "And him?"

Terry nodded again. "Yeah."

Jesus H, the poor bastard. I mean, maybe he's terrible. Probably. But...

Desperate people could do terrible things, Bob knew. He gestured with the pistol towards Vern. "Take off your belt, use it to tie his wrists. Make it tight... and I will check. Don't piss me off at any juncture, or you'll hate me even more than the pair of them, for whatever brief time you're still breathing."

Terry struggled to his feet, one hand cupping his swollen testes. He shuffled over to Vern and took off his belt. An alarmed expression crossed his face. "Is he..."

"Nope. If you look at his eyes, you'll notice they're still moving and, I'd say, have an angry edge to them."

"Yeah," Terry said balefully. "Yeah, that's about right. "

"Your belt first, his wrists behind his back. What's your name again?"

"Terry. Terry Perrine. Mister, I got a wife and two daughters..."

"Shut up. Do this right and I won't have to shoot you, Terry Perrine. Fuck this up even a little bit, and you'll never see that wife and kids again. Are we clear?"

"Uh huh, yeah." He finished tying his associate up. "Now what?"

"Your friends, they left in a truck a while ago. When are they back?"

Terry looked at his watch. "Be gone another two hours, as least."

"Good. I figure they keep plenty of valuables in that house, probably some meth if they're tight with Merry, probably some money, some trinkets and such. First, you're going to give me your phone, so you don't get tempted to scurry back to your abusers. Then you're going to take all that shit and load up the other car, and you're going to drive home. You're going to get your wife and kids, and you're going to keep driving. When you run out of gas, get some more... and keep driving. You go until Bakersfield is a memory... and that way I don't have to kill you. You understand me?"

Terry was nodding gently but his eyes danced around as if he was confused. "I never lived nowhere else..."

"Time to reinvent yourself. Phone! Toss it over."

Terry complied.

"Now go! Hurts talking right now!" Bob waved the pistol toward the doors.

Terry skittered towards the doors. As he reached them, he stopped and looked back. "They'll come back and kill you though..." he said.

"Not your problem. Go," Bob said, waving the pistol again.

Maybe that's why you hurt all over. Maybe when you lost your edge, you lost whatever it is that keeps the pain down, the adrenaline flowing, Bob thought as he watched Terry head towards the house.

But he was tired of killing people. That was reserved for cases with no choice. He turned his attention back to Vern. *Speaking of which...*

He didn't have to kill a man to take him out of the game, Bob knew. And Vern represented an opportunity.

It was time to find out just how much his brother loved him.

37

Tommy slowed the truck and peered cautiously through a silky haze of dust and low-beam headlights. The south entrance had been abandoned, the deck chair sitting empty.

"Something's wrong," he told Javier.

"He probably just went for a piss," Javier suggested. "Nobody's sneaking up on Vern."

Tommy just stared straight ahead as he pondered the possibilities. "Nobody loves my brother more than I do, and nobody else understands his limitations as much, neither." He shut off the engine. "Come on... grab your stuff. We'll walk it from here, see if we can't get a quiet look, figure out what's what."

They hiked up the slight slope. Near the top, Tommy slowed his pace. The lights were on in the house. But he remembered shutting them off when they'd left.

"Car's missing," Javier said.

Tommy drew his Walther PDP 9mm and released the

safety. "Something happened to Terry. He wouldn't run off on Vern. Don't have the guts."

They approached the house. Tommy pushed open the side door but stayed clear, anticipating a possible ambush. He poked his head inside. "Terry! Vern! You there?"

The kitchen looked normal, nothing amiss.

He closed the door as he ducked back outside. "Nobody there."

Javier nodded towards the barn. "Maybe...?"

Tommy nodded to the left. "You go around that side. If anyone got the drop on Vern, maybe we can surprise 'em."

The two men circled the barn slowly.

BOB HAD CONSIDERED AN AMBUSH, waiting behind the barn until Tommy and his associate returned, getting the drop on them.

But the whole point was to take them out without killing them, if possible. He had no doubt they'd be far less charitable if the tables were turned.

So instead, he'd taken advantage of Vern's incapacitation.

The two men rounded each end of the barn, Tommy coming into view a few seconds before his friend. Bob sat on the old wooden chair with Terry's pistol in his right hand, just inside the building.

Tommy stopped walking, his eyes widening in alarm.

His brother was three feet to Bob's left. The rope and hangman's noose had been slung over the old winch and around Vern's neck, the other end tied taut to the wall. The rope was supporting most of his weight, Vern's tiptoes perched atop the other wooden chair, barely touching its surface, offering just enough relief from his own weight to keep him from strangling. He was fighting to maintain his balance, the chair wobbling precariously.

"Dang," Tommy muttered.

His associate rounded the left side of the building. He saw Bob and Vern, and his pistol rose in an instant.

"Don't!" Tommy hissed. "Just... be cool, Javier."

Bob waved the pistol theatrically at his brother's helper. "Yeah, Javier, be cool. I've got cracked ribs and they hurt like hell. No telling how light the trigger pull on this is. I'm liable to have a spasm, start shooting the lights out or something."

"I can take him," Javier muttered to his friend.

"No," Tommy said, shaking his head vigorously, waving a palm in a downward motion at his friend. "Just... be cool."

"The reason Tommy's so nervous is because he's the smart one, if you can believe that," Bob said coolly. "That, or he's noticed the loop of string around the toe of my left boot."

Javier's eyes tracked downwards to the piece of string. As advertised, it was looped around the last two inches of Bob's boot then extended sideways to the other chair, where the string had been wrapped several times around one of the legs.

"Coño," Javier hissed loudly. "Is that—"

"It is," Bob said before Tommy could utter a word. "You shoot me, I go over sideways and, if my math is correct, Vern's neck snaps before he hits the ground. If I'm wrong, you'll have about a minute to get him down before there's a chance of brain damage—although having talked to him, that might be an improvement. And consider that if you don't kill me with the first shot, which we all know is likely, you still have me to deal with before you can rescue him."

"You dirty sum'bitch," Tommy muttered. Then he

frowned, the expression bordering on worry. "Is he bleeding?"

Bob nodded. "Uh huh. Long story short, he was briefly incapacitated by poison. Since I knew that wouldn't last, and that he'd eventually be up and around, I figured I could either just kill him, or I could reintroduce him to the concept of staying put. So... I put a bullet into each of his thigh muscles and another through each of his kneecaps."

From the chair, Vern tried to say something, but it came out as a strangled gurgle.

"I think he's trying to tell you both how much pain he's in. Don't worry, I was real careful not to rupture the femoral artery, so he's not going to bleed out on you or such. He's just not walking anywhere for a good few months."

"Gonna kill you," Tommy muttered. "Gonna kill you so god-dang dead..."

"Maybe," Bob said. "But I doubt it. And certainly not today. See, you guys are just an annoyance to me. After you put Mr. Feeney in hospital, I was half tempted to yank that string and let him dangle, take you two on the old-fashioned way. End you both, and all the problems you cause people in this community."

Tommy raised his chin defiantly. "But?"

"But Feeney's going to be fine. And the thing about twins—or so a little reading leads me to believe—is that you're real attuned to each other. As long as you know he's not dead, I figure you'd be willing to compromise. And when push comes to shove... You people ain't the problem. The problem is the guy you work for. You're just... an irritation."

Even from twenty feet away, Bob could see Tommy was grinding his teeth.

His friend strode forward boldly. Bob raised his pistol after two steps.

So did Tommy. "Stop! Just... stop, now," Tommy ordered him.

Javier looked stunned. "You raising your piece on me, Tommy Kopec?"

"Just... making the point, man. I ain't going to shoot you. You're like family. But Vern's my brother. We can't set this off. We... we just can't." He turned his attention back to Bob. "What you want, Bob? What do you expect to resolve with this?"

Bob wagged the index finger on his free left hand at the man, slightly taken aback to have been offered something approaching logic and reason. "Now... that's sort of life-affirming right there, Tommy. The two of you are darn close to sociopathic in your shittiness and willingness to hurt others. But you still give a damn about family."

He rose. The two men both shook in place, nervous tension making them jumpy as they glared at the string running from his boot to the chair Vern was tiptoeing on.

"Oh, don't worry, guys. I'm pretty focused on the pull there staying the same. My foot didn't move. But yours, better. First, toss your weapons over by Vern, there."

The men complied, the pistols thumping against dirt. "Good! Now, hustle on over here. Give me, oh, seven feet of space ahead of me, four feet apart."

They followed his instruction.

"Someday, we're going to revisit this," Tommy said. "Nobody gets lucky forever."

Bob nodded gently. "Yeah, true. You'd do well to remember it." He raised the pistol in a smooth motion, butt braced with his left hand. He shot Tommy through the left kneecap, aiming left of center to avoid the main artery. His target collapsed in a heap, clutching the wound.

Javier began backing away, trembling. "Ay, coño... No, please..."

Bob shot him in the same exact spot as his friend, the shot clean, the smaller man taking an extra moment to lose the strength and sensation on that side before also collapsing on his left hip.

He walked over to both men, the string pulled free from his boot, the chair yanked away from Vern's feet, his body dropping towards the ground.

"NO!" Tommy yelled.

Vern dangled realistically, but his expression barely changed.

"Oh, relax," Bob said. "I wasn't going to hang the man. He's still mostly paralyzed. The winch hook is looped through the back of his pants, supporting his weight."

"Dirty sum'bitch," Tommy moaned. "Tricked me."

"Yeah, real challenging," Bob said dryly. He shot each man through the rectus femoris muscle in the thigh, aiming for the fleshy middle. Tommy grunted loudly, Javier letting out a little yelp.

Tommy was breathing hard, almost panting. "Uhhh... Uhhhh... Motherfucker, I am gonna love killing you dead. Yes, sir."

Bob crouched, keeping his voice soft and to the point. "Now... don't tempt me, Tommy. I'm trying to be the bigger man here. I've shot you twice, and I'm going to make sure an ambulance comes for you. The second bullet, the one in your thigh, will make walking very painful for a long time. The first, through your kneecap, will require months of physiotherapy. Even then, I'd get used to limping."

"You should kill me, motherfucker," Tommy spat. "Cos if you don't..."

"I'll be long gone before you're running track meets."

Javier groaned. Then he stammered, "What... what'd you do with Terry?"

Bob sighed dramatically. "Yeah. Neither of you want to know the answer to that." He glanced over at the hog enclosure. "I told you, I'm trying not to kill anyone, but I figure by the time someone comes and helps you, there won't be much left, if anything. They eat bone, you know."

He began to walk back towards the field, trying not to show how much pain he was in. It was nearly a klick back to Sharmila's BMW, along the north road.

"Don't... Don't leave us here!" Tommy called out.

Bob took Terry's phone out of his pocket.

"911 emergency."

"Yeah, there's a couple of fellers who've gone and shot themselves several times." He offered the address.

"Sir, can you—"

Bob ended the call. He used his shirt to wipe down the phone, then tossed it back towards the scrubby field.

He needed his ribs strapped, the burns looked at, a healthy dose of painkillers.

And sleep. I need sleep.

Sharmila was not going to be happy. *But I promised I wouldn't kill them, and I didn't.*

Job done.

38

LAS VEGAS, NEVADA

Geert Van Kamp watched the five mechanical slot-machine horses race around the last turn. There was a small crowd gathered around the old gaming machine, the last version of Sigma Derby available to Vegas gamblers, in a corner of a downtown casino, just off the Strip.

Vegas famously had no horse racing of its own. It was one of Van Kamp's few vices, other than enjoying murder. His 'fixer' had promised him some action, nonetheless.

Very amusing, Renton. Clearly, you've forgotten I have no sense of humor.

He'd have to find a way to subtly punish the man, put the fear into him under ambiguous circumstances, so that he wasn't quite sure how serious Van Kamp was.

He smiled at the thought. *Now that would be fun, watching that little toad squirm for a while.*

His phone buzzed. He tapped his earpiece. "Go ahead."

"Sir." It was Renton. "I've been working on your request and I think I've got something solid."

"Details."

"When Singleton was working for the CIA, he may have been with a covert ops group called either Group Seven or Team Seven, depending on the source."

"I assumed as much. How does this help me? I'm paying for actionable intel, Renton, not a biography."

"Some of his early records were available through a Dark Web broker, from the CIA leak of about nine years ago. They're not substantial, but they do mention his championing a tech expert they'd contracted, a man named Nicholas Velasco."

"And this is the man—"

"In a roundabout way... I think so, yes. He's supposed to be serving ten years' federal time for wire fraud. Before he was sentenced, the FBI did up an extensive profile on him, noting he had a preference for running credit card impersonation scams, with the details obtained via elaborate email phishing campaigns."

"But... I thought you said he's in jail."

"I did, yes. Then I talked to an operator I met at Hackathon here in Vegas a few years ago who swore she'd seen him in DC not two months ago, running a phishing or wardriving scam at her husband's golf course. I had an algorithm running models to match his profile against current patterns of reported credit card fraud."

"And?"

"I got a pretty compelling match. I reached out to an associate with gang connections. They got me a cell phone photo of the man serving Nicky Velasco's sentence. And I don't think it's him. He's got a similar facial structure, but when I compare him with Velasco's old staff ID photo..."

"He pulled a switch somehow." Van Kamp was fascinated. "Could someone...?"

"This guy? Yeah. Getting into off-limits databases and manipulating them is his jam, especially banking institutions and government. His CIA sheet, attached to the Singleton disciplinary case, said he was the finest security breacher they'd ever run across, a guy so potentially dangerous they felt it better to recruit him, particularly, it noted, because he's immature and somewhat self-centered."

"And your pattern recognition match? Where?"

"Silver Spring, Maryland," Renton said. "If he's who I think, he's been running a security consultancy under the pseudonym 'Ray Edwards'. Just small-time stuff for nervous companies. But his office is based in a house that's almost dead-center the source of the phishing pattern."

"Book me a ticket."

"Already done. Tomorrow at nine in the morning. Emailing you the details."

"Good. Good work, Renton. It almost makes up for the other thing, but I'll probably get past that," he said.

"Yes, sir. Wait... what oth—"

But Van Kamp had already gone.

39

Bob woke suddenly, with no memory of having dreamed.

One moment, he'd had a moment of consciousness, the sensation of a hospital bed being lowered.

The next, he was waking up, blackout curtains shrouding the room. He sat upright, using his elbows. A sharp pain shot through his left side and he winced. He moved the sheet aside.

The burns had been covered with bandages, then covered once again by the thinner, tight wrap keeping his ribs immobilized. Blue-green bruising peeked out of the top and bottom of the covered area.

His face felt thick, swollen. Bob reached down the side of the bed and found the lift button, raising the head of the mattress up.

He glanced over to the side table to see if they'd left his phone nearby. They hadn't, but his clothing was neatly hung in a small closet.

The addictions clinic. He looked down at his left arm, a

slight itch on the underside of his elbow drawing his attention. An intravenous drip led back to a rack by the head of the bed.

He'd driven there directly from the Kopecs, the pain from his fractured ribs and the burns conspiring with fatigue and waning adrenaline to almost knock him out at the wheel. Then he'd dialed Sharmila. He didn't remember anything past that. She must've gotten him into the bed, had the painkillers administered.

Sharmila.

He'd barely registered the small figure curled up on the two-person sofa, next to the tall, open-faced closet. She had her knees drawn up to her chest, her hands grabbing her knees.

Bob pulled back the sheet and swung his legs out of the bed. They'd garbed him in a backless hospital gown, but he was in too much discomfort to care. He winced again, the mere pressure of standing sending shocks through torn cartilage, tired muscles.

Sharmila roused from her slumber. She stretched. "What... Bob! No! You're supposed to be in bed!"

Bob shook his head. "Nope. Too much to do."

"You have fractured ribs, and your face looks like you just fought a professional boxer."

"None of which changes the fact..." he took a deep breath, warding off fatigue, "...that the painkillers are averting the worst of it, and I have things to do. He squinted at the thin beams of light making their way between the curtains. "What time is it?"

Sharmila yawned and looked at her phone. "It's... oh boy, it's past noon. I need to get going..." She stared him down. "But *you* need to get back to bed."

"Not an option. You stayed here all night?"

"It was nearly four when I got here. I left around eight-thirty, came back two hours later. I've been out for a couple of hours."

"Help me get this IV out," he said.

"Keep your arm elevated," she said. "You need to rethink this."

"We don't have time. Merry Michelsen is probably a lot of terrible things, but stupid isn't one of them. If he thinks I had a role in what happened to Czernowitz, he'll worry I got something out of him, something linking him to Fowler or bribes, or Marcus. And he'll know from my visit to the Kopecs that I have no qualms about coming after him."

"So..."

"He'll come after me, hard. And you, and Czernowitz, possibly even Marcus, or his cheese factory associate, Greg Thomas. He'll try to clean house. Before he does, I need to figure out what that factory has to do with any of this. It had the hallmarks of some shady stuff, maybe a meth super lab of some kind."

"Gerry Tucker seemed pretty sure it wasn't."

"Records can be faked, ingredients hidden."

"He seemed pretty sure. They did surprise inspections twice after their initial visit."

"But it's something," Bob said. "If not meth, something equally illegal. And once I figure that out..."

"Then we take what you've got to the authorities," she said.

"Then... yes. Czernowitz can clear Marcus and implicate Baird. If I can get some leverage over Thomas or Michelsen, I can get them to explain what your dad figured out—and I'm guessing it's at that factory. Marcus goes free, the DA is handed motive, means, opportunity and a 'hero cop' witness who went undercover to bring them all down."

Her eyebrows shot north. "Witty? Undercover?"

"I mean... it's a narrative that will sell here while still getting a just result, right? So maybe we just go with what works."

"Uh huh." She stared down at her shoes for a minute. "Before I leave you to get dressed, I have to ask: do you want to talk about what happened to you last night? Those burns were quite bad. They're deep; enough that there's a risk of infection and poor healing without skin grafting. That warm sensation is Demerol."

He nodded. "I've worked through Demerol before, and third-degree burns. And... no, I'm not getting into the fine details."

"I don't think I want to know. The Kopecs. Did you..."

"Kill them? No. But wheelchairs won't be out of the question for a while."

"Wheelchairs?" She shook her head. "Now I *really* don't want to know."

"You really don't."

"Huh. Can you buy truck nuts and Dixie flags for wheelchairs?" Sharmila wondered.

"This is America," Bob said. "Of course you can."

Sharmila dropped him off at the bed and breakfast, on the promise he'd take it easy for the day.

As soon as she was gone, he got back to work, retrieving a burner from his soft-sided bag.

He waited for the call to ring through. It always took a

second longer than normal, Nicky's encryption doing its work.

"Bob."

Progress. Nicky actually used my name. "Nicky. Hope you're well."

"I am, but I'm busy. What's up?"

"The jagoff I mentioned, Greg Thomas. Baird's assistant. He's got some sort of interest in The Big Cheese. Can you do a quick hunt, see who owns the building, if there are listed investors?"

"When do you need this?"

"Tonight, if possible."

"You okay? You sound... strained."

"Broken ribs and a couple of burns. Nothing new."

"Ouch."

"It's nothing, just... uncomfortable. Listen, when I call back next I'll use the three rings, hang up, two rings code. I need to get a set of new phones."

"A set!? What did you do?"

"My soft-sided bag came along at a couple of crime scenes. The agency can get company location records, so... It's not earth-shaking, a handful of phones. I travel lean."

"Still Mr. Careful, right, Alph—right, Bob?"

"Yep. Speaking of which... you're keeping your head down? I'd hate to think you'd become so preoccupied with self-enrichment that the wrong kind of people start paying attention."

"Bob... That's going to take some getting used to, calling you Bob. Don't worry about it, okay? I'm the soul of discretion. Nobody's looking for Ray Edwards, solid citizen."

40

SILVER SPRING, MARYLAND

Nicky Velasco kept his hands in his pockets as he walked home along Dartmouth Avenue, watching golden leaves drift to the sidewalk.

Dinner had been perfunctory, a sandwich from Chick-fil-A. He'd wanted something more substantial and had planned to go to a nice steakhouse, lift a credit card from the first blowhard he ran into and run up a tab.

But Bob's warning about keeping a low profile had stuck with him. There'd been something in his tone. Real worry, perhaps, a sentiment Nicky was unaccustomed to experiencing.

The six-hour search for information on The Big Cheese had yielded little. It was owned by a holding company, which had purchased it and another outlet in south Bakersfield a year earlier. He'd run searches on dairy providers and matched up its suppliers, then dug deeper and found a reference in a government inspection report.

That had led him to a classified report on Gerry Tucker's

inspection team, a county crew going over the operation with a fine-toothed comb.

And... nothing. Nothing except that one anomaly.

He'd been extra cautious, pulling street camera images from the city's traffic network around the factory, then satellite images from every government agency he could access. There had to be something out of place if Alpha thought something was wrong. The man was rarely wrong.

Bob. Feels weird treating him like a mortal. Singleton had saved him from a homicidal co-worker at the CIA, even if it had cost him his legit career.

And all I've got for him is a tanker truck.

It had pulled up and parked behind the cage-like backyard. The satellite image didn't show a brand or marker, but the white dots around it indicated a small crew of men running what looked like a long, wide hose into the back of the building, two weeks prior.

Curious, he'd searched the traffic database for red-light camera images around the property that night. After nearly an hour of looking through images, he'd found a tanker truck of the same size, and had a plate number. The courts database had found the plate associated with a speeding ticket, unredacted, in the name of Jenkins Racing.

Jenkins was Thomas's employer. *So I've got him a tie. I just have no idea what it means.*

Hopefully, it would be enough. Eventually, Alpha—Bob—would come good and offer his services as payback. And Nicky had big plans.

At home, he felt the quietness immediately. The apartment was silent, empty and large.

He hadn't ever been a social person, not particularly, although there had been a time before high school when he'd wanted to be. Instead, Nicky had found himself pushed into the geek clique in school: the game nerds, the Dungeons and Dragons kids, the non-jock members of the computer club.

He'd discovered in his early twenties that he had a pain fetish and enjoyed being walked on by a woman in high heels. It had been an exciting discovery, a whim to try something suggested by a sex worker during a visit to Atlantic City. But it had gradually soured his already meagre attempts at finding a normal relationship.

But he tried not to think about that. Instead, he focused on the positive: self-enrichment at the expense of bad people, proving his mettle as an information broker and, in his spare time, leading an online guild in a turn-based fantasy roleplaying game.

He tossed his keys onto the telephone table by the door. In the adjacent living room, he headed directly for the computer desk under the back window.

"Hello, Mr. Velasco. You're not supposed to be here."

The man had an accent. *South African?* Nicky's training kicked in—as much as it ever did—and he glanced to his right, towards the bookcase.

"If you're wondering about the Ruger you had in the cigar box, it's presently in the side pocket of my jacket."

He turned around. The man in the armchair was older, maybe late fifties. He had scar tissue by his left eyelid and a thin line across his Adam's apple. In his right hand, he held a Glock 19.

"I think you've got the wrong apartment, sir," Nicky said, trying to keep his voice as wavering and uncertain as possible. "I'm Ray..."

"No, that's your cover. Why persist? I clearly know exactly who you are." Van Kamp gestured towards the opposite sofa with a shake of his gun. "Sit."

Nicky did as ordered. "How much?" he asked.

"How much what?"

"How much for you to go away and forget you saw me? I have access to a lot of money."

That piqued his captor's interest. "Really? How much?"

"Hundreds of thousands," Nicky said. "Like, within twenty-four hours, I can strip two dozen credit accounts for at least that much." *Use the delay. Find a weapon.* His eyes flitted back and forth across the room, looking for something obvious.

Van Kamp tilted his head, a curious expression washing over him, like a child trying to understand a puppy. "That much? So... how much could you steal in... say... two hours?"

Why is he asking me that? That's not good, is it? "Not sure. Maybe twenty thousand?"

Van Kamp smiled. "So... you'll do that for me, then."

"And you'll let me go?"

"No. But I will stop torturing you until you complete your work. That alone should make it an enticing offer."

He's going to kill me. Nicky felt a swell of panic, the realization like driving into head-on traffic. *Go. Run. Now. Before he gets out of the chair.*

He turned abruptly and sprinted towards the door.

At the last second, Van Kamp's foot shot out sideways, hooking Nicky's ankle. The hacker tripped, crashing face-first to the floor.

Before he could rise, Van Kamp was up, standing over him, a foot on his back. "I'm not going to kill you quickly. But

I'll speed it up if you give me something that helps me find Bob Singleton."

IN THE END, Velasco had been a weeper.

Van Kamp hated it when they cried. It was embarrassing to watch a grown man act like a frightened child.

After having the fingernails ripped out of three fingers on his left hand, he'd begun blubbering about how he had nothing that could help.

By the time the thumbnail was gone—Velasco's screams muffled by the balled socks stuffed into his mouth—he'd handed over the two things he had that could tie him to Bob Singleton: a burner phone and a list of phone numbers he insisted were the last five people Bob talked to prior to leaving Chicago and heading south.

Three of them were in Washington, DC, two in Chicago.

Velasco had clearly been unable to provide anything else. After his crying and begging for twenty minutes, Van Kamp shot the hacker through the back of the head, twice, leaving him slumped over his computer keyboard.

Then he'd called Renton. "I need you to run some numbers, tell me who I'm dealing with," he ordered.

41

Margaret Swain, District Attorney and noted "bringer of pain", stared at the treatment center hospital bed through the observation window, her legal briefcase held close to her body, her mouth agape.

"Sharm... this... this would be a good time to tell me I actually ate magic mushrooms or something, and am hallucinating deeply," she stammered.

"You're not hallucinating, no. I'd pinch you, but I don't want a punch on the arm. However... I can explain."

Swain turned her head slowly and glared at her with furious irritation. "The entirety of the Bakersfield law enforcement community is currently looking for this man, so it's going to have to be one hell of an explanation."

"Well... I did tell you after the boy was arrested that I didn't buy it. And Witty—David Czernowitz—is willing to testify his partner was working with Merry Michelsen, who was trying to scare my father away from his business."

"Was? And where is Officer Fowler now?"

"Marg—"

"Sharm... this isn't high school. You can't keep this under wraps. Not without consequences."

Sharmila sighed and pursed her lips, the weight of the tale unnerving her. "My understanding is that he's lying in the desert just south of the city, near Copus Road."

"He's *dead*?!"

"David will testify that Fowler murdered Professor Jenkins. They were going to try to get Marcus's first lawyer, Bob—"

"What!? Jenkins what!?"

"They were going to kill him. Fowler drove them out there and had Bob digging a grave, David says, to bury the professor, who was already dead and in the back of Fowler's cruiser. When David demanded answers about the professor and his own safety, Fowler shot him. Bob struggled with him for the gun, and while that was happening, David up and shot Jeb dead."

"Dang." Swain's expression had gone blank, the gravity of it all just a little too much to take in one shot. "Dang," she repeated. Her facial expression shifted, puzzlement settling in. "Why haven't you just taken this all to the police?"

"David insists Merry has other cops on the take. He doesn't know who, but he's bragged about getting information early on busts over the years, and that didn't come from them. And we still don't know why this is all happening. So..."

"So you're worried if we bring them in, somehow this gets pinned on Bob before he can figure it all out and help his... what, exactly? What is Marcus Pell in this? His client?

Or is there more to that? I noticed your cousin spoke to bail for him."

"He's a friend of Pell and his foster mom in Chicago," Sharmila said. "He's not even a lawyer. He came to help and got caught up in this."

Swain's head gently nodded from side to side as she tried to find the words. "I am at a loss for how you expect me to handle this, Sharmila. We've been friends a long time…"

"All we ask is for a few more days," Sharmila said. "Bob figures he's got a line on why this all happened. And at the end of that is whoever actually pulled the trigger."

"What if it was Jeb Fowler?" the assistant district attorney wondered aloud. "How do we square what happened to him?"

"We keep David under wraps and healthy until he can testify, that's how," Sharmila said. "He's pretty doped up right now, but they think in a few days, he'll be mended enough to lower the dosage, give you a formal statement. But… you know this town. If we tell his people, there's a chance the wrong ones hear. And then he's a dead man."

Swain crossed her arms and nodded her head slowly, staring through the window. "I didn't see any of this, in other words." She sighed. "A few days. Dang. No! No, Sharm. I can't do that. I can't believe I'd even consider it. I have to take this to the police. I have a working relationship with them that I have to respect."

"I get that, Margie, I really do. But if the wrong person hears any of this, David is finished. Bob figures this is a hell of a lot bigger than a run for sheriff. My father had something tying the new trailer park development in Oildale to the meth trade. Possibly a legit business."

"A legit business? Who?"

Sharm looked down and away quickly. "That's... complicated. We don't have evidence yet. And the owner's got friends in high places."

Swain shook her head. "Not good enough. You're asking me to withhold evidence in a homicide, Sharm. The only way that flies is if there's no other choice. Who has enough clout with—"

"Parker Baird, and Jenkins Mechanical. The professor's business partner."

Swain tipped her head back and started at the ceiling for a moment. She sighed deeply, then weighed the new information. "He's royalty to the local business community and a big police backer."

"Exactly. We go public on any of this without evidence, he'll walk and he'll sue. And if we tell the wrong people, David's done for."

Swain looked pained. "I know what you're saying makes sense. But you're asking me to trust a homicide suspect who lied about being someone's lawyer and may have already hospitalized four other people. It's too much."

Sharmila hung her head. "Then... you're going to blow this open?"

"No. But we need to get the police involved now, before there's any suggestion we're messing with their case, tainting the evidence chain."

"But... who? Like David said, we don't know who we can trust."

"The only guy I'd place my money on one hundred percent would be Staff Sergeant Gayle Dyche. He's been there for decades, he's got a scrupulous rep, he's even called out bad actors over the years. If he buys what your guy Bob is selling, I'll play along, at least for a few more days. Then he's an unofficial agent or CI, at least."

"Okay. That's as good as we're going to get, I guess."

"And until then?" Swain asked. "What do we do until then?"

"We pretend life is normal," Sharmila said, "and hope Bob gives us the people behind this."

42

The suitcases were packed and sitting by the front door, but Terry Perrine hadn't risen from the couch.

His wife Candy's frustration grew by the minute. She already had her heavy coat on, a pink fake fur that he always figured looked like something out of a rap video.

"The longer you sit there stewing, the more danger we're in! Don't you understand that, you useless..." Her voice trailed off. "You're goddamned hopeless, you know that?"

A few feet away, their twin six-year-old daughters stood by the back door, clutching glittery toy handbags ahead of them, embarrassed at the latest fight and glum.

Perrine reached forward and retrieved his cigarettes from the coffee table. He flipped the box open, slid out a smoke and lit it. "You keep talking so's I can't think, it's going to take even longer," he said.

"Think? Terry... God damn. You're my man and all, and the father of our girls. But this equation is real simple..." She stopped, realizing they were getting louder and louder. She glanced over at the girls. "Girls, room! I need to talk to your daddy in private."

They scurried down the hall to the back of the house.

"This equation is real simple, and it ends with the two of us getting hurt real bad! Get your ass off that couch. We need to get going, now!"

"But... what if I'm making a mistake? Now, hear me out on this before you go off all hot..."

"The mistake was ever getting involved with your old high school buddies in their drug business, not getting an honest job like your brother," she said. "The mistake now would be trusting that they actually like you. They ain't never done nothing but treat you like a worm, and you know that! How many times have you told me that greasy bastard gave you a hard time? Then you come home all covered in dog bites and scratches, and you don't think I put two and two together?"

"But... I know'd Merry my whole life," he pleaded. "Maybe if I tell him I didn't get no choice but to run, he'll forgive me, take me back."

"And? Even if he did—which he wouldn't—the man is crazy. The money's good, but it ain't that good. We ain't living in the lap of luxury or nothing. And chances are, he's just going to shoot you dead."

Terry's head dipped, his shame obvious.

He'd half expected his wife, who liked to spend their ill-gotten gains, would agree with him that it was a mistake, giving it all up. But... she wasn't wrong.

His head bobbed quickly. "Okay. Okay then, we'll go to your brother's in Modesto for now. But... you've got to realize what this means. We can't come back here. Can't see our friends or family. Probably can't even stay in California."

"I know. But I'd rather have my husband and kids healthy. That's more important than any of this," she said softly.

He got up. "Get the girls. We need to get this show on the road."

There was a knock on the door.

"That'll be the ride share," Candy said. She wandered over and pulled it open. "We'll be just..."

She didn't get a chance to finish the sentence, a mountainous figure shoving her backwards into the room so that his boss could enter.

"Terrance," Merry said. "We was told you'd been killed by our mystery man, then I heard you're back here, hiding out. We need to have ourselves a little chinwag."

"Merry... I swear..."

"Oh, you will," Merry said with a grin. "Your wife and kids, they ain't my problem. They can go wherever they want. But you and me? Well.... we're going to the park."

"To... the park?"

"Uh huh. We're going to play us a little game."

43

The six-pack of stock cars roared around the high dirt bank at Bakersfield Speedway, wheels kicking up mud as they braked and spun, before seizing traction, roaring out onto the next straight.

Bob wasn't paying attention. He'd arrived early, just before the noon race, to take a look at Jenkins Racing's team taking part in the sprints later in the day.

Sure enough, the same fueling tanker—or identical, anyway—that he'd spotted in Pahrump could be seen other side of the track, in the large open lot due south, at the far end of the public parking area, near the road. He'd rounded the grandstand to get a slightly closer look, able to make out "NITROMETHANE" in small block capitals, just above a series of cautions, a death's head and an explosion graphic.

A man in a white Stetson was leaning against the rail, chewing a toothpick as he watched the cars enter the next turn. Bob tapped him on the shoulder.

"Uh huh?"

"Yeah... apologies for the distraction but I'm new to all this. Can I ask a quick question?"

"Surely."

"Do they run Nitro Funny Cars here? I saw some pictures online, but they don't look like the stocks I see today."

The race fan frowned and took out the toothpick for a moment. "Different type of engine. They need straightaways for that, not a banked track. You'd have to go up to Famoso for that. That's the drag strip up by McFarland."

"McFarland?"

"Town north of here." The man went back to watching the race.

Same deal as Pahrump. Nitro Fuel at a track, but no cars that need it. He took out his phone and tricked Nicky Velasco again.

Still no answer. Nicky always kept that burner close, in his experience. That was worrisome.

He had another option, a source he hadn't intended to tap. *But he did say if I ever needed him...*

He took out his wallet and checked the number on a business card, then dialed it. It rang through a few seconds later.

"Sergeant Glebe."

"Sergeant. It's Bob."

"Mr. Fleming. Well, well. I confess, I didn't get the impression I'd actually hear from you again."

"How are you? How's Tucson?"

"Fine. Still weird, still hot," the officer said. "The struggle continues. But I assume you're not calling just to catch up."

"I'm working on a case for a friend. I keep running into two elements over and over and I'm trying to relate them."

"Shoot."

"Nitromethane 'Top Fuel' Funny Cars, and methamphetamine."

"And you're thinking... what? A business connection, a chemical connection..."

"The latter. Something specialized but not making meth itself. I figured I could wade through the internet and never find it, or I could call someone with good DEA ties."

"Huh. Okay, when do you need it? I'm off today..."

"As soon as possible. Sorry, but—"

"No, that's fine. I owe you big time for helping me put Carter Hayes away for life. Give me... well, I'll try to be quick, let me put it that way. Same number? You're coming up as unrecognized."

"No." Bob gave him the new digits.

"I'll get back to you."

"Appreciated." He ended the call.

The checkered flag was being waved furiously as two cars roared across the finish line in tandem, the inside track just inches ahead. A roar went up from the crowd.

A moment later, everyone sat down, freeing up his line of sight to the fuel truck. A truck had pulled up just a few feet away.

Bob squinted, trying to make out who it was getting out of the cab. He moved quickly without running, pushing through the crowd as he rounded the south end of the lot, the track obscured by the high bank. A minute later, he had a clear view.

Greg Thomas. Baird's assistant was giving two men in grey overalls directions, even as a second tanker backed up, its reverse alarm blaring, until it was parked parallel to the first.

Now what's going on here? Before he could get an answer, a third truck—an eighteen wheeler with a box trailer—

pulled into the lot off Petrol Road. It pulled behind the other two vehicles, obscuring the view of them from the grandstand.

This is some sleight-of-hand business right here. The two men were joined by two more, the crew running a corrugated hose between the two vehicles. He checked his watch.

It took fifteen minutes for anything to happen, at which point Thomas got into his pickup and drove off. Another ten minutes passed before they removed the hose from one truck and capped the tank, repeating the procedure on the other.

One of the four men rounded the tanker and climbed up into the cab. *I think he's moving.* Bob ran back to the other parking lot as quickly as his feet would take him. He threw the borrowed BMW into gear and hit the gas, the compact sports coupe barreling across the lot, tires squealing as it slid onto Petrol Road.

The tanker was just a block ahead. He followed it as it headed west. Within a minute, it turned south. Bob began to recognize the area. *We're near the cheese factory.*

The tanker passed the facility then turned right, the street adjacent to the factory's rear entrance.

Bob parked at the curb a half-block away and watched as the two men got out of the cab. They checked their surroundings for anyone watching. A moment later, a man exited the building with three workers. He directed them to the tanker.

Bob's phone rang. It was Glebe's number.

"That was quick."

"Easy request, as it turned out. Your Funny Car fuel can be used to make methamphetamine, albeit not directly. It has to be synthesized into an ingredient called methylamine first. Methylamine is relatively easy to make, but not in the quantities large producers would use."

"And it... does what? How does that relate to pseudoephedrine?"

"Different precursor chemical, same idea. The methamphetamine can be distilled from methylamine, and because it can be manufactured here—"

"It's easier than smuggling in controlled substances from Mexico," Bob proposed.

"Exactly. But that's where the volume issue becomes a problem. It's unstable and dangerous as hell to produce large quantities from ammonia distillation. But there's a process that can be used to extract it from nitromethane. Of course, most people don't have an easy source of that either, not without setting off all sorts of alarms, so..."

"And if someone had a near inexhaustible supply of nitromethane, one that was easily covered up in the accounting?"

"From what I hear? A lot of people would pay a whole lot of money for it. Millions. A good source for criminal organizations could be a nightmare for us." Glebe paused. Then he tactfully added, "This isn't something you should perhaps be sharing with local law enforcement, is it, Bob?"

"Oh... I'll get to that," Bob said. "Promise."

"Uh huh. This one falls heavily under the 'don't want to know' heading, doesn't it?" Glebe said.

"It was good talking with you again, Sergeant."

"Uh huh. Don't be a stranger, Bob."

Bob ended the call. He needed to get in touch with Sharmila, tell her and David he had their motive.

. . .

THEY MET at the diner they'd used for introductions on his first night in town. Sharmila was sitting in a booth, stirring a glass of ice water with a straw, a distant expression on her face.

She noticed him approaching. "Give me some good news, Bob. The clock is ticking."

"It's shrewd," Bob said as he sat down. "But it's not meth. The cheese factory is producing meth ingredients instead."

Sharmila squinted, puzzled. "But... wouldn't that be less profitable—"

"Nope. The more common precursor chemicals are what tip law enforcement officials off to meth production in the first place. They're only manufactured in America under strict licensing and regulation, so they're usually smuggled in from Mexico or central America, which is risky and expensive."

"So... instead of making the drug, they're making it easier for others?"

"My police source says every gang in the western US would kill for a steady, untraceable supply of methylamine. And it can be produced from Nitro Funny Car fuel. When I was in Nevada, one of the locals mentioned Jenkins fueling up at the local track... but they don't run at that track. Same deal is going on in Bakersfield. My guess is they're siphoning off product, labelling it as used in test and practice runs, then trucking it to the cheese factory."

"So they're creating a confined living environment for thousands of poor people next to Merry's existing turf with new trailer parks," she suggested, "then making it possible to massively ramp up both their own meth production and sell this precursor to others."

"It's millions and millions of dollars," Bob said. "That's motive enough."

"Okay. And my father?"

"I... still don't know who pulled the trigger. But we can prove it wasn't Marcus, thanks to David, and I'm getting closer. Once we have that..."

"Once we have that, we have everything," she said.

"Not quite. Parker Baird's still insulated."

"Why?"

"Jenkins Racing owns the numbered company that owns the cheese shop," Bob said. "But they're leasing it to a third player, which I suspect is owned by Merry. That gives Baird deniability; he can claim ignorance, as he's just the landlord. And unless we can get Thomas or another flunky to admit they pulled the trigger, we have nothing directly tying him to your father."

"But—"

"The professor was murdered by a rogue cop, he'll argue. That's evidence of nothing, really. David thinks Fowler was working for Michelsen alone."

"Okay." She scowled and crossed her arms.

"You're disappointed. I mean... Obviously..." Bob stammered.

"It's okay. Like you said, you're getting closer. But we have a bit of a problem." Sharmila relayed the assistant district attorney's demand. "You've got two days before she pulls the plug on David. And that's under one condition."

"I can work with that. I'll have to. Wait... what condition?"

"You have to meet with a cop."

44

Staff Sergeant Gayle Dyche gazed across the atrium towards the waiting room. A patrolman was sitting on one of the waiting area chairs, next to a very pregnant sex worker. They were comparing photos of their kids.

Dyche smiled gently. For all the heat they took, there were a lot of compassionate cops in Bakersfield, he figured. They just didn't get much press.

His desk phone rang. The call display number registered as 'unknown.'

He picked up the line. "Bakersfield PD. Staff Sergeant Dyche." He'd said it so many times it tripped without pause off his tongue. "With whom am I speaking?" It was veteran practice to ask for an ID on an unidentified caller. They were calling for a reason, and if they wanted his help, they'd usually acquiesce.

"I'm told you were expecting a call from me."

Bob Richmond. He'd wrestled with how to handle it. He'd known Margaret Swain's father, a respected officer in his own right and former military man, and he'd often praised her zealous pursuit of the city's criminal element.

"I'm giving you leeway, Mr. Richmond. I promised Ms. Swain I wouldn't try to trace the call or set you up to be scooped. She, in turn, says you have a lot of answers."

"And she says you're a straight shooter."

"Disappoint me and I'm inclined to believe you'll learn just how straight," Dyche said. "What are you offering?" He checked the booking area and nearby detectives' bullpen for anyone listening in.

"The motive for Hap Singh's death. The names of the men responsible, and a confession from one of them, a cop."

"Really?" Dyche couldn't hide the cynicism in his tone. "They just up and told you they did it, huh?"

"Something like that. We don't have time to discuss it now."

"Because..."

"You might be trying to triangulate a phone trace. You can tell Swain whatever you want; you and I don't know each other. So we get off the line quickly. We meet one on one."

"Look... if you're not even going to trust—"

"Where and when?" Bob said. "We're on the clock, Sergeant."

"Polo Park. It's a family sports park, where Noriega meets Old Farm Road. There are two big parking lots and you can see in all four directions. The one on Noriega. Also, people around, witnesses. Come after ten. I'll be there until ten-thirty, then I blow this off and have words with Ms. Swain. No weapons, or I hit my emergency beacon and you have a hundred officers down on you before you can blink."

"Okay."

The call dropped.

Dyche hung up the phone then checked his perimeter again. No one was paying attention, the young officer and the hooker chuckling happily as they waited to book her.

THE PARKING LOT was nearly empty as Bob approached. He'd parked at the lot on Old Farm Road then walked over, across the baseball diamond, past the small storage yard and three-bay garage.

The lot on Noriega was a slightly smaller rectangle but still a solid hundred yards long, with perfectly lined spaces for more than two hundred cars. But it was late, the handful of streetlamps casting a dull glow, a few cars pulling out for the night.

Near the far end of the lot, a white concrete path led to a small bandstand-style seating area on the property's east side. It looked deserted. Just before the path, a smaller sedan was parked in the shadows, a man leaning against the front end, his arms crossed.

Bob kept his head on a swivel. Dyche appeared to be alone. *Please tell me he didn't bring a police cruiser*, he worried. A police presence would attract attention from the surrounding housing developments. The park was book-ended by Patriot Elementary School and Freedom Middle School. Bob had no doubt worried parents might decide to wander over, and they might be armed.

Nope, looks like a Toyota.

Dyche was in civilian clothes. He uncrossed his arms and stuffed his hands into his jacket pockets. "Okay. You've got my undivided attention, Mr. Richmond," he said. "Talk."

"I have a witness who will implicate Officer Jeb Fowler in

two murders and clear Marcus Pell. I also have the motive behind Hap Singh's death."

"Huh. And how did you come about this information, Mr. Richmond? Because as you may be aware, most of the department is currently trying to ascertain your whereabouts."

"It was freely offered," Bob said. *Sort of. No money changed hands.*

"Just like that? With no coercion on your part? Because the last I heard, Jeb Fowler was looking to arrest on you on suspicion of assault."

"Entirely unrelated, I'm sure."

"Entirely?"

"Something... like that."

"I notice a hesitation on that point, Mr. Richmond. Let's not get this working relationship off to that kind of start. Did you coerce someone into a confession, or not?"

"I didn't, no."

"But someone did."

"Like I said... I didn't. Perhaps when you have them on the other side of a table, you can get them to tell you more."

Dyche's hackles were up. He could clearly tell Bob was holding back information. "And the motive?"

"I'll deliver you everything. I want reassurances my friend Marcus will get protection inside until he's released, and that neither I nor Sharmila Singh will be charged with interfering. In exchange, I'll give you the tape."

"Tape!?"

"Recording of our witness confirming everything. USB stick. You know what I mean," Bob said. *Jesus H, I'm old.*

"The Kopec brothers are in Memorial right now with multiple gunshot wounds. They aren't saying shit..."

"Without Fowler to do their dirty work, they're a little less inclined to work with the police, I guess."

"Richmond..."

"Sorry. But it's probably true."

"Just... don't push it, okay? We all know who and what Jeb was, but what little Margaret told me... that's going to cause a shitstorm of unprecedent proportions around here. Where's Officer Czernowitz?"

"Like I said, I need some guarantees first."

Dyche took a long, deep breath through his nose, his expression distant in the moment. He took off his glasses, then took a handkerchief from his coat pocket and began to clean the lenses.

"You know... I've lived here all my life, and there's a lot of truth in what people say about Bakersfield. People here came from hardship, and they're tough. They go after want they want, and sometimes... well, sometimes there's not a whole lot of consideration for legality. But... that's any city, I guess."

"It is," Bob agreed.

"All my adult life," Dyche said, "I've worked as a police officer, working to protect this town, these people. My people. And every week, I've had to go to church with my family and see guys I knew since they were in short pants driving up in Mercedes-Benzes, and Porsches and Cadillacs. And I know they're dirty. The congregation knows they're dirty. Heck, I imagine our pastor is fully aware of what they do when they're not putting on a respectable face."

"Frustrating," Bob said.

Dyche put his glasses back on and his hands back into his jacket pockets. "Very. Very frustrating indeed. Because nothing ever happens to the ones with money. I still like to believe most folk are good folk, Mr. Richmond. But I'm old, and I'm tired of fighting the tide."

Bob's hackles rose. *Where is this going?*

"Now... are you going to tell me who your information sources are, your witnesses? Because I expect you want me to take this seriously."

Something's off. I can feel it. Bob checked their perimeter, looking both ways, pivoting on one heel quickly to check his six. The painkillers were still doing a job of keeping his cracked ribs from screaming.

Nothing.

"When you talk to Swain and formalize a deal to release Marcus and protect the witnesses, I'll give you everything I've got," Bob said.

"That's... Ah, hell, son..." Dyche said, shaking his head gently. "That's not going to happen. You all might want to look down."

Bob's eyes flitted downwards for long enough to spot the red dot of a laser sight hovering over his chest cavity. It was moving too much to be a pro, but Bob knew that wouldn't matter.

"In case you're thinking of using me to cut off the line of sight," Dyche said, "There's two more aimed at your back right now."

Bob cursed his own naivete and Swain's reassurances. "Why am I guessing from that speech that these aren't Bakersfield PD SWAT?"

"You got that right. I'm sorry it had to be this way, son," Dyche said.

"Czernowitz figured Merry Michelsen had another source other than Jeb, someone else on the take."

"Like I said, I got old and tired," Dyche said. "Tired of never being on the winning team."

"So... they're going to gun me down right here?" Bob said. "In the middle of a neighborhood?"

Dyche shook his head. "Naw, I don't expect so. You've got information we need, Mr. Richmond, informant identities. I don't suppose whoever's snitching was ever a good soul."

"Justify murder to yourself however you want, Sergeant," Bob said. "Just don't expect a pass from me."

"Understood." Dyche withdrew a Glock 17 from his coat pocket. "Turn around, please."

Bob did as commanded. As stated, two more red dots took the other's place, wobbling around his sternum. He heard the slight drag of shoe heels on concrete.

Then the gun came down across the back of his skull, and his world plunged into darkness.

45

Bob woke to the sound of dripping water, a poorly secured tap somewhere nearby. His back was cold, the surface he was lying on flat, hard, possibly stone or granite.

The room was cool, strangely damp for the desert city. He tried to move, but his wrists and ankles were manacled to the surface. He craned his neck to lift his head just enough to look around. Pain shot through his cracked ribs and burned skin, and he winced, gritting his teeth.

His surroundings were dimly lit, the lack of windows suggesting a basement of some sort. They'd strapped him to what looked like a rectangular kitchen island, minus the kitchen, grey-and-cream granite or marble. The restraints were chain link, too strong to force.

His head felt slightly foggy. The pinching sensation on his upper left arm, near the shoulder, suggested they'd shot him up with something.

He lowered his head for a moment to rest his neck muscles, then lifted it again moments later, straining his stomach muscles to sit up as much as the chains would allow. It got him about six inches off the surface, a prolonged abdominal crunch. Bob looked around the room quickly.

On a ratty old sofa by the cinderblock far wall, a figure was sitting on his own, in a sleeveless t-shirt, his hands on his lap, a pair of Ray-Ban Wayfarer knockoffs covering his eyes.

Bob squinted. "Terry?"

It took a moment for him to reply. His voice was frail, tremulous. "Ah… y-yeah. Uh huh."

Bob leaned his head back. "What are you doing here? I gave you a chance to get out."

"Wasn't no chance," Terry said sullenly. "He came by my house, picked me up before we could leave."

There had to be more to it than that, Bob thought. The man had had nearly a day's head start.

"But you can't ever leave," Terry said. "Ain't no getting away from Merry. He's the Devil. Can't run from the Devil."

Bob looked up again. He had a terrible notion, a fragment memory of a colleague from Iraq who'd been blinded by phosphorus. "Terry… why are you wearing sunglasses?"

Terry hung his head for a moment. Then he reached up and removed the shades. The eye sockets were bandaged and bloody. One of the bandages came loose, the adhesive slickly defeated. It flopped to below his lid, a dark, blood-spattered hole signifying where his left eye had been just a day earlier.

"He… He took my eyes. He…" Terry began to sob, a wretched, guttural cough accompanying each bout of weeping. After about twenty seconds, he went silent.

A moment later, he composed himself. "Said he's going

to sell the cornholes or something... Wouldn't let me spin the Sig."

Bob had no idea what he was talking about. He'd seen plenty of war wounds and as horrifying as the act was, Terry's disheveled state was secondary to the questions running through his head.

"Why am I tied to this table, Terry? Is this where he did it?"

"I'm supposed to listen... yell if you try and escape. I don't know. Maybe making fun."

"Terry... is that what he plans to do to me?"

"He's going to make you play the game."

"Game? What game?"

"Never had a chance," Terry mumbled. "Why... why's it so hot in here?"

He's feverish. The wounds were probably infected, Bob thought. "Concentrate, Terry! What game?"

There was a metal clang from somewhere behind him, a deadbolt being drawn back. A squeaking of hinges followed.

"Terry! What game?!" Bob demanded. "Tell me what you can, before..."

"Before we join you?" The voice came from directly behind him this time, from the direction of the door. "I suspect Terrance has been referring to that old classic, Operation," Merry Michelsen said.

He walked closer and leaned over Bob. A bodyguard stood to either side. Bob recognized one as Diego, the wannabe MMA fighter from the motel showdown. The other was new, a big, bald side of beef with a spider-web tattoo around his right eye and temple.

"Seriously?" Bob suggested. "Please, for the love of originality, tell me you're not actually tying me to a table so that you can give me a villain speech. Because I'm all Netflixed out for today."

Merry glanced at his colleagues. "Will you listen to this feller, boys? He sure got a sack on him, don't he?" He looked down at Bob. "I kinda like him. I mean, not really. In reality, he's a pain in my ass that needs to be popped, like a big ol' pimple. But... you sure got some style, Bob, or whatever your real name is."

"It's actually Bob. It's annoying that nobody ever believes that, for some reason."

"Well, *Bob*..."

"The stressing it, like I'm lying? That too," Bob said.

"Huh. Well now, if you know so much and are feeling so talkative, why don't you go on ahead and tell me where they got Witty stashed, huh? Then we can get this over with in a more expedient and old-fashioned manner," Merry suggested.

Bob looked at the man next to him. "What the Hell is he talking about?"

Merry smirked and wagged a finger at him. "Nah! Now... you best be careful how you proceed, vis-à-vis all that bullshit and such. 'Cos we know what you told my good friend Sergeant Dyche, so we know you got a source and an alibi for your client, or friend, or just whatever the fuck the boy is to you. That's got to be Officer David Czernowitz. The one who's missing."

"I imagine Dyche pretty much always keeps you in front of him," Bob said. "He may be working for you, but I'm pretty sure he doesn't like you. And he sure doesn't trust you."

"Is that what you did with Jeb and Witty? Tried to 'divide and conquer'? Ain't going to work with me, son. For that to work, a man's got to care. Now... this is how this here is going to play out. I'm going to ask you one more time for information. Then, we're going to play a little game called Operation."

"Okay," Bob said. "Is that supposed to make me nervous?"

"I mean... It's Operation. Terry has no eyes. Are the ramifications not entirely clear to you?" Merry wondered aloud.

"Never heard of it," Bob said, which was true.

"Never..." Merry turned to Diego incredulously. "Did this A-One prime-beef bullshit artist just try to tell me he ain't never heard of Operation!?"

"Why would I lie about that?" Bob said. "I grew up in the fucking woods, okay? I have no idea what the fuck Operation is, except that it sounds vaguely surgical. Given that Terry's not going to be reading to blind kids again any time soon, I have to figure that's close."

"I wasn't never disloyal, Merry!" Terry whined. "I told you!"

Bob stayed silent, ignoring the urge to criticize his weakness. He'd known a parade of men who'd needed to belong to something, even at their own expense. *Hell, I was one of them.* Michelsen had beaten Terry down, like an abused dog, until he welcomed nothing else but a glimmer of hope that Merry would want him around.

You could say he lacked vision... but that would be grim even for you, Bobby.

"Uh huh," Merry drawled. "Ain't a problem no more anyhow, Terry. Can't snitch on what you can't see, you useless cripple." He turned back to Bob. "Operation is a board game. Usually, I let the person who owes me play it. Gives them a shot to walk away clean, or, if things go bad, to give me something in return. But for you? We're going to play for you, 'cos I don't trust you on the loose. In fact, I might just have Terry do the honors."

Diego chuckled at that.

The other bodyguard, the new guy, kept his eyes squarely ahead, swaying in place just enough to make Bob curious. *Is he uncomfortable? He looks it.*

"I take it this game requires some sort of visual acuity," Bob said, resting his neck once more by lowering his head back to the granite.

"Oh... it does, it surely does!" Merry said. "Terry's going to be manipulating a child-sized set of metal tweezers with his teeth, to remove toy organs from an electrified picture of a dude on an operating table. If the tweezers hit the side of the hole as he extracts the organ, the red nose lights up... and you owe me that organ. Just... the *real* version."

"You enjoy torturing people and organ theft, in other words," Bob said. "That's real original."

Merry sighed. "See? That kind of big-city, eastern judgment. We're used to that down here where real people live. I ain't going to do the deed myself! I've got a quack with a habit who handles that for me, former heart surgeon. Which, in your case, is ideal... because that's the piece Terry's going to play for first."

"And I'm guessing you won't be guiding his hand."

"Shit, son... I ain't even going to point him towards the board."

Diego chuckled once more.

Bob had dealt with his fair share of cruel people while serving and in the CIA. *But this guy's just demented.*

"Come on, Terry Perrine, get your lazy blind ass up!" Merry commanded. "Got the board right here. Going to put it down... ah! Don't you say nothing and help him, or I'll just go straight to taking out your ticker, okay?"

Terry rose from the sofa stiffly and took a nervous step forward. His shin hit the coffee table and he flailed for a moment to keep his balance.

"Ha ha! Heh heh heh!" Merry giggled. "Fellers, I do believe we have created ourselves a new slapstick comedy star."

Bob craned his neck to keep his head aloft, watching the newly blind man's struggle. "Take a step right and you'll have space," he said.

"*What* did I just say to you, Bob?" Merry demanded. "And still you're trying to help this treacherous moron not look stupid." He shook his head. "You are weak, son. You are a weak, weak man, feeling sorry for that crippled sack of shit. How'd someone like you ever get the drop on Tommy Kopec, huh?"

"Unchain me, and I'll gladly show you," Bob said.

"Heh! I don't think so. Come on, Terry, give it your best shot, blind boy!"

Terry took two steps forward, carefully, then another. He half crouched, reaching out with his hand, suddenly nervous. "I can't find it," he said. "I can't..."

Bob sighed and gently shook his head. "The pretense of letting him think he could help either of us is pretty cruel, Michelsen. Tell me, you ever fight a battle of your own? Or do you always rely on bigger men? I mean, in terms of courage."

Merry reached over and slapped him on the side of his torso with the flat of a palm. Bob winced and grunted.

"See, that's what you get for being fat phobic. I heard Vern busted up your ribs pretty good. Nah... I ain't going to fall for any of your macho, fair-fight bullshit, Bob, because I ain't a moron like Terry."

Terry slumped, cross legged, to the floor, sobbing once more.

"But I will save him any more embarrassment by just going next door and telling my surgically inclined associate to prep his stuff, get hisself scrubbed up and shit. That heart of yours is worth a lot of money to the right desperate sum'bitch on the Dark Web, and we don't want it getting infected or nothing."

46

The moment the door slammed shut, Bob barked at Terry. "Get up! He's gone."

"Can't. Can't do nothing," Terry moaned.

"Terry... man, you don't know me, but you do know I let you go."

"Yeah. Didn't have to do that."

"I didn't. But I did it anyway. So, believe me when I tell you: he's going to kill you. He's not letting you go blind as payback. That was just cruel fun for him. You're a witness, Terry, and one who was probably half out the door when he tracked you down. Am I right?"

Terry was silent for a few seconds, weighing how to think, what to say. "Wife had the bags packed, the kids ready. My daughters..." He began to sob again. "I can't see my beautiful daughters."

"But you can still be their father, if you get us both out of this. You just have to be strong. You have to get over here, following my voice, and help me out of these shackles. Then, we have a chance."

The room went silent. For a few moments, Bob worried the man was too sick from the infection, taken down by fever. "Terry? You there?"

He heard gentle sobbing again. "Can't. Can't hurt him. He always wins; always wins, and always gets his payback. Can't do it."

Bob yanked at the chains. The shackles were old-fashioned iron rings, the type of bracelet more commonly found in a museum. There was no give, no flex in the links. They couldn't be overcome. He tried to squeeze his palm closed, his fingers narrowed so that he could force them through the bracelet. But it was just too small, too tight to his wrist.

"Damn it!" he muttered.

"See?" Terry sobbed. "Just... just accept it. He's going to end us both."

Bob heard a creak from behind him, hinges gently squeaking. His eyes darted around and he tried to crane his head enough to see who it was, defeated by a limited range of motion.

"That was quick," he said instead. "You barely had time to scrub."

The man who leaned over him was massive, his forearms thicker than a firehose. "I ain't no surgeon, and you ain't dying today," he said quietly.

Bob got a glimpse of the man's face. His nose had been broken several times and he had scars, a gash across his forehead from long-ago violence, a spider's web tattoo around his right eye. He reached for Bob's right ankle and undid the shackle.

"What?" Terry demanded. "What's going on?"

"Not sure," Bob said.

"I'm cutting you loose." The man freed his other ankle then paused to look down.

"Why?" Bob said. "What is Merry playing at?"

"Ain't Merry's decision. I'm Lawrence," he said as he undid Bob's right wrist. He held out a hand and Bob reached up, incredulously, to shake it. "You got a friend in Lerdo who's a real good feller—Marcus Pell."

What the heck? "You know Marcus!?"

"Don't sound so surprised," Lawrence said, reaching over him to undo the other shackle. "He's a nice kid."

Bob grimaced against the stabbing pain in his ribcage. "Yeah, but..." He gestured to Lawrence. "You know..."

"What? I don't seem like a nice guy to you right now?" Lawrence growled testily. "I'm freeing your ass. I still have to get out of here in one piece. Show some fucking gratitude!"

"Apologies." Bob swung his legs off the kitchen island and down onto the floor.

"HEY!" Terry screamed. "HEY! THEY'RE TRYING TO ESCA—"

Before he could finish the thought, Lawrence took two quick steps towards him and hammered the smaller man in the jaw with a meaty fist. Terry slumped to unconsciousness.

"Asshole," Lawrence muttered. He nodded at Bob. "We need out of here, but the only way is through Merry and Diego," he said. "Can you fight?"

"I've been known—"

"I'm not asking if you're capable, dude. You're in pain, stupid. Can you fight?"

"Yeah. Yeah, I think so. You got a piece?"

Lawrence shook his head. "Doing this as a favor because I owe Merry money. He just wanted muscle. Didn't say nothing about a gunfight."

That didn't help. Diego and Merry would both be armed, Bob knew. He looked down at Terry, unconscious and sprawled on one side. "We can't leave him here. They'll kill him."

Lawrence looked at him strangely. "Are you touched in the head? He just tried to warn them."

"He's a beaten, frightened animal at this point," Bob said. "He's just trying to survive, and nothing on this Earth scares him more than the guy in the next room. And he has a family."

Lawrence crossed his arms. "Man... we don't have time for this shit. They're going to notice I've slipped out any moment."

"Help him up," Bob said. "Please."

Lawrence did as asked, but he was muttering, unhappy. "This ain't smart."

"It's what Marcus would do," Bob said. It was unfair, but he figured the man had to have taken a significant liking to the boy, or he wouldn't be there.

"Yeah. Yeah, okay, I get it. Marcus..."

"What?"

The bigger man shook his head. "I don't rightly know. Something spooked me when I got out of Lerdo. There was no word on a new cellmate. He called me collect his morning, said he spent the whole night in cells alone and no word on anyone coming today."

"So? Is that a problem?"

"That place... it's usually overcrowded if anything, man. Felt like maybe someone was trying to isolate him. It was better with me in there, looking out for him."

Terry stirred to consciousness, held upright, one arm draped over Lawrence's shoulders. "Wha–?" he muttered.

"He's concussed," Lawrence said. "Come on, stupid, we're taking a walk."

The three men covered the fifteen feet to the door. Bob scoped their surroundings properly for the first time. It was clearly a basement room, with no windows. In the back right corner, an old porcelain basin sat with the tap slowly dripping. In the left corner, a gas boiler piped hot water to the rest of the house.

"Where are we?" he asked quietly.

"Merry's bunker, under the trailer park," Lawrence whispered. "It's how he's kept his lab secret all these years. The DEA and local narcotics cops are looking above ground, looking for heat sources in trailers and such. There's another room past the steel door, then a big open cook room, where they make his product. Stairs are beyond that."

"Where are they? Next door?"

"Just the doc. He was about to scrub about when I—"

The sound of the latch turning interrupted him. They stepped back and to one side, letting the door swing open.

The man who walked past it wore green surgical scrubs, rubber gloves and a face mask. He was older and slight, with a dark complexion and silvery hair. He had a leather roll-up pouch, like an old tool kit. He took two steps past them and saw the room was empty.

The surgeon pivoted on his heels to look around, not seeing Lawrence's fist until the split-second before it connected with his chin. He slumped to the floor.

"He won't be out long," Bob said. "We need to move."

He opened the door again just enough to check the next room. It was a sparse lounge, with a sofa, a six-person table and some magazines. One corner was blocked off by a washroom.

"Break room for the cooks who don't smoke," Lawrence whispered.

They crossed the room to the next door. "And in the lab? Will the cooks defend him?"

Lawrence's eyes narrowed as he considered it. "Most owe him money. My guess? The second Diego draws his piece, they'll run scared."

"How big is the room? What are the sightlines and exits?"

"Big, about thirty yards long, a ton of tables, burners, the usual shit," Lawrence said. "Exit at each end, a door on the south wall to the bathroom, but... underground, so no windows."

"Numbers?"

"Excepting Merry and Diego? Maybe thirty. I didn't count."

Bob worked the handle slowly and gently. He gradually pushed the door open until the crack was wide enough to check inside.

Diego had his back to them. Merry was following one of the two lines of tables, commenting on the cooks' work. The cooks were a mix of men and women, naked other than white aprons, surgical hair covers, gloves and filtered facemasks.

"The key you used to free me," Bob asked, "is that the only one?"

Lawrence nodded. "He had me shackle you up in the first place, when they brung you in."

"Give it to me," Bob said. "When I throw the door open and run in, you take Terry out along the left side of the room, which is mostly clear. Take him directly out the door on the other side, and get him out of here."

"Man... you're pushing this favor thing a whole long way, ordering me to do shit," Lawrence muttered. "I'm trying to do right here, but..."

"I'll apologize properly later, when we have time," Bob said. "But for now, he has a wife and kids, and he's pathetic, not evil."

"You're going to handle them two on your own?" Lawrence sounded doubtful.

"I'll manage," Bob said. "Ready? Okay. We go on three. One... two..."

47

The door flew open, slamming into the near wall as they burst into the cook room. Bob ran straight ahead, towards Diego.

The noise drew everyone's attention, the cooks looking up. Diego turned quickly. He drew a pistol from the back of his waistband.

The gun had the predicted effect; a cook nearby screamed, and suddenly the room was a madhouse, people panicking, fleeing past the bodyguard and pushing around Merry, who clung to one of the tables with his fingertips.

Diego tried to aim over the group, but Bob ducked low, using the fleeing mob as cover.

The sea of bodies parted enough for Diego to sight him. Bob glanced around quickly, his hand going for a large glass flask, grasping it by its long, skinny neck and flinging it, backhanded, towards the guard.

Diego raised his hands to protect his face, the glass bouncing off him and shattering on the ground.

He lifted the pistol again, but Bob was on him, driving a

palm punch at his elbow joint, pushing the gun wide, the shots skewing off target.

Diego tried to regain his balance, swinging the gun back towards Bob, even as the ex-agent lashed out with a low side-kick, driving the ball of his foot through the big man's knee joint. Bob felt a crunch and Diego screamed, collapsing to his other knee, the gun dropped in a moment of agonizing pain.

Bob scrambled to retrieve it. The weight came down on his back unexpectedly, a sharp pain stabbing at Bob's shoulder blade as Merry plunged the knife in once, twice, three times in quick succession.

Bob half turned at the waist, grabbing the heavier man's jacket and waistband, pivoting at the hip and using his thigh to trip Merry, the judo throw tossing him near-effortlessly to the ground, the drug dealer's weight doing most of the work. Adrenaline was firing, the pain in his ribs temporarily forgotten.

Merry slammed to the ground, the switchblade skittering away. Bob crouched down quickly and hammered the man in the side of the chin, where the mental nerve resides. It compressed, Merry losing consciousness, his eyes rolling back even as he blacked out.

The gun. Bob rose and turned in time to see Diego, on one knee, reach down to an ankle holster.

Bob threw himself forward, skidding across the slick tile floor, his hand reaching the Glock. He turned as Diego's snub-nosed revolver came free, aimed directly at him.

Bob fired four shots center mass, the bodyguard going over backwards.

Diego lay unmoving. Bob got up, keeping an eye on Merry while walking over to the bodyguard. Diego was coughing up mouthfuls of blood, one of the bullets having pierced a lung.

Damn it. A year. More than a year without having to... He looked down at the man choking on his own blood. One of the wounds was pumping fluid in irregular gasps, an artery hit somewhere, possibly the heart.

A haunted sensation struck Bob, memories of being young, alone in the woods, watching a deer he'd trapped accidentally suffering.

No chance he makes it.

Do it quickly, Bobby, don't let him suffer.

He shot Diego twice through the head.

Merry woke suddenly, his arm twitching several times before his eyes snapped open, the Operation board he'd been carrying upside down on the floor beside him.

"Who–?" he mumbled bleakly.

"Me." Bob reached down and snapped a quick jab from the shoulder, knocking the man out again.

He looked up. On the far side of the room, Merry's surgeon was frozen in place, one hand against the wall, bracing himself and shocked.

"It's okay," Bob said. "I'm not going to hurt you."

The man stared, unblinking, unmoving, terrified.

"But I need your help. First, you're going to patch the stab wounds in my back. Then, the dolly in the corner... bring it over here." Merry weighed more than he could handle alone, Bob knew. "Help me move this useless tub of shit, then I'll let you go."

Time to get Mr. Merry Michelsen talking. And I have just the right incentive in mind.

. . .

BOB THREW the flask of cold water into Merry's face. He woke with a start, shaking his head, trying to expel the droplets, unsure of what was happening.

"Where–?" He tried to lift his head and look around. Then he tried to raise his arms, feeling the shackles bite at his wrists. "Fuck."

"Appropriate," Bob said.

"*You*! You..." His rage was flaring, his face flushed and contorted into a snarl.

"I strapped you to the same table as you did me," Bob said. "I had to get help getting you in here, and even then we needed a dolly. I'm not one to judge, but you ever think about laying off the burgers for a week?"

"Man... you gonna kill me, just kill me," Merry whined. "I got a condition. It's glandular."

"My heart bleeds for you."

Merry turned his head. "Chained me to the dang island."

"Yep. Now, you get to feel how much fun your game is. We're going to play Operation, Merry, only this time I'm going to pick the organ for you."

Merry's expression transformed in an instant, from irritated to haughty. "Bleeding heart like you? You ain't got the stones, son."

"But what I do have," Bob said, "is this very large buck knife that your friend Diego had in a sheath on this belt. It looks really, really sharp. I had to amputate a swabbie's arm at the elbow in Afghanistan; he had it trapped under a burning Humvee and we had heat coming down, necessitating a rapid evac. Made a hell of a mess, too."

Merry turned whiter than white. "Now... you just take it easy, okay?" He was trying to maintain his authoritarian tone, but the look in his eye was sheer panic.

Bob reached down to the board game propped between Merry's legs on the marble counter. "Okay, let's see. Suppose I go for the testicles first, huh? I mean, I figure, of the items you've got here, it's the one least likely to make a sale later. But this isn't really about the financial opportunity, is it? I doubt Terry's corneas were going to make you a whole lot richer."

"I got money. I got lots of money," Merry said. "You let me go, it's yours. All of it. This don't have to get ugly."

"Oh... I think we crossed that threshold quite some time ago." He took the knife and leaned down, tracing its tip up the inside of Merry's leg from the ankle, past his calf, up to just short of his groin. "I'm thinking at this point, I do this just on principle. I had to kill someone tonight, Merry, and I haven't had to do that for a while."

"Then don't!" Merry spat. "You don't have to—"

"If you think your death is going to bother me nearly as much as poor old Diego over there," Bob interrupted, "you've got a real weak grasp of your situation. You're an animal. Most people would see putting you down for good as a favor to society."

He placed the flat of the blade under Michelsen's groin, then used it to lift the man's testicles slightly. "Or..."

"*Or*? Or what? The money? I ain't lying. I've got—"

"Or you confess to every shitty thing you've done and take your punishment like a normal human being, which clearly you aren't. The jacket that I had on when I met with Dyche. Where is it?"

"The... what?"

"Someone took off my jacket. Where is it? I need the recorder that was in my pocket. Come on, fess up." Bob juggled Merry's testes with the blade, lifting them up, then letting them drop. "Unless you feel like becoming a eunuch, I'd tell me real quick."

"*The office!*" Merry blurted. "The office on the other side of the cook room."

Bob withdrew the blade. "Good boy. I'll be right back. Now, don't you go nowhere, you hear?"

He followed the dealer's instructions. As advertised, the jacket was draped over the arm of a leather sofa in the small, sparsely furnished room. Against its far wall, he noticed the stairs up to the ground floor.

Bob put his jacket on and retrieved the recorder. *How long did that take? A minute?* He paused and waited. *His first reaction on me leaving would be relief. But the longer I wait to go back, the more he'll think I've left him chained there. Give him another two minutes and he'll be near panic.*

Bob sat down on the sofa's edge. He checked for missed calls, finding three from Sharmila and another from an unknown number. He watched the clock on his phone until three minutes had passed.

He walked back to Merry's torture room. The dealer was kicking at his bonds, unable to get loose.

"You can't leave me here," he croaked. "Not with my boys all gone."

"Oh... I'm sure someone would find you eventually," Bob said. "You must have a real friend somewhere... right, Merry? Of course, that could be weeks from now, long after you've died from dehydration and cardiac arrest. Or worse, starvation."

"There's... there's got to be some dang thing you want," Merry pleaded. "I got three million dollars. *Million.*"

Bob set the digital recorder down on the slab, next to Merry's head. "If I'd been thinking in the moment, I'd have used this to record your crooked cop friend, Dyche," Bob said. "But I was suckered from behind before it occurred to me. So now what's going to happen is you're going to talk, Merry. You're going to tell me shit you never told anybody, as well as the entirety of your business with Parker Baird and Greg Thomas."

"They ain't going to buy it," Merry said. "It's coerced."

"Yeah... but they're not going to know that," Bob said. "Because every time you even hint on the recording that you're being forced to talk, I'm going to turn it off and start over. But first... I'm going to take a payment for your dishonesty, in the form of something I remove from your body. Maybe we'll start with the big toe on each foot. You know it's basically impossible to walk without one, right?"

Merry closed his eyes tight, the stress obvious.

He's beaten, and he knows it.

"Good," Bob said. "When we're done, you'll get a chance to live, a chance nobody gave Hap Singh. I'll leave you here."

Merry's brow furrowed, a sadness setting in. "Won't be nobody back here, not after this. Won't come for days, if ever. You can't leave me here."

"Ah, don't worry. I'll be sure to let the police know where they can find you. Eventually." Bob glanced around. "Between whatever I give them and the lab next door, the methylamine production at your cheese factory... I imagine they'll be along before you starve. Maybe. Now... let's get started."

48

Sharmila Singh threw the wheel left, taking the corner quickly and at the last second, without a turn signal. She looked up at the rearview mirror.

The truck was still on her tail. It had been following her since a block from outside the clinic, and they were now fully across the city.

Is he even following me? He must be, right? The truck had stayed back, as if it could be a coincidence that it had taken four identical turns to hers. It didn't appear to be trying to catch her, or force her off the road.

She'd tried Bob's number twice already. She'd called him the evening prior, late, expecting a report on his meeting with Dyche. But he hadn't picked up any of the three calls.

Maybe he's hurt. She shook the thought off. There was nothing to be gained from assuming the worst.

Her phone rang through the car's speakers. She hit the answer button on the wheel console. "Bob?"

"Sorry, I got tied up," Bob said. "Look, we have to act

quickly. I've got a confession out of Merry Michelsen. But he doesn't know who pulled the trigger on—"

"Bob, I'm—"

"He says Baird arranged your dad's death. He admitted to the lab and the housing scam but—"

"Bob, please, I'm—"

"He says whatever led to Marcus being busted was last minute, maybe a reaction to your father meeting with—"

"Bob! Please let me talk!"

"Sorry."

"I'm being followed. A grey or pale blue pickup, ever since I pulled away from the clinic twenty minutes ago. Why? Why would someone be after me?"

"They probably aren't. I've been driving your car regularly for the last three days. They probably think it's me. Where are you?"

She checked the sat nav. "We're approaching the intersection of Stockdale Highway and Village Lane."

"Is there a restaurant in view, a chain, something that will be busy?"

"A what!?"

"A restaurant. You need cover and witnesses. These guys aren't audacious. They're not going to try to shoot a witness in front of dozens of people and cameras."

"There's a steakhouse a block up."

"Go, now," Bob said. "If you can't find a spot near the door, just park illegally. Better to get towed than to have to make it across a lot without cover. I'll be there soon."

"Okay, but—"

"No buts! Don't argue. Just do it," Bob commanded. He ended the call.

Sharmila checked her mirror. The truck was still nearly

two blocks back, the restaurant approaching quickly. She undid her seat-belt and got ready to bail and run.

Bob kept his head on a swivel as he crossed the trailer park towards the entrance.

The hire car pulled up a few seconds later. Bob opened the back door and climbed in.

"Bob?" the driver asked.

"One and the same."

"Good to meet you."

Bob pulled up his trouser leg and reached into his boot to retrieve his money clip. He peeled off a hundred and held it over the division between front and back. "This is yours if you get me there in fifteen minutes or less."

The driver's eyes widened. Then he frowned. "That's impossible. I'd have to go sixty the whole way there, or more. I can't risk my ride privilege."

Bob withdrew Diego's Glock from his waistband. He leaned it on the seat partition. "Wouldn't it be better to do it for money than under threat?"

The driver glanced quickly at the pistol.

Bob held up the money again with his other hand.

The driver snatched it.

"Smart," Bob said. "I assume you're going to call the cops once I'm out of here, and that's okay. None of this is on you, man. I'm just in a tight spot. Hit the gas."

The car peeled away from the curb, tires shrieking on the hot asphalt.

49

The hire car took Route 99 to Stockdale Highway, the kid behind the wheel stepping on the gas pedal like it might escape.

"The steakhouse, on our left," Bob said.

The driver began to slow down for the left turn, across the opposite lanes.

"Just stop us here!" Bob barked.

The car shuddered to a halt. A split second later, the traffic signal turned yellow, then red.

Bob took out forty dollars and handed it to the car's owner. "Again, sorry about the gun."

The kid stared at him, wide-eyed and terrified, as he climbed out.

Well... that was less than ideal, Bob thought as he jogged across the road. In the moment, it was necessary, he told himself. But he didn't feel good about it.

The steakhouse was an upscale chain. Bob threw open the main doors. A couple were waiting at its reception for a table. He walked past them, ignoring the tall, thin greeter looking for their reservation.

The restaurant proper was decorated in dark wood and equally dark paints, offset by small globe lights above each booth and tall table. It was busy, families in for an early dinner, waitresses carrying trays of drinks and platters of T-bones, onion blossoms and baked potatoes.

Bob scanned the room. It took a moment to spot Sharmila, stuffed into a back-corner booth. Her purse was on the table, clutched between both hands. She looked frightened.

He looked over at the row of booths by the windows, across the aisle. They were all empty save one, two booths up. The smoked glass wasn't giving away much but it looked like the back of a man's head.

He kept his pistol in his belt. There were too many civilians in the line of fire to be comfortable.

If I move quickly and quietly, I have the drop on him. Bob strode casually up the aisle. Five feet ahead of the man's table, Sharmila looked up and saw him approaching, her expression shifting from bleak to hopeful in the blink of an eye.

Her pursuer rose and turned to lean around the booth divider, the pistol leveled at Bob from less than ten feet away.

Bob dove sideways as the gunshot shattered the eatery's peaceful blather, patrons in an instant panic, diners ducking, sprinting for the door. He reached out in midair, grabbing the oversized pepper shaker from the nearby tabletop, tossing it hard, from the shoulder, the half-foot-tall wooden implement striking the gunman between the eyes. The gunman staggered a foot back, his legs colliding with the edge of the table, the pistol flying from his hand.

Bob pushed off hard, rising to his feet, then turning and running at the man, leaping into an elbow drop. His target rolled away from the table top, scrambling to regain his balance.

"SHARMILA, GO!" Bob screamed. "Get out!"

The two men squared off.

Greg Thomas.

Bob reached for his back waistband, but his hand came away empty. He glanced sideways quickly.

The pistol was under the opposite table.

Before he could move for it, he saw the glint of the blade in his periphery, Thomas aiming a slashing backhand at him, the switchblade glinting under the dome light. Bob ducked away from it, anticipating the return swipe and stepping around it. He locked the man's passing arm up at the wrist and elbow, the force jarring the knife loose.

Thomas was already turning, as Bob caught the switchblade handle first and drove it down, hard, through the man's free hand and into the tabletop. Instead of panicking, his opponent screamed and pivoted the other way, throwing a hard elbow backwards, catching Bob square in the solar plexus, his wind driven out in an instant.

Bob fell to one knee. Thomas pulled the knife out of his hand. Both men glanced towards the gun. Before either could react, a police siren blared from somewhere near the front of the restaurant.

Bob dove for the gun and reached it before his opposite number could react. He turned and rose, levelling it. Thomas had a gushing wound, the switchblade in his free hand, the blade slick, his expression rage-filled.

There was something hard and L-shaped in his front pocket.

"Don't even—" Bob began to say, another gunshot interrupting his thought, a glass booth partition to his left shattering.

From behind both men, an older man's voice called out. "I am affecting a citizen's arrest!"

Oh, for crying out loud...

"Put the gun down, or I will shoot," the man said. "Do it! Now!"

Thomas grinned toothily. He had wild blue eyes, the smile almost a sneer. He turned and sprinted towards the kitchen doors.

Bob looked over his shoulder. "I can't let him get away, sir."

"You can just stay put!" It was an older customer, well into his late sixties or seventies. "And don't think I don't know how to—" The customer's attention was drawn by the clanging of the main doors being booted open.

Bob took the opportunity, sprinting towards the kitchen door and barreling through it, the galley-style entry swinging free behind him, the customer's gunshot wild.

The back door was open and ajar, the kitchen staff having cleared out after the first shot, he supposed. Bob ran through it and turned left. He looked cautiously around the corner in time to see a blue Nissan pickup screech out of the bays and towards an exit, smoke spewing off burnt rubber.

A split-second later, Sharmila's BMW screeched to a halt in front of him. "GET IN!" she screamed.

Bob did as instructed.

"DUCK!" she bellowed.

He pushed his torso as low as he could go, practically kneeling under the dash, just as the column of three police cars sped past, lights flashing, klaxons blaring.

Bob felt the car turn right onto Village Lane, then left onto Stockdale and into traffic.

He lifted his head. "Are you okay?"

She nodded twice.

"That was Greg Thomas, Baird's assistant," Bob said.

"I know. Once he walked into the restaurant and I got a look at him—"

"Let me guess, you went to high school together."

Sharmila glared at him. "He was at Marcus's arraignment. He's at least forty. How old do you think I am, exactly?"

"A day older than yesterday," Bob said wearily. "And thankfully, a day younger than tomorrow."

She pursed her lips, as if warding off tears, the implication setting in. "Well... I'm sorry," she said. "But that was really scary."

She's not built for this. Say something nice. "It was good thinking, driving past the back door."

She sobbed a little. "I didn't. I just saw you at the last second, is all."

Ah, Hell. "Still, good timing anyway," Bob said. "And you were very brave, sitting there trapped by him."

She shook it off, wiping a tear away with her sleeve. "What now? The police are going to have camera footage from the restaurant."

"He attacked me without even confronting you," Bob said. "They'll think it's between us, and they're already looking for me. If you're lucky, whoever reviews it doesn't recognize you. It's not that small a city, right? If nothing else, we know Baird's using his own guy for heavy lifting. That gives us another viable suspect."

"You think he killed my father?" Sharmila said.

"Given what just went down, it's seriously possible."

"So we need to find him, make him talk." She said it with the zeal of a Grand Inquisitor. Then she frowned. "How?"

"Modern medicine," Bob said. "That and a visit to your clinic."

"Because…"

"We need someone with access to Jenkins's medical records, and you mentioned the clinic handled their medicals last year."

"And…"

"And his records will have his home address. And we know he'll have medical records, because based on the inhaler in his top pocket, Greg Thomas has asthma."

50

CHICAGO, ILLINOIS

Dawn Ellis stood at the clinic exam room basin as the warm water doused her hands and she stared off into space. She was tired, worried about Marcus, worried she still hadn't heard anything from Bob after two more days.

What if something happened to him, with Marcus still inside? No one would be there for the boy.

It seemed less convincing every time Bob told her to stay away. She knew his history, had seen the death and pain that could surround him. But it had been nearly a year, and he'd hardly kept a low profile. Where Bob went, trouble followed or quickly reared its head.

And yet, no arrest, no government team hunting them as in DC.

She'd prayed on it the night before, asking God whether a guy like Bob could ever have a semblance of peace. Usually, just asking the question, looking for the answer, offered some measure of comfort. But this time, she'd wanted a definitive answer, and it hadn't been apparent.

Even if he could just be left alone, enough to have real friends. To make his own family.

"You okay, girl? Dawn!"

"Hmmmnh?"

Her co-worker at the community clinic was snapping her fingers. "You're tripping about something."

Dawn shook her head briefly to clear the cobwebs. "I had a poor night's sleep, Joceyln. My apologies.

The other nurse pointed to the tap. "You're going to wash your fingers off if you don't turn that tap off sometime soon."

Dawn blushed and did as suggested.

THE DAY SPED BY, and Dawn found herself walking home at twice the normal pace.

The burner phone was in the bottom drawer of her clothes chest, nestled under some old slips she didn't wear anymore. She'd made up her mind to call back hours earlier but had spent the day worrying Bob would be annoyed.

It had only been forty-eight hours, after all. But he'd promised he would talk to Marcus, and she'd assumed he meant he'd call back and tell her what the boy said.

She got home and hung her coat before the door had swung shut. She hustled back to the bedroom and retrieved the burner from the bottom drawer, then speed-dialed Bob's phone.

The phone rang twice, then went to a recording. "The number you are trying cannot be reached. Please hang up and try your call again."

She ended the call, fairly slapping the red button on the screen.

That wasn't good. He was too careful to just let the phone die. That meant he'd abandoned it.

Or that he was in trouble and couldn't get to it.

She took her purse off her shoulder and fished for her regular phone, throwing the purse on the bed. She dialed a number.

"Dawn. What's up?"

"Hi, Del. Sorry to get you after hours. I need to book a few days off. Parent stuff." Her boss knew she'd adopted Marcus, that it came with challenges.

"You've still got hours in lieu owed. I can get someone else in."

"Thank you. It's greatly appreciated. Just until Tuesday, I expect."

"You're a great nurse, Dawn. We all appreciate you."

"Good night, Del."

"You let us know if you need anything else."

"Uh huh... and thank you again."

She ended the call and scrolled to a travel website.

ON THE ROOF of the Greektown apartment block, Geert Van Kamp removed the earpiece and stashed it in his side pocket.

Renton had been right about tapping the woman's apartment with video. He'd gone in through the kitchen skylight while she was at work. The tiny cameras were attached to the door jambs in three rooms, feeding video back to his phone.

The call to her boss had come moments after trying a number several times without success. Her expression had been pure dismay, as if she fully expected an answer that hadn't come.

He tapped the Bluetooth set in his other ear. A moment later, Renton's voice rang through. "Go ahead, sir."

"Renton, get me on the next available flight from Chicago to Bakersfield, California," he said.

"Sir? She gave something up?"

"She's taking a trip. Something spooked her, or disappointed her, and it was impromptu. It may be coincidence, but I'm not a great believer in them."

"She could just be visiting family."

"Did I request supposition, Renton? No? Then keep any opinions to yourself, mate. The video caught her retrieving a burner phone from a drawer. It definitely was not the phone she used to call her boss moments later. Unless she's the most undercover drug dealer in history, Ms. Dawn Ellis is hiding something. And Bob's friend had her number on his list."

"There's a red-eye at four forty-seven in the morning. Or, I can—"

"Put me on it," Van Kamp said.

It was time. He could feel it in his bones, the calm before the storm, the sense of a battle in the offing.

51

They sat in the parked BMW, across from an undersized bungalow on Pine Street, in Riviera/Westchester.

It was an older neighborhood by Bakersfield standards, the lots non-uniform in size and shape, the homes as well. The street had been repaired hundreds of times, a spider web of asphalt patches covering much of its surface, stretching out like shadow tendrils under the tall streetlights.

Traffic had slowed as the evening progressed, so that by eleven o'clock, barely a car was passing. The other two- and three-bedroom homes were quiet, lights out at many, no one venturing out.

"I don't like that you're here," Bob said. He yawned deeply.

"And I don't like that you're clearly exhausted," Sharmila said. "Are you sure you can do this?"

"I'll be fine," he said as nonchalantly as possible. The

truth was he was so tired he was nearly seeing double. They'd given him something after knocking him cold at the sports park to keep him unconscious, his head still slightly woozy.

"Just stay in the car," he ordered. "As long as we're clear on that. This guy is dangerous, and he didn't give a rat's patootie about firing off a loaded pistol in a busy restaurant. He's not going to worry about what his neighbors think."

"If this man killed my father, I have a right to be here," Sharmila said.

"Yes… in the car," Bob stressed. "When we stopped at your house…" He paused, unsure how to be diplomatic.

"What?"

"I didn't ask why. I was worried you were maybe going to get a piece."

She glared at him again. "A 'piece'? I don't own a gun, Bob. I'm not going to shoot him. I'm a grown woman, for crying out loud, a physician! And… you're not going to shoot him either, right? He has to be punished. We deserve justice. My father deserves justice."

"I'll do what I can," Bob said. Then he noticed her growing consternation. "Seriously, I'm not planning to kill the guy. We need his statement, for one. Without him, everything relies on Merry's confession. And the recording sounds like he's gone three rounds with Tyson in his prime. I'm not even sure they'll accept it as evidence."

"But Marg will believe it. She knows who he is," Sharmila said hopefully. "That's almost as good, you figure?"

"Yeah, I think so. Combined with whatever David picked up from Jeb Fowler, it should be enough for her to recommend clearing Marcus and myself with respect to Fowler.

But it won't be enough to put a guy like Baird away, a guy with money and friends. Thomas, on the other hand…"

"He spends all of his time with Baird. He probably knows everything," Sharmila said.

"Which…" Bob said, undoing his seatbelt, "…is why you're staying put." He opened the passenger door a crack.

"If you're gone more than a half-hour…"

"Stay in the car," Bob said. "If it's taking longer than expected, I'll let you know. Deal?"

She didn't sound convinced, but nodded nonetheless. "Fine. Deal."

THE PALE BLUE pickup was in front of the home's one-car garage. It was a modest single level, the kind of kit they built in the fifties, when estate subdivisions offered even a modest employee a route to ownership, with gyprock facia in a fading shade of coral.

Light streamed out of an ajar window to the right side of the front door. Bob craned his ear, the faint sounds of canned sitcom laughter drifting into the night.

He checked the street in both directions, paying close attention to front windows for any movement, any sign of onlookers. Satisfied it was clear, Bob ducked low and moved under the window to listen.

A woman was chuckling, her lilt older, pure country. "…time you come up from the holler with that godawful rat, telling your daddy you wanted to keep it as a pet. And he brung it out back and shot it, and you blubbered like a tap gone off in your head or something." She laughed at the memory.

"Aw, Mama... I didn't know no better, you know that. And besides... he shot the dog, too. Weren't like it was just because it was a rat. Pa just liked taking away things I liked, is all."

"He was a tough old piece of leather, your father. You want another beer?"

"Surely. I'll get it. You sit right there."

The woman was a complication, Bob figured, but also an opportunity. Even a nasty piece of work like Greg Thomas had a mother he loved, evidently.

Leverage? Maybe. You do what you need to do. There would be heightened risk, a chance of the woman being hurt. But Thomas was key to putting Baird down and saving Marcus. *You know how it works, Bobby. It's only a problem if you're not paying attention.*

He followed the dark path down the home's right side, towards the back yard. At a side door, he climbed a step to the square landing pad, then peeked through the inset half-moon window.

In the kitchen, Thomas was taking items out of the fridge, moving thing aside as if hunting ingredients. A loaf of bread sat nearby on the counter, along with two open beers, a tall wooden pepper mill and an empty plate.

Bob turned the handle slowly, pushing gently on the door to maintain the same pressure at the hasp and prevent a loud click as it popped open. He pulled the door open slowly and gently.

"...got ham and mozzarella slices, if that's what you feel like." His target was stooped, his head practically inside the boxy old fridge.

"Anything," his mother's voice came from the other room. "My tummy's sure growling something fierce."

Opportunity knocks, Bobby.

Bob took two steps closer and tapped Thomas on the shoulder with his left hand, even as his right grasped the fridge door and swung it closed, the hard edge slamming into the top of Thomas' skull as he turned to look up.

The blow dazed him, and he stumbled two steps sideways. Bob gauged the width of the man's second step and led his movement with the follow-up punch, his fist catching Thomas on the side of the chin.

His target dropped to one knee but didn't go down, a hand flashing towards his waistline. Bob lashed out with a straight kick, catching Thomas flush in the chest, knocking him on his back, the pistol flying from his grip before he could raise it and skidding across the tile.

Bob ignored the pain in his ribs and jumped on the younger man, trying to pin his arms with both knees, a 'ground and pound' maneuver that left Thomas's chin unprotected.

He loaded up a right cross, but a tiny, withered hand grabbed him at the wrist, the old lady jumping on his back, her other hand raking at his face and neck. She wailed like a banshee, "AIEEEEE!" her free hand clawing at his eyes.

"Get off!" Bob barked, standing and stepping backwards, trying to throw her.

"You leave my boy alone!'

Bob threw himself backwards out of instinct, coming down full weight on the elderly woman, feeling something under him pop. She bellowed in pain but didn't let up, trying to scratch and claw at him from every angle. He rolled away... directly into the path of Thomas's kick, her son recovered and coming to her defense. The sneakered foot caught Bob square in the right side of his ribcage, a lightning bolt of pain shooting through him. He slumped onto one side, bile rising from his stomach.

The pain was so intense he thought he might pass out. His vision blurred for a moment. He was barely able to register Thomas striding over to the corner of the room, stooping to pick something up.

The pistol.

Bob knew he had no strength, his mind cloudy from pain and fatigue.

Thomas pointed it at the top of his head.

I'm done.

After everything... I'm done.

Thomas's finger curled around the trigger.

Then Thomas slumped forward, his eyes momentarily rolling back and up as he lost consciousness. He collapsed rigidly, thumping to the floor.

Behind him, Sharmila stood holding the wooden pepper mill aloft.

The room sat in stunned silence for five seconds. Then, Thomas's mother gasped, a free hand coming up to her face in shock. "My boy!" She tried to rise but couldn't, settling for pulling herself four feet across the tile to his prone body. She practically flung herself atop her son. "Don't you hurt him!"

Bob rose unsteadily, using the kitchen counter for support. He hobbled over and picked up the gun. Then he looked over at Sharmila. "I thought I told you to stay in the car."

Her eyes widened. "Are you kidding me?"

He nodded curtly. "Yes, completely. Sorry... the more tired I get, the dryer everything comes out. And I am, excuse my language, fucking exhausted."

"Now what?"

"Now? Now you're going to restrain Mrs. Thomas so that she doesn't get any crazy ideas, and I'm going to do the same to her boy. And then he and I are going to have a little chinwag."

52

District Attorney Jerald Valenzuela watched through the glass block window as Assistant DA Margaret Swain continued her lengthy interview with Greg Thomas. He was clothed in an orange prison jumpsuit, his wrists manacled to the tabletop via a chain through a large iron loop.

Valenzuela's expression was grim. "The problem we have, Mr. Richmond, Ms. Singh, is that all we have is his word."

"I don't understand," Sharmila said.

"Yeah, well... it's a real mess." The DA looked at his watch. "One thirty in the morning." He sighed. "My wife's going to kill me."

"Surely Thomas's confession is enough, when you combine it with what Michelsen told me about Baird's involvement, to pick him up," Bob said.

"That tape of Michelsen won't stand up in court. There's no chain of evidence and it sounds, from his gasping and sobbing, that you scared the right holy hell out of him. As envious as I am after a decade of him terrorizing this town that you had the opportunity to put the fear of God into him, no judge is going to give that much weight."

"So what about Thomas?"

"Thomas will turn on Baird, but that's problematic. He also stole Hap Singh's wallet and money, and he has nothing in writing from Baird, just his word," Valenzuela said. "He has given us chapter and verse of Mr. Merry Michelsen and his attempt to branch out from meth to real estate. Apparently, Mr. Thomas was seen meeting with Merry Michelsen a few days before Mr. Singh's death. Someone reported it to him, and told him Thomas worked for Professor Jenkins."

"So he confronted them."

"And he pulled corporate and tax papers on everything he could find associated with Jenkins... including Jenkins Racing and The Big Cheese factory."

"So he'd figured it out."

The DA took a deep breath. Bob could sense the bad news coming immediately.

"But it still doesn't prove Baird knew about any of this," Valenzuela said. "His lawyers will argue he tried to invest, innocently, in a housing development. And he innocently rented a factory space to Michelsen, who was using a numbered front. Equally, Officer Czernowitz's statement pegs his former partner for killing Professor Jenkins... but Czernowitz doesn't know Thomas, and he can't tie Baird to Hap Singh's death. Thomas has lost credibility by robbing the victim. The only person who can corroborate his version is Michelsen."

"Then bring him in!" Bob declared. "Interview him properly. Get him to admit it on the record."

"The police department is in the process of arresting him

as we speak, as I understand. But getting him to help us with Thomas? That," the DA said sullenly, "will require cutting a deal, almost certainly. But we already have him dead to rights on the meth lab, a major felony that can put him away for life."

Sharmila crossed her arms defensively. "What are you saying?"

"I can't in good conscience risk that conviction on the chance of a 'he said, he said' with Parker Baird. Baird has a scrupulous reputation, a lot of money, political friends. It would be his word against a major drug dealer getting a break for his participation, to confirm the word of a confessed murderer. You see my problem here. I can put one dangerous felon away for a long time, or I potentially go easy on him and still not land Baird."

"Land", he says, like he's going after a trophy fish. Bob wandered a few feet to the far wall and slumped down on the old leather two-seat sofa. He leaned back and closed his eyes momentarily, the weight of the week catching up to him.

"Sharmila's father is dead. Professor Jenkins is dead. I have two broken ribs on my left side, another on my right, at least one third-degree burn. My friend, Marcus Pell, is isolated in pre-trial custody, possibly because Baird pulled strings to make sure he stays vulnerable. And you're telling me the guy responsible is going to walk?"

In the adjacent room, Bob saw Swain pass in front of the window briefly on her way to the door. She joined them.

"I've been filling Ms. Singh and Mr. Richmond in on the Baird situation," Valenzuela told her.

"He's letting him walk," Sharmila spat angrily.

"I know," Swain said. "Shar... sometimes these things are complicated."

"No!" Sharmila said. "No, it's not complicated! He ordered this man to shoot my father. This man has admitted it. But we get no justice for the man who is actually responsible, because the state wants to bust another meth dealer!?"

Bob couldn't remember the last time he'd been so tired. He nodded Swain's way. "Why there, in the alley?"

"Thomas knew Marcus took that route home nightly. He needed a patsy. So he carjacked Singh in the parking lot and ordered him to drive down the alley and park behind the pawn shop, where he'd be unmissable. He left the car door ajar so that the interior bell would alert Marcus even if he somehow didn't see the Cadillac. Then he exited the alley through the pawn shop, as if he'd never been there. No sign of him entering because he was in the car, or leaving, because he cut through the store."

"And Fowler and Czernowitz were ordered to wait nearby," Sharmila finished the line of thinking. "But... what about motive? Surely a jury would believe someone ordered Thomas to do it? He works for Baird..."

"But he also stole the money from your father's wallet," Swain said. "In that moment of greed, he accidentally gave himself sufficient motive—a robbery gone wrong."

Sharmila was shaking her head steadily back and forth, the realization of what was happening sinking in. "This cannot happen."

"I'm sorry, Shar," Swain said. "We can give everything we have to our federal contacts, see if it's enough to trigger a racketeering investigation of Baird, but beyond that, there's nothing—"

"I have an idea," Bob interrupted.

. . .

Parker Baird rose at six thirty every morning.

His schedule was identical; a traditional calisthenics routine of push-ups, sit-ups and deep knee bends; a hot-then-cold shower, to stimulate mental alertness; followed by a breakfast shake of protein powder, kale, blueberries and vitamin D powder with skim milk and no-fat yogurt prepared by his housekeeper, Consuela, who arrived at six.

Typically, he listened to Wagner throughout the house, the Teutonic composer's gothic opera filling every room, controlled via Bluetooth and his phone, imbuing him with a fervor to win the day.

But he found himself taking out his phone to pause the song as he left the bedroom, a concerned expression on Consuela's face as she walked up the left side of the curving double staircase.

"Mr. Baird, sir, you have a visitor. It's Mr. Greg."

Thomas? At such an early hour? "Let him in," he instructed.

He followed her downstairs. Consuela pulled open the door.

Thomas rushed in. He had a crazed expression on his face, his hair mussed, eyes bulging. "Parker, you have to help me, man!" he gasped.

Baird leaned past him to close the door. "That's all for now, Consuela. If you could see to the kitchen..." He let it hang there and the housekeeper took the hint, leaving the room. "Now... just calm down and—"

"Hell no, I won't!" Thomas exclaimed. "You have to hide me, man!"

"What? Stop blathering! What the hell are you yammering about?"

"Sharmila Singh's friend, the so-called 'lawyer', Bob Richmond. He killed Merry, and he's after me." He was panting, wild, leaning on his thighs with both hands. "Been on the run all night. I did what you said... went after him. But he's like a machine. He's lost it, says he's going to take out everyone responsible for the professor and Hap Singh. Took a shot at me in a crowded restaurant! You..." He looked up at Baird, then straightened up and grabbed his boss by the lapels of his jacket. "You have to hide me, Parker!"

Baird felt his blood rising. "Calm down! You're a grown man!" He grabbed Thomas by the wrists and wrestled him loose from the cloth. "Get hold of yourself! Where is he now?"

"I... I'm not sure. I think I lost him downtown."

"You *think*?" Baird was tempted to go upstairs to his study and get his .357 Magnum. He looked past Thomas to the front door. Bob Richmond had avoided killing anyone up to that point, as far as they could tell. But he had been a consistent thorn.

Would he actually show up on the doorstep? Baird couldn't be sure. "How long since you last saw him?"

"Maybe... thirty minutes. He came for me this morning, after I got out."

"Got out... wait... what?"

"Police picked me up yesterday. This all started because he got away from your boy Merry and took a potshot at me in a restaurant. Cops questioned me about it. Then, when I got out this morning at five, he was waiting for me outside the police. I took off up north, see if I could stay at my friend's place in Oildale for a few, but he kept on my tail. I slipped him near the speedway, I think."

"There's that expression again, as if you ever thought a goddamned thing through," Baird muttered.

"I stopped home and grabbed some stuff, got some money out. I figured if anyone owes me a little protection, it's you."

I need to get this lunatic out of here. "Did you call Dyche?" Baird demanded.

"Yeah. He said he'd be here!" Baird began to pace back and forth across the lobby. "Why isn't here here?!"

The doorbell rang again. "I've got it, Consuela!" Baird yelled. He moved to the door and checked the small window next to it to see who it was, then opened it.

Sgt. Gayle Dyche looked fatigued. "Gentlemen," he said. "I had a heck of a long night..."

"I thought you were supposed to be taking care of all of this!" Thomas spat.

"Now, I did what I was told, so you just hold on there," Dyche said. "Last I heard, Merry had him tied to a table."

"Last you heard?" Baird said. "You mean you didn't stay and make sure?"

"Merry didn't pay me to stick around!" Dyche groused back.

"Clearly, something went wrong in your plan," Baird said. "He's at large. Greg says he took out Merry and his boys."

"Shit," the cop said. "I should find out what the latest is from one of my contacts." He took out his cellphone. Then he frowned. "This is my work phone. I can't use this for this type of call, shouldn't even have it on while I'm here. You got a landline somewhere?"

Baird rolled his eyes. Both men were just incompetent enough to worry him. "My study. Be quick about it," he said.

Dyche jogged up the stairs.

Thomas watched him go, then turned back to his boss. "You need to protect me. You said if anything went wrong—"

"I said if you ever got arrested, I'd bail out one of my employees. I didn't tell you to get into a shootout with a lunatic."

Thomas looked around frantically. "You have men? Protection?"

"That's why I pay the two of you," Baird said.

"That's why—" Thomas started at him incredulously. "He's going to find us, Parker! He's going after everybody involved, one by one! He knows about the lab."

Keep it cool. You're insulated from all of this. "That's none of my concern," Baird said. "I'm just an investor in a project, remember?"

"Oh, cut the bullshit, Parker! Damn!" Thomas exclaimed. "You know damn well you—"

"I don't know a damn thing," Baird said, cutting him off. "Whatever problems this feller has, I'm sure it's not with me or Jenkins Mechanical."

"He doesn't give a shit about alibis, Parker! He's going to kill us. He's going to kill you, too, you can bet on that. Your name was on his list."

"Then we stay calm, we call the police—"

"Can't."

Parker turned towards the voice. Dyche was coming down the long staircase.

"Why? You're a sergeant."

"Because I just checked with one of my guys and he says they've got a warrant out on Mr. Thomas here for his role in a shootout in a steakhouse yesterday afternoon. If they find him and me here, they'll start asking all sorts of questions, maybe start looking into my bank account. If Bob then shows up, there's no way they'll believe we aren't all tied into this somehow. And then they'll really start digging."

Baird felt his annoyance growing. *It's one man.* "And your proposed solution?"

"We run, and you get out of town for a few days."

"Not an option," Baird said. "I have business, appointments to keep."

"Then we kill him when he gets here," Dyche said. "After that, we have someone inside pop his friend, close the book on Hap Singh's killer as a poor unfortunate outsider who tried to rob the wrong guy, and then pissed off someone inside the joint even worse."

"Oh sure, just like that," Thomas said, still pacing. "Sure."

"Yeah, just like that," Dyche sneered. "Man, I don't know where you found this one, Baird, but he's more gutless than a jellyfish at low tide."

"I should go," Baird said. "If I go before he gets here, it's breaking and entering, maybe, and you're a cop who just happened to be passing, saw a disturbance…"

Dyche shook his head. "They'll never buy that I previously just happened to have dealt with the guy who just happened to break into your house when I just happened to be walking by, even though I live across the city. That's not going to work."

"Then what do you propose?" Baird said.

"Easy: we ambush him," Dyche said. "I got his phone number off Merry while he was unconscious. You call him, tell him you're waiting in your study if he wants a face-to-face. We wait until he enters, guarding front and back, and put a bullet behind his ear the moment he walks in."

"He'll be expecting a trap."

Dyche nodded. "Sure. That's why we funnel him through the back door. Lock the front and back, but give him a window of opportunity—literally. Leave one of the back windows unlocked. He'll check those adjacent to the door and use what we give him…"

"And if he doesn't? If he suspects that it's too easy?"

"Then he'll find another route in… but it'll make a noise, whatever it is, and we'll be right here. Right, Greg?"

Thomas kept pacing and said nothing, his doubt writ large.

"I said, *right, Greg*?" the sergeant stressed.

"Hmm? Sure. Sure, right."

Baird waited until his assistant was halfway back to the door before speaking up quietly. "He doesn't sound confident."

"You know him," Dyche said. "Should he be?"

"Point taken."

Dyche nodded towards the stairwell. "Go on, go get ready. Lock the study door. You still have that .357 I gave you?"

Baird nodded.

"Keep it handy, just in case. He could be the most determined lunatic on the planet; still won't stop a bullet. He'll come. But we'll be ready for him."

53

It took less than twenty minutes before Baird heard the first gunshots.

And then the house went silent again. He stood away from the study door and held the pistol aloft, pointed at it, his hand shaking slightly.

Can't miss from this range... right?

He looked down the iron sights. *Just like Dyche showed you. Breathe in for two seconds, then hold it and squeeze naturally.*

After another few quiet moments, his curiosity kicked in. He moved over to the door and opened it a crack.

The move was well timed. He could see just enough of the staircase to catch Dyche backing up it. The veteran cop turned back towards the downstairs and fired two shots, then a third. Then he checked over his shoulder and saw the crack in the office door.

"GET INSIDE!" Dyche bellowed, a second before his chest plumped at the impact from a pair of bullets, blood spraying from the wounds as he collapsed onto the stairs.

"Oh fuck!" Baird exclaimed. He slammed the door and locked it, then backed up several feet, the pistol extended.

The door lock had no chance, the force of the kick sending the door flying open.

"BAIRD!" Bob bellowed.

Baird closed his eyes as he squeezed the trigger once, twice, three times, the blast from each deafening. He opened his right eye, his left held tight in a terrified squint, and looked down.

Bob was lying just ahead of the door.

Is he—

In answer to the silent question, Bob labored to turn himself over, so that he was lying prone on his back.

Baird walked over to him and pointed the gun at his face. He had a seeping chest wound, based on the spreading blood stain on his shirt.

I did it.

I actually did it.

I actually got the sum'bitch.

Another bloody patch was growing near Bob's shoulder, another on his left thigh. It wasn't exactly clean, Baird figured, but it had done the trick.

Arrogant bastard, Baird thought. *Thought he could come into my town, hassle me and mine.*

Bob was grimacing in pain. "Almost... almost had you."

"But you didn't," Baird said, lowering the revolver for a moment. "Made a big mistake, biting off more than you could chew. Somedays, you eat the bear, son. Sometimes, the bear eats you."

"Surprised... Didn't think you had it in you," Bob said through gritted teeth. "Damn... hurts getting shot."

"I bet it does. But the next one's going to make that all go away." He raised the gun again. "And all that anyone will remember is how I bravely shot a cop-killing intruder, another scary outsider."

"Why? Why Singh? Why get Thomas to shoot him? That..." Bob grimaced. "That I don't get."

"Not much to it," Baird said matter-of-factly. "He was a nosy kind of feller. I expect you know most of the details already."

"Methylamine... Seems a little cheap for you."

"It's a growth industry. Demand outstrips supply. And we have all the supply."

"So... it's just about money, then."

Baird scoffed at the notion. "It's always about money, son. What isn't?"

"Uh huh." Bob pushed off the floor and began to rise. "Did you get that?"

"What?" Baird said. *What the hell...*

A figure stepped around the corner of the study door.

"We did."

Baird's eyes widened. "Margaret Swain?"

Bob opened his shirt to show the wire and blood pack harness. "Bringer of pain," he said.

Two police officers stepped past her and into the room. One had cuffs in his hand. Baird was frozen in place, dumbfounded. "I don't... What?!"

"Hands behind your back, please, sir," the first officer intoned, grabbing the gun right out of his hand.

Baird did as ordered.

"You look surprised," Bob said. "But like you said to Mr. Thomas and Mr. Dyche—who were also wearing wires—you were insulated. The sergeant was kind enough to pop up to your study when he go there to 'use the phone', and switched your rounds for blanks."

"You were insulated, but they weren't," Swain said, nodding back towards the stairs. "Murder, conspiracy to commit, an entire truckload of other charges."

"Dyche..." Baird began to say, flummoxed.

"Had a whole lot of money in a bank account he couldn't explain," Bob said. "But as a law enforcement professional in California, he has to be able to."

Baird glared at him. "You... You..." He began to shake his head slowly, rage building in him.

"Now, Parker..." Bob said. "Just accept it. Like you said... Sometimes you eat the bear. Sometimes the bear eats you."

The second officer took Baird by the cuffs, a hand on one shoulder to guide him towards the door. "Parker Baird, you have the right to remain silent. Anything you say can and will be held against you in a court of law..."

OUTSIDE THE HOUSE, Bob watched as they loaded Dyche and Thomas into the back of one squad car, uncuffed, and led Baird towards the other.

"Thank you, Mr. Richmond," Swain said, coming up behind him. "Dyche wouldn't have been enough. As you suspected, most of his money came from an account that seems to be controlled by Merry Michelsen, not from Baird directly."

"As long as he had Michelsen as cover, we needed an admission," Bob said. "Now what? When does my friend get released?"

"He should be out by this afternoon," she said. "And then we can sit down and talk about your testimony."

"My what now?"

She smiled ruefully. "You didn't think you could just walk away from this, did you? You're our key witness."

"But you have him on tape admitting it. And you said I'd get confidential informant status. And you have Dyche, Thomas *and* Czernowitz. You don't need me. What does confidential informant mean to you exactly, Swain?"

"Your name won't be entered into the record and only the judge will know your identity."

"The rest isn't enough? The tape?"

"Technically, probably, yeah. Nothing you said personally changes the statements he made. But it will greatly help the credibility of the sting if you're there to confirm it in person. It was your idea, Bob."

That's not going to work, Bob thought. *I need to extract myself from this.* "I take it you're going to want a longer debrief, then?" he said.

"We will. We can do it right now, if you want to come back to the station with us…"

"Can I take a raincheck until tomorrow? I have a ton of things to catch up on."

She peered at him curiously then and Bob had a momentary fear she was on to him.

Then, she turned her attention to the cruiser carrying Baird as it pulled off down the driveway. "Do what you need to do, Mr. Richmond. Just don't go anywhere, okay?"

Bob gave her a genial thumbs-up… and even that felt bad in the circumstances.

54

Dawn Ellis sat in the otherwise empty public waiting area at the Lerdo Pre-Trial Facility and played with her thumbs. She'd been there for nearly an hour, and, beyond a cursory "We'll be with you shortly," from the counter clerk, had no idea what was going on.

Finally, the same clerk reappeared at the counter.

"Ma'am..." Dawn asked, waving a hand to get her attention.

"We'll be with you—"

"Shortly, uh huh. I did understand you when you said that an hour ago, ma'am. Will someone please tell me what in the heck is going on?"

The woman looked puzzled. "You mean you don't know? We assumed that was why you were here."

"Because of..."

"Your dependent."

"My friend," she said. "He's nearly nineteen."

"Be that as it may, he describes you in his file as his stepmother. Is that correct? You're his next of kin?"

She felt a chill rush through her. "Next of kin?"

The woman recognized her fear and raised both hands. "Oh, Land sake's, no! Nothing bad. He's getting out today."

The fear subsided to a wave of relief, her head slumping slightly as she exhaled deeply, a hand raised to her beating heart. "Oh... thank you, Lord," she whispered. Then, louder, "He is?"

"Marcus Pell, correct? Charges against him were dropped his morning. You're lucky; it can take twelve hours or more to get this all done, typically. Figured you were here to pick him up."

"I... guess I am."

"Well, you just wait a few more minutes and he should be making an appearance."

She felt stunned, elated, as if the world weighed a little less. "Thank you." She wasn't sure what else to say.

The clerk's expression was measured, as if she'd heard it before. "Well, you are most welcome, dear."

She'd worried about him so much, not just after the arrest but even before that. She'd worried every minute, she figured, since he'd left Chicago. It hadn't been fair, because Marcus was kind, and smart. But then something terrible had happened anyway. And then something proper and fine had happened, because...

Bob.

It had to be. He'd gone silent, but then two days later, Marcus was being released. He'd done something, somehow.

He always did.

She looked up. *Thank you for looking out for him, Lord. I know he says he doesn't believe in you, but he's a good man.*

The tears came out of nowhere, gently rolling down both cheeks, the relief washing through her. She felt the guilt again, then, just for a moment, her mind drifting to her late son, Maurice, and the life he'd never have.

But I couldn't have saved him. I tried my best, son, I really did. It was the first time the thought had occurred and truly felt accurate. Maurice's death had been meaningless, because he was a good boy caught up in someone else's violence. *And there was nothing, Dawn Marie, nothing that could have prevented that.*

She looked up again to the Heavens. *I hope you understand that, son. I hope...*

I know you know how loved you were.

A buzzer sounded to her left and she turned to see the barred gate by the front desk swinging open. Marcus was in his civilian clothing, grinning as the sight of her.

They ran toward each other, the hug held for full value, Dawn intent on never really letting go.

THEY WERE HALFWAY to the car when his voice behind them caught Dawn by surprise.

"You two look fit and rested."

They both turned. "BOB!" Dawn practically yelled. She threw her arms around him.

Bob hugged her right back. "I'd get mad at you for being here, but your timing has never been better," he said, ignoring the screaming pain in his ribs. He held out a hand and Marcus shook it. "Young man. You look none the worse for wear."

Marcus shook, but his expression was considerably more

concerned. "You... don't. Brutal! What happened to your eye?"

Bob raised his left hand to self-consciously feel the swelling. "Yeah... I went a few rounds with an angry redneck. I imagine it looks worse than it feels."

"Are you all right?" Dawn said. "You flinched a little when I hugged you."

"A few minor bumps and bruises," Bob lied.

She put her hands on her hips and glared right through him. "Uh huh. I'm a nurse, Bob. I know when someone's in pain."

"Then the direction this conversation is headed should be setting off all sorts of additional signals," he said dryly. "Besides... I'm on antibiotics, I've got painkillers. I'm okay."

"Sure."

"You have wheels? I have some stuff to pick up."

She nodded and smiled. "A rental. Are you going to let me in on just what the heck happened down here, or..."

"Come on. I take it you have a hotel room somewhere?"

"I do."

"I'll explain on the way."

They'd stopped for a burger for lunch and a chance to discuss the week before heading to pick up her stuff. There was a flight that evening directly back to Chicago.

Dawn was enjoying being behind the wheel; she hadn't owned a car in more than a decade, which made driving herself a treat.

But even more, she was subtly enjoying the relaxed, almost placid expression Bob had on his face, despite her ongoing sense he'd left out major details.

He noticed her staring. "What? Do I have something..." He felt around his mouth for stray food.

"It's not that. You just look—I mean, you look like a meatloaf who got beat up by a brick, really—but a happy meatloaf."

"I was thinking about my mom," Bob said. "I don't do that enough."

"You've never really talked about her," Dawn said. "Your father, I know, was difficult."

"Yeah, he was at that. Hard, suspicious, difficult. She wasn't like that at all, though. If anything, I always sort of thought she was with him because he was someone who needed fixing. She just wanted people to get along and care about each other. She spent a lot of time she could have spent on herself on us instead, either trying to make him happy or keep me from being unhappy. He'd be trying to drill something home—he was drill instructor in the Marines—and she'd try to undo any damage by telling me to do what I love. The trouble was, by then, I didn't know what that was. I just knew what my old man had taught me."

"But now you know what you love: helping people," Dawn suggested.

"Eh..." Bob didn't sound so sure. "I wish that was it. But I kind of think it's a little more selfish than that."

"How do you figure?"

"Sorting this all out... it took a lot of hard work, days of graft and personality management, keeping my temper under wraps, dealing with bad boys. And throughout—and I guess I should be more ashamed of this, but it is what it is—throughout, I didn't really think much about Marcus at all." He looked over his shoulder to the backseat. "No offence, kid."

"Then... why?"

He shrugged. "I like punishing bad guys. I like what I do, I guess. I mean, I've spent a lot of years bitching and crying about my time in Team Seven, but when push came to shove, I just went right out and started doing the same kind of things, just on a smaller scale and on my own targets. I have to be more empathetic, more understanding of people trying to maintain normalcy. I get that. But what it's all been about, really, has been making life difficult for difficult people. I'm nobody's savior. I just fix problematic people."

"Ah," Dawn smiled and nodded.

"What?"

"And you've just figured out you shouldn't feel guilty about that. That as long as it's helping good people and hurting bad ones, it's not wrong to do right it for its own sake, not because of how other people see it or judge you."

"Exactly."

"And that's what your mom wanted: for you to pursue what you love, and not feel bad about it."

He nodded, then leaned on his hand and stared out the side window. "She'd say, 'Do right, but do right by you also'. I don't think, until very recently, that I understood that. Then a friend I'd made in Arizona died suddenly."

"Oh... I'm sorry, sweetie."

"It's okay. The last thing she'd told me before dying was that she felt blessed, to have that second chance at not just doing the right thing, but being the person she was supposed to be, the person she felt like on the inside."

"She sounds lovely."

"She was. She was a nun. And before that, a former corporate raider who laid off thousands of people."

"That's..." Dawn cocked her head a little, weighing the dichotomy. "That's quite the role reversal."

"You would've liked her. She kept telling me that I needed to stop worrying about who I am and accept myself. She also got pissed at me every time I swore."

From the backseat, Marcus chimed in, "It's like you have a type or something."

Bob closed his eyes tight, then pincered them with his right thumb and forefinger. "Yah... I don't want to even try to unpack that right now."

Business was brusque in the hotel lobby, guests checking in for the weekend. There were a few more Stetsons on display than was typical for the town, Bob figured, and a sure sign some of the visitors were there for the town's country music legacy, the Bakersfield Sound.

They took the elevator to the third floor and followed the fading faux-Persian runner carpet to Room 312. Dawn reached out with the keycard and put one hand on the handle.

Then she stopped. "Hmm."

"What?" Bob's hackles rose a little.

She stepped back from the door. "Well now, I was sort of angry with you before I left Chicago. I thought all of these precautions that kept us all apart were paranoid. And I even got mad that you'd conditioned me to put a hair across the door jamb, so I could tell if someone had broken in."

Bob was perplexed. "So?"

"So... I put one across the crack of this door, and it's gone."

Bob's hand went to his waistband and the Glock 19 at the

small of his back. "Go," he commanded. "Run. Put distance between yourselves and here."

"We should get help," Dawn said. "The police cleared you—"

"They cleared a stolen identity for a man still being sought by the federal government. I can't call the police, Dawn," Bob said. "Keycard."

She handed it to him.

"Go, please, now. For once, no arguments."

She nodded quickly and led Marcus towards the stairs.

He waited until they'd rounded the corner. He stood to one side of the room door, reaching across it to work the lock, turning the handle gently, then shoving the door open full force.

It was weighted, but even so managed to smack into the wall behind it, next to the bathroom door. He drew the Glock and peeked around the corner.

Nothing.

He leaned against the door as he entered, the pistol braced. He pushed it nearly closed behind. The bathroom door was open and he glanced inside.

Empty. He swung the gun back to his right, towards the room proper, taking small, cautious steps until he could see more of the room in the mirror above the television set.

Clear? His angles were cut off slightly. Bob leaned down and around the corner, going wide, until he could see between the beds.

No one. The hall closet had no doors, so that had been out of the question. He glanced towards the windows, wondering if there was a balcony he hadn't—

Behind the bathroom door.

He caught the faintest glint in the windowpane as the

titanium cord necklace looped over his head and around his neck. He tried to get a hand up, between it and his Adam's apple, but his attacker was too quick.

The man leaped onto his back, wrapping his legs around Bob's torso, the chain cutting into his carotid artery, blood flow stopped, a leaden fog hitting his brain almost immediately.

Bob threw himself over sideways, crashing them both into the faux-wood desk next to the TV. But the attacker clung on, even as Bob clawed at him, trying to pry him loose.

"You'll start to lose consciousness soon, Singleton," the man said. "But rest assured, it will be a good death. A warrior's death. You can take pride knowing you died at the hands of Geert Van Kamp, the world's greatest assassin."

Bob struggled to cough out an answer.

"Wh...who?" he choked.

55

The man's grip around his neck relaxed ever so slightly. "What do you mean 'who'? You know exactly who I am." The grip tightened.

Bob tried to bend at the waist, just enough to let his head nod forward a few inches. Then he threw it backwards with all his strength, Van Kamp too close, the back of his head smacking into the other man's face, nasal bone snapping.

Van Kamp shrieked, the garotte momentarily loosened. Bob rolled away and up to his feet. Pain shot through his right ribcage and he staggered for a moment, even as his opponent also came to his feet, clutching his broken nose.

Bob looked both ways quickly, trying to spot his pistol. Van Kamp was faster, drawing his weapon and raising it before Bob could move.

"Pathetic," Van Kamp spat. "You are so embarrassed that you cannot admit being beaten by me."

"Buddy," Bob said, gently shaking his head, "I have no idea who the fuck you are."

"RUBBISH!" Van Kamp raged. "That is nonsense, mate, and you know it. I am the world's—"

"Greatest assassin, yeah, I heard you. I mean... I still have no idea what the fuck you're talking about."

"You have a lot of enemies—"

"Tell me something I don't already know. Let me guess, you're an Andrew Kennedy special."

"Enough!" Van Kamp spat. "Turn around, and down on your knees."

Bob complied. "Well... we've established one thing: you're not the world's most original assassin."

"That you have the gall to still pretend—"

"I'm not pretending," Bob said. "I've never heard of you. Do you really think everyone in the game is keeping a tote board going on who's killed the most people for money? Or however the fuck you judge your status?"

"YOU SHOT ME IN THE FUCKING FACE!" Van Kamp ranted.

Bob frowned, puzzled. *I've never seen this guy before in my life. I'd remember it.* "I what now?"

"You know what I'm talking about. You saw a chance to take out the competition and complete your objective."

"I think I know my own past."

"Somalia, fifteen years ago," Van Kamp said. "I was protecting the warlord Dalaal Gurmad Qayaad in Mogadishu. There was a raid on his complex by US Marines. But I got him out. We were clear, free, making our way over the rooftops to his helicopter."

Bob's mind drifted back. "Dalaal. The former long-distance guy, the one who'd been to the Olympics. I shot him with a BAR .50 from nearly two klicks away. With strong wind, no less, and him moving. Best shot I ever made."

"But not the first bullet. The first two shots, the tracer rounds you used to gauge your target lead? One of them took down his bodyguard. You remember? Turn around. Ah! Don't get up, just shuffle on your knees."

Bob did as ordered. Van Kamp was a strikingly ugly man, his cheeks broad but flat, his nose broken at least twice. He had a burn scar covering the outer edge of his left eye, scar tissue partially covering it.

"You did this to me, Singleton," Van Kamp said. "You made me look like a freak. And when your former employers came looking for the best, it was practically destiny."

Bob stared at the damage. "Ouch," he said. Then he shook his head gently. "Nope, still can't place you. And... man, if you were really as famous as you think, I'm pretty sure I'd remember a mug that ugly."

Van Kamp seethed in place, his face contorted, his head bobbing about as he tried to decide how to act. "Gyeaargh!" he ranted. "If I shoot you in the gut, to make it slow and painful, there's a chance maybe an ambulance saves you. If I shoot you in the head, I don't get the profound satisfaction of throttling you to death, or to watch you suffer for what you did to me."

Bob nodded. "It's almost as if even though *I'm* the guy on his knees and *you're* the guy with the gun... you're still just some anonymous psycho."

"SHUT UP!"

"Unloved and uncared for by the world, still basically running across rooftops for warlord creeps, with the guy who shot you not caring if you even exist."

"And that resolves that question," Van Kamp said, lowering the gun to point it at Bob's stomach. "I'll shoot you in the gut, watch you suffer for a few minutes, then put two in your head. And I'll still be out of here long before the police arrive."

"Are you going to talk the entire time?" Bob said. "Shooting me in the gut is one thing, but five more minutes of this self-pity fest is more than anyone could take."

"You... You are so self-righteous, Singleton! You call me a psychopath but at least I know who and what I am. You're no better than me. I know you; I've seen your CIA file. And you're going to die here, like you say, an anonymous loser, unloved, uncared for."

The door flew open, crashing into the wall once more. Van Kamp pivoted on his heels, instinct and training kicking in.

But not quickly enough, the leads from the stun gun in Dawn's hand flying ten feet across the room, burying themselves in his face, fifty thousand volts coursing through the South African's body.

He shook in place, the current holding his muscles rigid as they filled with lactic acid. Then he collapsed to the carpet.

"So much for that theory," Bob said.

Dawn studied the prone assassin bloodlessly. She put the stun gun in her purse. "Are you going to help me tie him up, or what?"

"Nurse Dawn... you've changed," Bob said. "I mean... in a good way. But... in the face?"

She did not sound impressed. "Your ability to try and be funny a at entirely the wrong time continues to amaze me. He had a leather jacket on. Not a great insulator, but enough that the stun gun might not have worked."

"Thinking ahead, even. I am impressed." Bob rose unsteadily, wincing.

"Your ribs?"

"Yeah, lots of pain. Good thing you came back. Second time someone has saved me in the last two days."

"We'll have to get you some more Demerol," she said.

Bob nodded towards the door. "Go. I need to finish up here alone."

She frowned. "And that means what, exactly?"

He gave her a weary look. "Thank you for coming through for me. Again. But you can't be here for the rest of this."

"Bob…"

"Dawn, this man is a psychopath and a paid killer. All he does is end lives prematurely. All he causes is pain."

"And you want to behave exactly like he does, to resolve something? Is that what I'm hearing?"

Van Kamp had begun to stir. Bob bent at the knees, picked up the pistol next to the hitman and clobbered him across the side of the chin with it. He slumped back down, motionless once again.

"If I leave him alive, he'll find me again. Worse, he'll find you. Given that he was in your room, he probably followed you to Bakersfield from Chicago. It's everything I warned you could happen if we saw each other," Bob said.

Dawn pursed her lips, a tear appearing in the corner of her left eye, rolling down her cheek unabated. "No, Bob. Don't kill him. I… I can't live with that. Not when he's beaten. No more death. Please. Look in your heart. If nobody ever stops, then it never stops."

He stared at his shoes for a few moments. She didn't need the guilt, he knew, didn't deserve it.

"Okay. Fine." He walked over and put the pistol down on the desk. "But... I still have to stay with him until the police can get here and take custody. And it's not safe for you to be here with me. You must know that now. It's not safe for you, and it's not safe for Marcus. Besides... I'm going to be out of Bakersfield by the end of the day, and then they'll be looking for a material witness, at least in this county, probably state-wide."

"I know."

"So... it's not going to change. None of it. Not any time soon. I need to get running... and you need to be somewhere else."

He reached down and flipped Van Kamp over onto his stomach. Bob took off his belt and used it to bind the assassin at the wrists. Then he got up and walked over to her.

They hugged, holding each other tight for as long as felt right. "Go," he said. "Take Marcus home."

"And you?"

"I'll be in touch when I can. You know the drill."

She pursed her lips once more, warding off more tears. "Yeah. I know. Goodbye, Bob."

"Until later," he said.

She turned and hurried out of the room.

BOB WATCHED his battered old Seiko wristwatch until five minutes had passed. He went out and checked the hallway.

She was gone.

He went back inside and closed the door.

"You're really going to hand me over to the police?" Van Kamp said. "My God, Singleton! What a pathetic, tormented individual you must be now! To have ended so many lives, and yet to care so damned much! So conflicted by things as everyday as living and dying!"

He raised himself to his knees, his eyes darting around the room. Bob watched him without intervening.

"You won't kill me. You're the good guy in this silly narrative. Me, I don't care either way. I never had a bloody thing. Never had family or love or the silly sentiments people like your friend seem to find so important in their silly lives. You won't kill me, but you know what, Singleton? I wouldn't care if you did."

Yeah, Bob thought. *You don't care about dying at all. That's why you're frantically searching the room visually right now, looking for any way out of this.*

"What? Cat got your tongue, Singleton? Nothing clever to say in your moment of triumph?"

Bob walked over to the desk and picked up the pistol.

"Be serious!" Van Kamp scoffed. "For all your reputation, you are the civilized one now, right? A bleeding heart, helping out those people in New Orleans, then again in Tucson. I killed your paper maker there, you know. He screamed like a stuck pig in hot oil. And I killed your tech friend in DC, as well. He cried even longer."

Bob walked over and stood behind him. "Nicky?"

"Very dead. I ripped out his fingernails first." Van Kamp raised his chin, jutting it out haughtily. "He was even weaker than you. And that's the difference between me and you. You're weak."

Bob considered him stoically. *What a waste of a person.* "I'm weak because I care about others? Then why the fuck are you the one kneeling and nervous?"

His head shook slightly as he searched for justification, a

narrative for his narcissism. "Bad luck. You got lucky, Singleton. And I fear nothing, not even death."

But his eyes continued to flit around, looking for an escape. His rambling held a slight hesitancy, the tone getting shakier. "You've killed plenty of men, Singleton, but still you cannot revel in your power, the power those of us who are strong have over others, over life and death itself. When we exercise power over life and death, we are made Gods! We are... we are powerful beyond belief. Beyond all concern."

Bob raised the pistol and pointed it at the back of Van Kamp's head. "Or, you know... you could just have chosen to have friends, be a decent person."

"More weakness! You could kill anyone, take anything you wanted! You... could have been a legend! A legend..." Van Kamp's eyes darted around, tongue moistening his dry lower lip. "Like me."

Bob pulled the trigger, the gun's report blistering. Van Kamp pitched over, face first.

He leaned over the man's body and shot him through the head once more, then used his left foot to flip the contract killer's torso. He shot him twice more, through the heart.

Then he stared at the man's body for a moment, the blood seeping out onto the carpet.

The utter waste of it.

"The difference between us," Bob said softly, "is that you'd have enjoyed this."

He pocketed the pistol. A 'do not disturb' sign would only buy him a few minutes. The gunshots would likely have prompted calls to the front desk, the possibility of someone looking for the source.

He needed to get moving.

EPILOGUE

Sharmila Singh slammed the driver's door on her BMW and slung her purse over her shoulder. She headed for the sidewalk, glad to have found a spot less than a block from the rooming house.

She'd had a day to consider everything. Bob had dropped into their lives out of nowhere, basically. Sure, he was helping a friend, but he'd also given her peace, helped her avenge her father, helped put a dangerous man behind bars.

It had curbed her cynicism, the growing sense since her father's death that there was nobody good left out there, nobody who would be selfless. Not just Bob, but Mr. Feeney, Margaret, even David, who'd found the strength to be better.

Mel Feeney was standing outside the rooming house's front door, leaning on a crutch. "He's not here," he said. "The owner said he packed up and left about an hour ago."

"Where...?"

Feeney just shook his head gently.

"He... just left?"

"It seems so."

"But... I don't have a number for him. He changed phones. I don't have any way to contact him, to thank him."

She felt suddenly empty.

"I suspect that was by design," Feeney said. "He was a private sort of feller. I tried getting the lowdown on him a little, but he was reluctant to talk."

"But... why?" she said. "He did nothing but put his own life on the line for me, for my father, for a week. And then he just leaves? It doesn't make sense."

"Maybe there's history there we don't know," Feeney said. "Some of the most helpful folk I ever knew had a ton of guilt behind it. Maybe... well, maybe the reason he cleans up so good is that he's spent a lot of time in the mud."

Sharmila felt a tear track its way down her cheek. "I didn't even get to say goodbye."

WASHINGTON, DC

EDDIE STONE KNOCKED on the ajar office door, waited a moment, then entered.

"Don't wait for an answer or anything. Just come right in," Andrew Kennedy said dryly. He was seated behind the ornate, carved mahogany desk, the chair turned slightly sideways to accommodate his midsection girth.

"The door wasn't completely closed. I didn't realize you were having a private moment." Stone looked around the office. He hadn't seen it in... months? Years? It had been long enough that he couldn't be sure. "Rare seeing you behind a desk, even your own."

"There are... pressures from above right now," Kennedy said.

"You saw the paper this morning? Benji Usmanov bit the big one."

"I heard. Heart attack in his sleep."

"And how are we feeling about that?"

"He was a friend. It's a shame. But he was in his eighties."

"He was a Russian asset," Stone said, "and a willing one at that. You know as well as I do that he signed the checks on the failed Tehran mission. There are a few folks who think he had more than two of Team Seven on the payroll."

"It doesn't matter now, does it?" Kennedy said wearily. 'It's history."

"Perhaps," Stone said. "Although maybe it's still too early to say."

That got his boss's attention. Kennedy straightened up and turned head on, leaning on the desk. "And what does that mean, exactly?"

"Well... Singleton's still out there, for one. He's the last of them, the last guy who might still have questions. Discounting the two of us, of course. And I'm certainly not worried about my ties to Usmanov."

"And you think I should be?"

"Only you can answer that, Andy. We've worked together a long time. Maybe, sometimes, the Singletons of the world are unavoidable, an avenging conscience that always shows up, to right old wrongs."

"Perhaps. But perhaps for not much longer. Our outside contractor—"

"Is dead. Again."

Kennedy winced. "How?"

"In a hotel room in Bakersfield, California."

"Singleton?"

"Would be my guess, sure. But we have no indication it was even related. I have a line on a freelance handler out of Dallas who might know more."

"Anyone familiar?"

"Adam Renton. He was a digital spook over at NSA a few years back. My sources say he was working a lucrative freelance gig for a South African hitter. Can't be too many in the US right now meeting that description at that level."

"See what you can find out."

"And then? Do we keep this up? I mean, sure, chances are eventually one of them catches him cold. But Van Kamp cost us two million dollars, a spend so large we had to create paper and be inventive to wash it. And he did no better than those who went before."

Kennedy looked uncharacteristically befuddled as he considered the question, Stone thought. *Shaken, almost.*

The older man took off his glasses and rubbed his tired eyes. He ran his fingers through his thinning silver hair. "Leave it for now," Kennedy said. "This is going to take a more creative fix than just throwing money at assassins. He's too unpredictable, too much of a survivor for that to be the best approach. If nothing else, after fifty years in this business, you'd think we'd both know when to cut our losses."

"Sure. You'd think. But... we're both on the wrong side of seventy, both working on an age exemption. You ever wonder if maybe we shouldn't have both stepped aside a long time ago?"

Kennedy just shrugged. "What else is there?"

LOS ANGELES, CALIFORNIA

THE HIRE CAR dropped Bob at the LAX departure terminal. He tipped the man an extra ten dollars for respecting his desire for silence on the long drive.

It beat taking the bus. He'd seen enough of them, from DC to Pahrump, Nevada, to last a lifetime.

The flight to Seattle wasn't scheduled to leave for another two hours, but he was content to grab a tea, find a new book. Anything to take his mind off Dawn and Marcus.

It ate at him. He didn't understand why, really. Outside of his mother and Maggie, he'd never had caring relationships. And those had been different. A mother's love was something unique, and Maggie had been as much about crazy passion as anything likely to last. They were like puzzle pieces that had found each other.

But this was different. This was...

What? Family? From all other accounts, that was how it seemed. He loved them both, and he worried about them. But he knew he'd worry more if all three were in the same room together.

It wasn't even about penance anymore, paying for his terrible judgement in working for Team Seven, or the horrors experienced and meted out in warzones.

It was just about doing what was right for them. Dawn was always so worried about others, and not herself, that she'd walk into the line of fire for the people she cared about. Marcus required the same support, the same mentoring, as anyone his age. But Bob knew if he was present, the boy would also need constant protection.

He slung his soft-sided bag over his shoulder and walked into the terminal. It was typically busy, passengers lining up to check in, scouring departure boards, hugging loved ones.

She would know, or at least suspect, what happened to

Van Kamp. She wasn't naïve, despite her wholesome approach to just about everything. That was difficult, to know that at least a small part of her might begin to doubt him.

But it couldn't have been avoided. Van Kamp had been of a type, a man he'd met more than once while in the military, someone there as much for the deranged nature of combat as any sense of service. He'd have kept coming until the job was done.

The difficult part was accepting the collateral damage. She'd cried at the notion of him killing Van Kamp, because she was normal, and healthy, and the idea of ending a life shocked her.

Maybe that will make it easier.

Maybe she'll stop worrying and let me go.

It was the best-case scenario, Bob knew, all he could hope for. Life on the road wasn't bad, but it wouldn't ever be good.

And maybe that was how it had to be.

THE END

ABOUT THE AUTHOR

Did you enjoy *Hard Country*? Please consider leaving a review on Amazon to help other readers discover the book.

Ian Loome writes thrillers and mysteries. His books have been downloaded more than a half-million times on Amazon.com and have regularly featured on the Kindle best-seller lists for more than a decade. For 24 years, Ian was a multi-award-winning newspaper reporter, editor and columnist in Canada. When he's not figuring out innovative ways to snuff his characters, he plays blues guitar and occasionally fronts bands. He lives in Sherwood Park, Alberta, with his partner Lori, a pugnacious bulldog named Ferdinand, a confused mostly Great Dane puppy named Ollie, and some cats for good measure.

ALSO BY IAN LOOME

A Rogue Warrior Thriller Series

Code Red

Blood Debt

Dead Drop

Hell Bent

Hard Country

Printed in Great Britain
by Amazon